D0786414

Mr & Mrs Pond
17 Twigworth Road
Leadworth
Gloucestershire

POSTA ROMANA

HOJPERIA

101011100-1111010100101

Canton Everett Delaware III
773 Fort Elm Drive Northwest
Brightwood Park
Washington DC
USA

THE
BRILLIANT
BOOK 2012

EDITED BY **CLAYTON HICKMAN**
DESIGNED BY **PAUL LANG**

BBC
BOOKS

THE BRILLIANT BOOK 2012

CONTENTS

WELCOME
TO **THE
BRILLIANT
BOOK OF
DOCTOR
WHO 2012**

Stop. Look behind you. What did you see? Nothing. Really? Maybe there was nothing there. If you're lucky...

You see, the Silence has come for the Doctor. Who are the Silence? No one can remember – but they've been waiting for a very long time...

You see, the Doctor is the most dangerous man in the universe. He doesn't look it. He likes to think he's a stylish chap, all floppy hair, tweed jacket and bow tie. But the Doctor is the last of an ancient race – the Time Lords – who travelled in fantastic craft called TARDISes. They spent so long in the Time Vortex they became nearly immortal, able to regenerate their bodies – a secret that died with them... until the Doctor met Amelia Pond.

Amy Pond was the girl who waited. The Doctor met her as a child and promised her adventures. But it was only many years later, on the night before her wedding, that he finally whisked the now grown-up Amy away on amazing voyages in time and space.

But in the end Amy got married to Rory Williams. Only after she'd managed to restart the universe, pulling the Doctor out of her dreams in time for him to dance at her wedding. And after Rory had been a plastic duplicate in an alternate timeline for 2000 years. They had a lot in common.

While travelling through the time vortex Amy realised she was pregnant – and at first she was worried about the effect time travel could have on her baby. And then she forgot all about being pregnant.

Which wasn't as strange as you'd think, as suddenly, everyone was forgetting a lot of things – because the Earth had been infested by a powerful alien race, the Silence.

As soon as you look away, you forget them. And they've been in the shadows for such a long time – nurturing a weapon to defeat the Doctor. And that weapon was a child.

It took a long time before the Doctor realised what was going on. Amy had been replaced with a psychically linked replica – she was actually far away, on the asteroid of Demons Run, getting closer and closer to giving birth to a baby that would grow up a killer.

Amy's daughter was called Melody Pond and the Doctor raised an army to rescue them both. It wasn't enough. Melody was taken by Madame Kovarian, a servant of the Silence.

And then the Doctor found out who Melody would grow up to be. For some time he'd been crossing paths with River Song, a mysterious woman who claimed to know him in his future. She refused to say more – but the aftermath of Demons Run brought her secret to light at last.

River was revealed as the woman Melody would grow up to be – the Silence's secret weapon. She led an amazing life – trying to kill Hitler, studying archaeology, regenerating... and along the way, she fell in love with her victim. So, when the day finally came to kill the Doctor, she couldn't.

And all of time stopped.

It was up to the Doctor to restart time and marry River Song. Not necessarily in that order. And now the seconds are ticking away to a terrible revelation. What will happen on the fields of Trenzalore?

The Doctor wants the universe to think he's dead. But River knows he's not. How safe is the Doctor really...?

The Brilliant Book of Doctor Who 2012 gives you the whole story of the Doctor's recent adventures – from a NASA lanchpad to a pirate ship, from Nazi Germany to a department store. It's packed full of secrets, hidden details, and things that never made it to TV. It's going to be the ride of your life.

Just don't look behind you...

'The Doctor is a *thrill-seeker*. He's *addicted* to it'

The Doctor himself, **Matt Smith**, takes us on a personal journey through his second year at the TARDIS controls and looks to the future...

M att Smith is waxing lyrical about *Doctor Who*'s eponymous hero. 'The Doctor is still having fun,' the 28-year-old actor tells *The Brilliant Book*. 'No one wants to tune in and see some guy moaning about saving the world. "Oh, everything's so bad, and I'm so dark, and I've got this great weight on my shoulders..." Yeah, well, we don't want that. Fine, if he's feeling it. He is, and that's great. But, by the same token, he can impersonate a spitfire, put on a fez, and just be silly. He flirts with the threat, and he likes it. He's a thrill-seeker. He's addicted to it.'

These days, Matt seems to spend a lot of his time talking about the Doctor. Talking and *thinking* about the Doctor. As acting roles go, this one is all-consuming. It's just as well that Matt is so in love with this 'madman in a box'. He embodies the character like no other actor. Whereas most Doctors

were playing the part, spend five minutes in Matt's company and you realise that he pretty much *is* the Doctor. 'Casting Matt,' *Doctor Who* supremo Steven Moffat once said, 'was the easiest decision in the world. Because, let's be honest, Matt *is* unselfconsciously nutty. That's what he's like.'

Today, the part-time TV star, full-time Time Lord appears laid back and in high spirits. He's wearing a snug black T-shirt, and slim-fitting jeans tucked into leather boots that look oddly familiar; his pompadour of hair hidden beneath a blue knitted beanie, which slides off every time he throws back his head in laughter. Which is quite often. He's four parts nerdy eccentric to six parts rock star. And this man loves his job...

You said once, 'I think about the Doctor every day. Every single day, I consider him. It's what I'm paid to do. He's an interesting man to live opposite.' So as the

man who lives with the Doctor 24/7, he must wind you up sometimes, too?

No, he doesn't annoy me. I mean, I can see how he would annoy others with his incessant madness. But I just love him. I love how brave and clever he is. I think he's someone to set your morality by, in many ways. He tends to make good choices, for the right reasons. Also, what I love about my Doctor is just what an out-and-out liar he is sometimes. You're going, 'Is he telling me the truth?' And often he isn't. Do you think he seems more immoral than other Doctors? I quite like the idea of that, actually, so please don't worry about sugar-coating your answer.

It's perhaps harder to trust your Doctor. You have to hope that what he's doing is for the greater good, because he can come across as more reckless than earlier Doctors. Thoughtless, even.

Yeah, to get what he needs. I kind of like that, though – the good of the universe and all that. I always wanted to push the Doctor into areas that were difficult for him. He can spin a lie to serve the greater good – or what he believes is the greater good. It might not be that for everyone.

He's the Doctor one feels is most likely to mess things up.

I think you're right. My Doctor could be saving the universe, then trip over, break his nose, and not be able to see. I was always interested in making him fallible. He doesn't know everything, and yet purports to. The idea that someone else would know more he finds preposterous. 'I am the cleverest man in the world! How could you possibly know more than me?' And then he'll do something

stupid. [Laughs] Hopefully, that gives him a sense of humour about himself.

How far can the show go in portraying the Doctor's manipulative side?

That's a good question. I think you probably could take it too far. But in Steven Moffat's hands, taking it too far could be really interesting.

The Doctor has gone on quite a journey this series.

Yeah, it's been a roller coaster. And I really like the fact that Steven is pushing that. That's part of the reason the show is doing so well in America, I think. I like the idea that it's serialised. You learn a bit more every week. Great science fiction is detailed and layered, and there have been many layers to explore and indulge in this year. But then you also get romps. You get pirates. You get Hitler. You get Cybermen. It has a bit of everything in there, really. Perfect example: *Let's Kill Hitler*.

Were you as excited as the rest of us when you first heard that title?

Definitely. That was *so* exciting. I thought, 'Oh, Steven, you clever old thing.' And the episode is fantastic, isn't it? Alex Kingston [River Song] regenerating is just brilliant.

And the scene straight after, in Hitler's office, where you're both –

– trying to kill each other! Yes! I mean, a) it's a joy to do it with Alex, because she's brilliant, and b) the writing is so good, because the beats are really clear. A lot of that scene was fast editing – cut, cut, cut – which actually takes a lot of the pressure of the pace off you, but I really liked having all that to play. Another example is *A Good Man Goes to War* – really great writing, a great

> ❝ **MY DOCTOR COULD BE SAVING THE UNIVERSE, THEN TRIP OVER** ❞

cliffhanger, a homage to *Star Wars* at the end there, if you're a fan of that sort of stuff. 'I am Melody Pond. I am your daughter!' None of which I knew, I might add.

You didn't know that River was going to turn out to be Amy and Rory's daughter?

Not until I read the script. Absolutely no clue until the read-through – where we had a false ending anyway, for everyone else – and then Steven took us outside afterwards, me and Karen [Gillan, who plays Amy], into the corridor at Upper Boat studios and showed us the real ending. We went, 'Whoa, that's cool! Oh my God!'

In the series finale, at long last, the Doctor makes an honest woman of River.

Yes! She *is* the Doctor's wife! Steven, you clever man. I love the way it's been teased out this year. You have to give that storyline the whole series before it's all explained, and that allows Steven to deliver something huge in the finale. Episodes 1 and 2 make much more sense when you've seen Episode 13.

In Alex's interview [see p94] she points out that your Doctor will flirt with anyone.

[Laughs] Did she now? As characters, I think that's true. Alex is a wonderful flirt. We're really good friends, so that helps. Steven once said to me that it's better if you don't flirt off set, because it means you can flirt on set. The Doctor is either really good at it or really bad at it. He can sort of be both. In that scene in Hitler's office, with River, he starts off being quite bad at flirting, and gets better. As soon as the Doctor realises it's about her trying to kill him, he's at ease. When it's her being nice, that's what freaks him out.

The Doctor can deal with people wanting to kill him –

Yeah, he gets that. He can flirt with that.

– but not with actual flirting? Ha! Do you think you're a good flirt?

In real life? I like to think so. I think Daisy [Lowe, Matt's girlfriend] would probably say I flirt with her quite well. We flirt, me and Dais'. It's good.

What advice would you give readers of the *Brilliant Book*?

On flirting? Be brave. Don't be afraid to be stupid.

Surely being rich and famous must help?

I don't think wealth or fame has anything to do with it. Either you can flirt or you can't. Well, I guess... if you're famous, if you're meant to get whoever you're flirting with and you don't, then not only are you a failure as a flirt, but you're a failure at using your fame to win you something over... which some people choose to do. Of course, I've had a girlfriend for the whole time I've been in the public eye.

In general, do you think being famous has made you a more confident person?

No, because there's more to consider. There's further to fall, in many ways. It's quite hard to have a clear and intelligent perspective on fame, because... I don't really know what it is. I mean, I do, but it's quite hard to define. It's totally transient. It's different for everyone. David Beckham is really famous. He's famous to me. Then again, I am, to other people. If anything, being famous can strip you of confidence, because everyone has an opinion on you, and it's not really real. Confidence is about satisfaction in what you're doing, and I enjoy what I do, or being unsatisfied, but chasing it anyway and working hard. In playing the Doctor, I have something that I can work hard at, get better at, and explore – be satisfied creatively. The Doctor gives me confidence.

Do you watch yourself on TV, or do you find it unsettling?
It can be unsettling. You're worrying about if you're rubbish, or interesting, or if you've made good choices, or the wrong choices... but I'm far too vain to care what other people think. It's only difficult with bedroom scenes. I watched *Christopher and His Kind* [a BBC Two film, broadcast in March 2011, in which Matt played gay novelist Christopher Isherwood] with Daisy, which was weird. But it's just pretend.

Since last year's *Brilliant Book*, as well as 14 episodes of *Doctor Who*, you've also appeared in two episodes of *Doctor Who* spin-off *The Sarah Jane Adventures*, opposite Elisabeth Sladen, who passed away earlier this year.
Yes. It was so sad. It happened so quickly as well.

What are your memories of working with Lis?
Oh, she had real *grace*. Yes, that's the word. And youth. To have such youth when you're a woman in your 60s is... I hope I seem that youthful when I'm that age. She'll be missed, especially in Cardiff. The crew was really upset because they'd become good friends with her, and I can see why. I was honoured to work with her, and thrilled to meet her. That's

the weird thing with me now – having gone from someone who didn't really watch *Doctor Who* that much, now that I'm a fan, having watched loads of it, you can never really... well, *I* can't really switch my fan bit off when I meet people like Lis.

Welcome to our world.
I know! [Laughs] It's weird, that. Does that mean I'm a proper *Doctor Who* fan now, then?

Yes, Matt. You're infected.
Brilliant! There is no show like this one. To be part of something this devoted is wonderful. I mean, not only Lis, but if you look at what happened with Nicholas Courtney [who played *Doctor Who*'s Brigadier Lethbridge-Stewart, and passed away in February 2011] – it seems like the *Doctor Who* family really gathers around, be that online or wherever. It really pays tribute. That's remarkable.

Looking to the future – have you read the 2011 Christmas special yet?
Not yet. Steven is still writing it.

Do you know anything about it?
I know the pitch and the story. I don't know who's in it yet. I know when we film it. Apart from that, I can tell you very little.

Does it worry you when the scripts are delivered so close to filming? Or does it make life more exciting?
I don't know if it makes it more exciting. It doesn't bother me, because it's the nature of the beast. It's the nature of our schedules on *Doctor Who*, really. Steven hasn't had a day off in two years, and he's working as hard as his fingers and his mind can possibly work, so we get the scripts when we're meant to get them and we go from there. But actually, it's fine because Steven is an absolute genius, so let him do his thing, I say. Give him time to make it as brilliant as it can be. The effort that goes into making this show is extraordinary. It's important to get that right.

There are going to be fewer episodes of *Doctor Who* in 2012. How do you feel about that?
Well, I mean, in some respects, for me, it's quite nice. It gives me a sort of mental break from it, and the ability to go and do other things. We're still going to shoot 14 episodes, so there is still a whole series of *Doctor Who* coming, just maybe not all in 2012. And, of course, I get to go into the 50th Anniversary in 2013, which is really cool. That's incredibly exciting. I hope the break next year is a good thing, because it seems that the anticipation is still around for the next series. It's a risk, I guess. But a good one.

Can you give us any hints of what's in store for the Doctor in the next series?
Steven told me the pitch for Episodes 1 and 2 of next season, yesterday, and I just... oh man, it's so brilliant! I got really excited. It involves lots of things I like. I literally can't wait. Trust me, there are some extraordinary times ahead...

❝ I WAS HONOURED TO WORK WITH LIS SLADEN. SHE HAD REAL GRACE ❞

A MESSAGE FROM
Madame Kovarian

Oh, *there you are!*

No, this isn't a dream. This really is *The Brilliant Book of Doctor Who 2012*. Relax, it'll be all right. You're doing fine. It's real.

My word, you look just about ready to pop with excitement, don't you?

Well, don't worry. It'll all start in a minute. We've got quite an army massing on these pages. The Papal Mainframe informs me that we've the true history of a Silurian warrior-woman, a guide to the Flesh that I've personally found invaluable, Handbots, Cybermen and a Minotaur... all of them fighting for attention. Steady now, don't lose your head – although who could blame you if you did?

Of course, there's a complete guide to all the latest outrages caused by the Doctor, and lots of information on my most remarkable project, Melody Pond. I'm so very proud.

I must say, you're handling all this very well. You've taken in quite a lot in just 15 pages. But I know you're just burning with excitement to know what will happen on the fields of Trenzalore. Well, you'll just have to keep wondering – unless one of our hapless interview subjects lets a detail or two slip out whilst under interrogation.

It's been a privilege to bring all this to you, it really has. But study these pages very carefully.

Although every care has been taken at the printing press, some of the paper may be psychic. Look out for the signs, won't you? I know you'll be most careful.

It's going to be quite a journey. But I'll be with you every step of the way.

Now then, let's not try and hold it in for any longer, shall we? Grip the book in your hands, and spread your arms nice and wide. Done that? Good.

OK then. Take a nice, deep breath, grab this page in your hands... and PULL!

A Christmas Carol

BY STEVEN MOFFAT

THE STORY

Amy and Rory's honeymoon cruise has taken a turn for the worse. The spaceliner on which they're holidaying is plummeting, out of control, through the misty atmosphere of a storm-shrouded planet. The thousands of passengers and crew on board are in mortal danger, and Amy and Rory can do nothing to help – so it's time to call in the Doctor...

Arriving on Christmas Eve, the Doctor finds his rescue attempts blocked by the miserly Kazran Sardick, ruler of Sardicktown. He controls the ice clouds that cover the city, and refuses to clear the skies so the ship can land. Cruel and cranky though Kazran is, the Doctor is convinced he can melt the old man's heart.

In a bid to rewrite the past and shape Kazran into a better man, the Doctor travels back in time, where he and the young Kazran meet a beautiful woman called Abigail. For most of each year, she is kept frozen in an icy casket deep beneath the Sardick family mansion – but each Christmas Eve, the Doctor brings Kazran to visit Abigail. Love soon blossoms between the pair but just as it looks like Kazran's whole life may have changed for the better, Abigail reveals that she is dying – and breaks his heart.

Back in the present, grief has made Kazran as bitter as ever. The Doctor has failed. It really does look like Christmas is cancelled – and time has run out for Amy and Rory...

Where Have I Seen?

MICHAEL GAMBON
Kazran Sardick
Michael's many roles include King George V in *The King's Speech* and Professor Dumbledore in the later *Harry Potter* movies.

KATHERINE JENKINS
Abigail
Abigail was Katherine's first acting role. As a classical singer she has performed for Pope John Paul II and the Queen.

NUMBER CRUNCHING

4,003 *The number of passengers facing death*

1 The number of hours left to save them

A CHRISTMAS CAROL

▶▶ This story borrows its title from its main inspiration: Charles Dickens's *A Christmas Carol*, the tale of Ebenezer Scrooge and the Ghosts of Christmas Past, Present and Future. (The Doctor met Dickens and a bunch of sort-of ghosts in *The Unquiet Dead* (2005).)
▶▶ Kazran's cloud-controlling equipment features isomorphic controls, programmed to respond only to his touch. The Doctor has been stymied by such technology before: in *The Last of the Time Lords* (2007), the Master's laser screwdriver was isomorphic. In *Pyramids of Mars* (1975), the Doctor claimed that his own TARDIS's controls were isomorphic, and in *Spearhead from Space* (1970), the same was said of the TARDIS key – though, given how often we see his companions using both these things, he presumably reprograms the TARDIS regularly to allow his friends access. Or lies a lot. ▶▶ The Doctor manages to sneak back into Kazran's mansion because all the servants have scarpered, having mysteriously and coincidentally won the lottery at the same time. (And this despite the fact that there is no lottery in Sardicktown.) He first used this trick in *School Reunion* (2006), ensuring

Fantastic Facts!

that a teacher would resign so he could take over his job. We've also seen the Doctor use his time-travelling lottery cheats to do a favour for a friend: he left Donna Noble a jackpot-winning ticket as a wedding present in *The End of Time, Part Two* (2010). ▶▶ It turns out that the Doctor is friends with singer Frank Sinatra and Nobel-winning physicist Albert Einstein. It's unclear whether Einstein met the Eleventh Doctor before or after he was kidnapped by the Rani in *Time and the Rani* (1987) and rescued by the Seventh Doctor.
▶▶ The Doctor manages to get hitched to movie star Marilyn Monroe – and this isn't the first time he's wed a famous woman from Earth's history: he explains at the start of *The End of Time, Part One* (2009) that he took so long to respond to the Oods' call partly because he was marrying Queen Elizabeth I – and we saw in *The Shakespeare Code* (2007) how well that turned out. ▶▶ Amy and Rory must have been, erm, holding their own private fancy dress party in the honeymoon suite. She wears the police outfit first seen in *The Eleventh Hour* (2010), while Rory sports his Roman get-up from *The Pandorica Opens* (2010). ▶▶ There are 4,000 passengers and crew on the ship, plus Amy and Rory. But 4,003 are reported as facing death. Hm. You don't suppose one of them might have been, say, *pregnant*...?

MAGIC MOMENT

Kazran raises a hand to strike a child for throwing a lump of coal at him. But he stops himself, struggling with his anger. The Doctor notices this...

THE DOCTOR: What am I missing?
KAZRAN: Get out. Get out of this house.
THE DOCTOR: The chairs! Of course, the chairs! Stupid me, the chairs!
KAZRAN: Chairs?
THE DOCTOR: There's a portrait on the wall behind me. Looks like you, but it's too old, so it's your father. All the chairs are angled away from it. Daddy's been dead for twenty years – but you still can't get comfortable where he can see you. There's a Christmas tree in the painting, but none in this house – on Christmas Eve. You're scared of him, and you're scared of being like him. And good for you, you're not like him, not really. Do you know why?
KAZRAN: Why?
THE DOCTOR: Because you didn't hit the boy. Merry Christmas, Mr Sardick.
KAZRAN: I despise Christmas!
THE DOCTOR: You shouldn't. It's very you.
KAZRAN: It's what? What do you mean?
THE DOCTOR: Halfway out of the dark.

DELETED!

THE DOCTOR: *[working at Kazran's cloud-controlling apparatus]* Now, this console is going to solve all my problems, or I'll eat my hat. If I had a hat. I'll eat *someone's* hat. Not someone who's *using* their hat, I don't want to shock a nun or something.

BEHIND THE SCENES
STEVEN MOFFAT
Writer

This was your first time writing the *Doctor Who* Christmas special – did it require a different approach than a regular script?
It was especially strange for me cos I was stuck in Los Angeles in April when I was writing *A Christmas Carol* – and you can't get less festive than that. I was listening to all the Christmas albums I could find just to get me into that frame of mind.

But the whole spirit of Christmas and the spirit of *Doctor Who* are kind of in tune, so it's not a show that needs much tailoring for that Christmas Day slot. The Doctor is really just a big kid, so the notion of Christmas is really exciting for him. And I've never had the chance to write a Christmas special before, so it's also exciting for me. I love the specificness of a Christmas episode – you just want it on one day of the year. So it had better be properly Christmassy!

UNSEEN ADVENTURES

>> There are plenty of 'not quite unseen' adventures in this episode: through a series of photos, we see the Doctor, Kazran and Abigail visit Egypt, Australia, France and the USA.

Welcome, traveller, to SARDICKTOWN

A GUIDE FOR THE DISCERNING VISITOR BY MESSRS CROOK, BLIGHT AND BANCOCK

Warm greetings, friend, and welcome to Sardicktown, named after the forebears of our kind and most generous benefactor, the honourable Kazran Sardick, Esq.

During your stay here, you will find all manner of entertainments and diversions to while away the hours.

Miss Garglespike's World of Pins is home to the largest collection of antique and decorative pins in the Horsehead Nebula. *(Note – If blood is drawn, seek a Physic with haste.)*

The Duckchester Tanneries provide Sardicktown with the finest leather goods. The tanners there can strip the hide off a giant Camoose in less than five minutes – an impressive and entertaining sight for all the family. *(Note – Keep your own children away from the many young employees you will meet here. No substitutions accepted.)*

The galaxy-famous *Scratchington Fish Market* is where you will find the finest selection of fresh fish, plucked from the skies that very morning! *(Note – if weather is bad, then your fish is guaranteed to have been caught within a week. Or so.)*

Dr Henry Fizzog's Museum of the Macabre is home to the mummified remains of King Zadok the Gory, the perfectly preserved larvae of a giant Gastropod, and a wide variety of torture and executional implements from across the galaxy. *(Note – not for those with a weak constitution. Children half price.)*

Sardick Towers. Residence of the venerable Kazran Sardick, Esq, and to the esteemed Sardick family for several generations, this Modern Gotho-Baroquezantine architectural masterpiece should form the vital cornerstone of any sightseeing trip around Sardicktown. *(Note – Sardick Towers is not open to the public. You can see it from most streets if you crane your neck.)*

Enjoy your visit! But don't linger too long. *WE HOPE THAT'S CLEAR.*

WORDS TO THE WISE

● Anyone wishing to meet with Mr Kazran Sardick in person may apply to the Assistant Deputy Sub-Manager of Administrative Assistance at the offices of Sardick, Sardick & Sons - 91 Throttleby Lane, Sardicktown. Please be aware that replies to correspondence may take 12 to 18 working months and that not all correspondence will receive a reply. Mr Sardick's decision is final. (Always.)

● Visitors are further warned that, due to atmospheric conditions, Sardicktown is frequently subject to infestations of airborne fish. While many are quite harmless, others are larger and more carnivorously inclined. You are urged, for the sake of us all – **DO NOT FEED THE FISH!**

When you're alone,
Silence is all you know.

A CHRISTMAS CAROL

Dear Doctor,
Rory and I having a bit of a time of it. Watched Rom. + Jul. @ the Globe last night. V. romantic! (Even though London theatre audiences stink and the play ends with loads of death.) Shakespeare says 'Hi'. Well... Actually, it was more like 'Hey nonny no', then he tried to touch my bum, but you know what I mean. Then King James 1st or the 6th or whatever turned up, found out we knew you (thanks to bigmouth husband), and tried to have us arrested and chucked in the Tower. What exactly did you do to/with his cousin? Can you pick us up from the wine cellar of our hotel, please. We'll be the ones secreted in empty barrels.

Amy xxx

LONDON
JANUARY 13
1605

2ND

The Doctor
The TARDIS

GALACTIC TELEMESSAGE SERVICE:
Transcript of voicemail from the Gardens of Zul-Thep, 9 July 3104

Hello? Doctor? Can you hear me? This is Rory. Oh... It's the answerphone. Right. Well, you see, thing is, these gardens. Turns out they're full of killer bees. And I'm not even talking about little killer bees, like in that film with Michael Caine. These things are enormous. And they can talk. Anyway... They really don't like humans, so we were wondering if you could maybe swing by, pick us up, take us somewhere else, yeah? Cos, right, we've got a whole picnic here and there is a dangerous amount of jam in it. Amy likes jam. Do they like jam? Bees I mean. Sorry! Coming Amy! Doctor - really, hurry up. They like jam a lot... argh! 〖message ends〗

Instant Message from Drago14, 3 May 2698:
Doctor - Amy and I both alive. Beach holiday slightly ruined by acid-spitting land squids. My Terry Pratchett book got kind of melted. I checked with the bookshop here but it turns out it's been out of print almost four hundred years. And they no longer sell 'books'.

Anyway, look, we really appreciate all your ideas, we honestly do. But we'd really like to go somewhere less squiddy next. With no royalty, bees, aliens, sheriffs and definitely no spiky plants of any kind. See, we've found this brochure for a cruise ship. Well Amy found it. In a travel agents next to the shop that sells acid-proof towels. Only it's a spaceship. So, like, a space cruise ship. Looks nice. No dangerous wildlife of any kind. Just nice. Anyway, can't text much longer, due to painful acid burn on my thumb. But Amy told me to write 'lots of love', so... Lots of love. Rory. (You're not getting kisses.)

CLASS OF SERVICE
This is a full-rate Telegram or Cable-gram unless its deferred character is indicated by a suitable symbol above or preceding the address.

LC=Deferred Cable
NLT=Cable Night Letters
Ship Radiogram

The filing time shown in the date line on telegrams and day letters is STANDARD TIME at point of origin. Time of receipt is STANDARD TIME at point of destination

Wyatt Earp nothing like in the films STOP Not a very nice guy STOP Tried to shoot Rory STOP Rory v upset STOP Also aliens STOP Lots of aliens STOP You never see that in the old movies do you? STOP You never see that STOP the aliens STOP And So get here pronto and STOP the aliens STOP And the randier cowboys STOP And please bring Savlon for Rory's cactus accident STOP Amy x

PLAY AMONG THE STARS, AND COME ABOARD THE

THRASYMACHUS

With room for over 4,000 passengers, the *Thrasymachus* is the largest cruise ship in the Solaris World Holiday fleet.

Why not enjoy an authentic Earth Peen-a Collah-Da on our Tropical Paradise observation deck, complete with realistic sand and palm trees, plus live music from resident bio-calypso band, the Flaming Bongos.

Or perhaps you'd prefer something with a Neo-Latin Flava? Well how about a dance lesson in our 2,000 capacity ballroom? Whether it's the rumba or the cha-cha-cha, our instructor Raoul will show you some moves!

Is fine dining your thing? Our head chef is none other than Gourmandroid X7, star of hit TV shows *Robochef* and *Robochef's Software Nightmares*. Whatever you

want, Gourmandroid X7 can create stunningly authentic food substitutes to satisfy any palate.

Or perhaps you're just looking for a quick bite? In that case, you'll find everything you could want in our food court. Tear up your Space War II ration books and clog those arteries at Greasy Bob's Authentic Mid-20th Century Café, where it's almost always 1953! Or how about grabbing yourself a McClintock's Candy Burger? You're never

more than 6 metres from a McClintock's booth aboard the *Thrasymachus*!

If you missed Halley's Comet last time it passed Earth, fear not – the *Thrasymachus* makes a scheduled fly-by of that dirty galactic snowball every single week. Twice.

Cabin fever is never a problem, as our organised space walks will leave you feeling pathetically small and insignificant as you float helplessly against the vast canvas of infinite space!

On a family break but want to get away from the kids? Gobo the Clone-Clown's World of Fun has the largest ball pit ever constructed, with a volume of over four cubic kilometres! Kids can lose themselves for hours – even days – in Gobo's World of Fun!

With prices as low as GB$46,500 per person, a trip on the *Thrasymachus* is guaranteed to be out of this world!

DISCLAIMER: Solaris World Holidays is not responsible for the extra-vehicular off-world injury, death, or impersonation by shape shifting organisms of any passenger.

HONEYMOON SPECIAL

Just married? Why not literally have a 'Honey Moon'? Our romantic Newlyweds Package takes you to the nearest moon with a suitable gravitational force and the lowest number of hostile life forms. There, you and your spouse/life partner can enjoy an afternoon of tea, cakes, and yes... you've guessed it... plenty of honey! We simply couldn't help ourselves!

"WE'LL NEVER FORGET OUR THRASYMACHUS HONEYMOON!"
Mr and Mrs P, Earth

McLintock® CANDY BURGERS

EPISODE 1

The Impossible Astronaut

BY STEVEN MOFFAT

THE STORY

A date, a time, a map reference. Amy, Rory and River have all received invitations, summoning them to the deserts of Utah in the United States of America in 2011. There they meet the Doctor for a picnic on the shores of Lake Silencio – and it seems the Time Lord has something important to show them.

As his friends watch from a distance, the Doctor walks to meet an astronaut rising from the waters. The astronaut lifts its arm and suddenly sky-shattering bolts of energy thud into the Doctor's body. Our hero starts to regenerate but, with a final, thundering shot, the astronaut fells him for good. The Doctor is dead.

Or is he? It turns out there was one more invitation: this one was sent to the Doctor – an earlier Doctor – and he's arrived just in time to bump into his mourning friends.

All the clues point to Earth's past. The Space Race. The Apollo 11 mission, and the desperate battle to put a man on the moon. Travelling back to 1969, the Doctor starts to uncover a centuries-long manipulation of human history. Finally, he comes face to face with a force that's been following him for years. And Silence will fall...

Where Have I Seen?

MARK SHEPPARD
Canton Everett Delaware III
Mark has appeared in a number of hit US shows, including *24*, *Battlestar Galactica* and *Supernatural*.

STUART MILLIGAN
President Nixon
Jonathan Creek star Stuart previously voiced a character in the *Doctor Who* animation *Dreamland* (2009).

NUMBER CRUNCHING

2 DOCTORS 200 *years to save one of them*

THE IMPOSSIBLE ASTRONAUT

>> As we found out in *The Time of Angels/Flesh and Stone* (2010), River Song currently resides in the Stormcage Containment Facility, where she is imprisoned for the murder of a 'great man'. **>>** River describes her chronology, relative to the Doctor's, as 'all back to front – my past is his future', adding that 'we're travelling in opposite directions'. Just look at Jim the Fish: the future Doctor knows all about Jim, but the earlier Doctor has yet to meet him. River, coming from a time after both these Doctors, knows Jim the Fish well – just as she knows what's going to happen to the Doctor and who the astronaut is. (But, as she'll explain in *The Wedding of River Song* (2011), those facts are spoilers.) Each time we meet her, River is a little younger and the Doctor is a little older. Her meeting with the two Doctors here does, however, wrinkle her neat 'opposite directions' assertion: the Doctors we see are presented to us in reverse order, but within a single 'instance' of River's relationship with him, during which she is travelling – very conventionally – forward in time. So, still opposite directions – they've just swapped trajectories! Furthermore, the Doctor/River meeting in *Let's Kill Hitler* (2011) features a much earlier River (earlier than any the Doctor has met up to that point) but a Doctor who comes from a time between the two Doctors seen in *The Impossible Astronaut*. Keeping up? Finally, in *The Wedding of River Song*, both characters are older than during their last on-screen meeting, thoroughly debunking her claim. 'Opposite directions'? River should know by now: things are never that simple in a Steven Moffat script! **>>** River also mentions that 'the day is coming when I'll look into [the Doctor's] eyes and he won't have the faintest idea who I am – and I think it's going to kill me'. This day was chronicled in *Silence in the Library/Forest of the Dead* (2008).

Fantastic Facts!

>> The Doctor – both of him – calls Amy's husband 'Rory the Roman', a reference to *The Big Bang* (2010) and Rory's long life as the Auton facsimile-cum-Roman centurion who guarded Amy while she was trapped in the Pandorica for 2,000 years. **>>** During the astronaut's attack on the shores of the lake, the Doctor starts to regenerate – before a final shot terminates the process and ends his life. River explains: 'It killed him in the middle of his regeneration cycle. His body was already dead. He didn't make it to the next one.' We've seen this happen before – in an alternate timeline, anyway – in *Turn Left* (2008), in which the Tenth Doctor, while battling the Empress of the Racnoss (see *The Runaway Bride* (2006) for the official version), was killed before he could regenerate. **>>** In *The Invasion* (1968), we learn that the TARDIS's visual stabiliser circuit is part of the technology which controls the appearance of the ship's outer shell. When it's damaged and removed in that story, the TARDIS becomes invisible. Presumably, it's through manipulation of this circuit that the TARDIS is rendered invisible in this episode, too. **>>** The Doctor asks the President's security team for Jammie Dodgers (as

seen in 2010's *Victory of the Daleks*) and a fez (2010's *The Big Bang*). And while we're on the subject of the President: although *The Impossible Astronaut* doesn't dwell on Richard Nixon's unpopularity, it doesn't dodge the issue either – chiefly in the rather cool treatment he receives from Canton. Cut lines from the script refer to both the Vietnam War and the Watergate incident, following which Nixon became the first, and so far only, US president to resign from office. See page 30 for more on 'Tricky Dicky'. **>>** When they first appear in the script, Steven Moffat's stage directions describe the Silents as like 'Munch's The Scream', referencing the famously disturbing painting by Edvard Munch. **>>** Although she knows she has to tell the Doctor something, Amy seems remarkably unsure about her pregnancy throughout this episode. One minute she knows what secret she's hiding; the next, it's as if she's not pregnant at all. As we'll find out in *The Almost People* and *A Good Man Goes to War*, this is because it isn't actually Amy in these scenes: it's her Flesh duplicate, receiving flashes of memory and experience from the real Amy, who is actually being held prisoner by Madame Kovarian.

MAGIC MOMENT

Amy tries to persuade the Doctor that he has no choice but to follow the summons back to the US in 1969...

AMY: You have to do this. And you can't ask why.
THE DOCTOR: Are you being threatened? Is somebody making you say that?
AMY: No.
THE DOCTOR: Are you lying?
AMY: I'm not lying.
This is so hard to do, goes against everything. Agony. He's still staring so hard at Amy, right into her eyes, reading her soul.
THE DOCTOR: Swear to me. Swear on something that matters.
AMY: ... Fish fingers and custard.
A silence. He just looks at her.
THE DOCTOR: My life in your hands, Amelia Pond.

WHERE IN THE WORLD?

>> Although shots for *Daleks in Manhattan/Evolution of the Daleks* (2007) were taped in New York, this episode marks the first time scenes for *Doctor Who* featuring the series' stars were filmed in the USA, in and around the Valley of the Gods in Utah.

UNSEEN ADVENTURES

>> We catch a snippet of saucy under-the-skirt action with noble folk Charles and Matilda in the 17th century, plus the Doctor escaping the Germans in World War II (see p31).

DELETED!

Amy desperately wants to find a way to save the future Doctor, but River points out that some moments in history are just too big...

AMY: Time can be rewritten.
RIVER: Not all of it.
AMY: Says who?
RIVER: Who do you think?
AMY: He also says bow ties are cool.
RIVER: Fair point.
AMY: Look at him. Would you let your husband out looking like that?
RIVER: Who says he's my husband?
AMY: But if he was – would you?
RIVER: Who says I'd let him out at all?

BEHIND THE SCENES
STEVEN MOFFAT
Writer

The series really hits the ground running with the death of the Doctor. How vital is it to keep making big splashes with the series' wider story?
I don't know if it's important, but it's one way in, and one we haven't tried before. A big, impossible conundrum that will motor under the next 13 episodes. It's not the way to do it every year, but it's exciting, and refreshing to do it this year. We've always tended to start with fun romps, to remind and reboot, so it's even more of a shock.

Everything about this episode is big – including the locations. Was it satisfying to film such a significant moment in the epic setting of the Valley of the Gods?
Size is tough on television, so yes, very satisfying. And we were doing America, for real, actually going there. We all just felt we need to give it cinema scale – a blast of blue sky and big mountains!

Though you're not blatant about it, you don't dodge the issue of President Nixon's unpopularity. Is it important to acknowledge that the Doctor can't only meet history's 'good guys'?
It was an accident. I wanted to use the moon landing, so I just checked who was president at the time. And damn, if it wasn't the rubbish one. For a while I thought about a fictional one – a standard-issue, unnamed President, like in *The Sound of Drums* [2007] – but that didn't feel right for a story partly about real events. Then I thought it might be fun to use Nixon. There was something comically awkward about him, and it always gives the show a bit of spice if there's someone in it the Doctor doesn't like.

THE IMPOSSIBLE ASTRONAUT

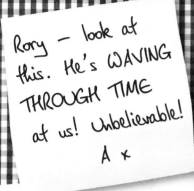

Rory – look at this. He's WAVING THROUGH TIME at us! Unbelievable!

A x

as you will see. The final decision rests with you, the reader. Are there rational explanations for all these events? Or do some things defy our understanding? Read on and find out...

'THE UNNAMED DOCTOR'

One of the most intriguing and compelling of all the documented historical impossibilities I have come across in my studies so far is what I like to call 'The Strange Case of the Unnamed Doctor'. Nearly a dozen incidents of this mysterious, dark-haired young man cropping up in wildly varying locations and periods of our history makes this one of the most mysterious cases herein. Some have called him the 'Bow-Tied Boy', others the 'Time Drifter', but whoever he was, or is, he certainly seems to get around...

The Bayeux Tapestry – though, of course, not actually a tapestry – has fascinated scientists, historians and the public alike for centuries. Of all the images depicted in this fascinating commemoration of the events surrounding the Norman Conquest, none is more difficult to comprehend than the seemingly anachronistic figure in the bow tie pointing towards what is now widely thought to be Halley's Comet. Could he be our Unnamed Doctor? And what of the strange words 'Cooee pond'? Certainly not Latin. A joke by the nuns who embroidered this masterpiece, perhaps? We may never know.

* * *

As was often the case with the speedy turnaround of the famous *Carry On* comedy films, publicity pictures were sometimes taken before the cameras even started rolling. Though the actor pictured here (identified as 'John Smith' on the back of the photograph) did not end up playing the role of the Khasi of Kalabar in Peter Rogers' 1968 camp classic *Up The Khyber* – the role eventually being filled by veteran *Carry On* star Kenneth Williams – he clearly got as far as a costume fitting.

In an entry from 12 March 1968 in Kenneth Williams's diary, Smith is referred to briefly.

'Costume's far too big,' complains Williams. 'Daft idiots offering the role to Smith. Who's heard of him anyway? Should never have turned it down in first place... Met JS briefly yesterday at Pinewood. Nice looking chap. Checked for him later in Spotlight directory – no trace! Very strange. Dinner at Biagi's with Louie. Bowels playing up again.'

No other clues remain as to why or how this 'John Smith' was hired or fired from the movie.

This is a facsimile of a recently discovered contemporary transcript of a 1601 production of William Shakespeare's *Hamlet*. A character simply named 'Medic' interrupts Hamlet's famous 'skull' speech with lines that in all other folios are given to Horatio. It has been widely dismissed as a forgery, but I have other ideas.

> HAMLET: Alas, poor Yorick! I knew him, Horatio.
>
> MEDIC: It's not Horatio actually. He's just popped off to, er, the olde privvie. Tis I, m'lord, your old mucker the Doctor.
>
> HAMLET: A fellow of infinite jest, of most excellent fancy, he hath borne me on his back a thousand times.
>
> MEDIC: Hold on a sec. (Loudly) Hey Pond, it's me! The Doctor! Remember? Making a little Shakespearean cameo. (To Hamlet) Sorry, carry on.
>
> HAMLET: And now, how abhorred in my imagination –
>
> MEDIC: (Musing) Funny name 'Hamlet'. Is that your surname? Always wondered. So, are you, sort of, Dave Hamlet? Or... Marcus J Hamlet? Oh, of course, it's Danish. More like Jørgen Hamlet then? Jørgen Dave Hamlet. That works.
>
> HAMLET: Wilt thou shut up?

28

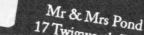

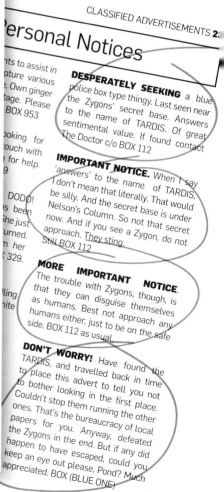

PROFESSOR CLIFFORD MEASEY

*   *   *

This I stumbled across in an 1819 book entitled *Mrs Molbury's Collected Rhymes Both Ancient and Modern*. Though the first verse is the same as those usually found in texts of this period, the rest of the tale is very different indeed. What could a 'Sontaran' be? Considering a 'humpty-dumpty' is supposedly a 17th-century beverage of boiled brandy and ale, might this Sontaran too have been an ancient cocktail of some kind? And could the 'Fool' in question be the Unnamed Doctor?

> Humpty Dumpty sat on a wall,
> Humpty Dumpty had a great fall.
> All the King's Horses and all the King's Men
> Couldn't put Humpty together again.
>
> But then came a cry, 'twas from the King's Fool:
> Opining that bow ties look fashionably cool.
> He stepped from a blue box and said with a grin:
> 'What a terrible pickle you've got yourselves in.'
>
> 'Humpty,' he said, 'is far more than he seems.
> No egg but a monster beyond your worst dreams.
> So I would suggest, you give him a wide berth
> He's a Sontaran Trooper who's stranded on Earth.'
>
> The Fool waved his wand, and Humpty awoke,
> Then the Fool knelt beside him and in hushed tones spoke:
> 'I've saved you from death, so we must face the facts –
> You are now in my debt, and I've work for you, Strax...'

Further references to our Doctor crop up in even more unexpected places, among

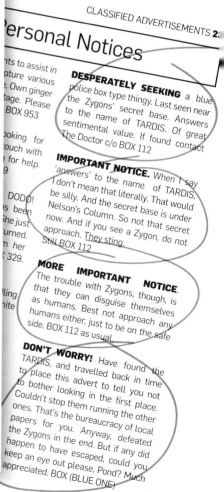

CLASSIFIED ADVERTISEMENTS 2:

Personal Notices

...nts to assist in
...pture various
... Own ginger
...tage. Please
... BOX 953

...ooking for
...ouch with
... for help.
...9

... DODO!
...s been
...she just
...urned.
... her
...X 329.

...lling
...ite

DESPERATELY SEEKING a blue police box type thingy. Last seen near the Zygons' secret base. Answers to the name of TARDIS. Of great sentimental value. If found contact The Doctor c/o BOX 112

IMPORTANT NOTICE. When I say 'answers' to the name of TARDIS, I don't mean that literally. That would be silly. And the secret base is under Nelson's Column. So not that secret now. And if you see a Zygon, do not approach. They sting. Still BOX 112

MORE IMPORTANT NOTICE. The trouble with Zygons, though, is that they can disguise themselves as humans. Best not approach any humans either, just to be on the safe side. BOX 112 as usual.

DON'T WORRY! Have found the TARDIS, and travelled back in time to place this advert to tell you not to bother looking in the first place. Couldn't stop them running the other ones. That's the bureaucracy of local papers for you. Anyway, defeated the Zygons in the end. But if any did happen to have escaped, could you keep an eye out please, Pond? Much appreciated. BOX (BLUE ONE)

29

CLASSIFIED ADVERTISEME...

...nal Notices

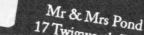

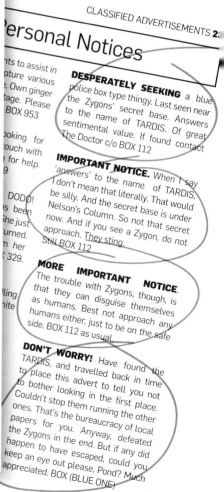

Thank you for shopping at
FOODFARE

APPLES	£1.27
MIXED NUTS	£1.35
YOGHURT	£0.49
INSTANT MASH	£1.12
TEA BAGS	£2.99
SKIMMED MILK	£0.89
MARGARINE	£1.10
EMMENTAL CHEESE	£1.82
TOILET TISSUE	£4.49
HONEY	£1.99
EGGS	£1.25
DEODORANT	£2.65
ORGANIC SHALLOTS	£1.19
COD IN BATTER	£2.79
TOOTHPASTE	£1.29
ORANGE JUICE	£0.89
RICE CAKES	£0.69

Mr & Mrs Pond
17 Twig...

Tricky Dicky

JUST WHO WAS RICHARD NIXON?

Richard Milhous Nixon was the 37th President of the USA. Born on 9 January 1913 in Yorba Linda, California, Nixon served in the US Navy in the Second World War, rising to the rank of Lieutenant Commander. In 1952, after serving as a junior senator, he became Vice President to Dwight D Eisenhower, making him one of the youngest Vice Presidents of all time. However, when he tried running for President in 1960, he found himself up against the younger, cooler, more photogenic John F Kennedy. In a televised debate between the two, Nixon refused to let the make-up assistants work their magic, and so appeared before the nation looking noticeably pale and sweaty. Many think it was this that lost Nixon the election.

Eight years later he made another run for it – and this time Nixon won. America, however, was a troubled nation, and Nixon was now President of a country mired in the Vietnam War.

Perhaps his greatest achievement as President came in 1972, when Nixon visited China and met with Chairman Mao Zedong – the first time a US President had visited the country since the Communist Revolution.

But back in Washington, things were about to turn very nasty indeed. Nixon's cronies paid five men to break into the rival Democratic Party's headquarters at the Watergate Complex. The plan was to steal information that might ruin the Democrats' chances in the next election, but the five burglars were busted, and investigators eventually linked them with Nixon's Committee to Re-elect the President (known as 'CReeP' – we're not making this up). Amazingly, Nixon held on to the keys to the White House for a further two years, famously telling the nation, 'I am not a crook!'

Investigators begged to differ, however, for Nixon, it turned out, had recorded many Oval Office conversations, and these tapes proved he'd tried to cover up his involvement in the burglary and lied to the world.

Perhaps he shouldn't have taken the Doctor's advice to tape everything and trust no one quite so literally...

Nixon quit as President in 1974 – the first and, to date, only time a US President has ever resigned. He was succeeded by Vice President Gerald Ford, who then pardoned Nixon for any federal crimes he may have committed while he was President, letting him off the hook completely.

Three years later, Richard Nixon was interviewed by British TV presenter David Frost, who directly accused the former President of lying and committing a crime. The interviews were watched by over 45 million people, and later turned into the film *Frost/Nixon*. With the ex-President a seemingly never-ending source of fascination to the viewing public, Nixon has rarely been out of the limelight. Another film, *Nixon*, was made in 1995, with the title role played by Sir Anthony Hopkins, while in Matt Groening's animated series *Futurama*, the villainous, disembodied head of Richard Nixon is elected President of Earth in the year 3000.

The real Richard Nixon died in 1994 at the age of 81. His presidency was one of the most dramatic the USA has ever seen, and Watergate remains the most infamous political scandal of all time. Some might argue that Nixon should be remembered as the man who oversaw the moon landings, or helped open diplomatic relations between the USA and China. However, many more will remember him, now and forever, as a crook.

He did help save the world from the Silence, though. Not that anybody will remember *that*...

TOP SECRET

INT. EARTH TUNNEL - NIGHT

Darkness and torches, a section of low wood-
scaffolded tunnel, like you see in POW movies.
CAPTAIN SIMMONS, streaked in mud, the tunnel behind
him receding into darkness. He's flat on his front,
at the end of the tunnel. He is calling up into the
vertical section, which is clearly the tunnel exit.

                    CAPTAIN SIMMONS
              Doctor, what can you see?
              Are we past the wire? Are
              we in the woods?

Abruptly THE DOCTOR's face appears in front of
him, hanging upside down from the vertical tunnel
sections.

                    THE DOCTOR
              Is the Commandant's office
              painted a sort of a green
              colour, with a big flag on
              the wall?

Now angry voices in German, and lights snap on around
the Doctor, as from a room above.

                    THE DOCTOR
              I think the answer is
              probably 'yes'.   CUT TO:

INT. AMY AND RORY'S FLAT - DAY

RORY slumped watching telly, AMY is snuggled
next to him, still with her Myths and Historical
Impossibilities book.

                    AMY
              Six months later, every
              allied prisoner escapes from
              the camp in a single night
              - during a production of
              a musical show that hadn't
              even been written yet. Even
              the Germans were taking
              part. By the time the SS got
              there, the Commandant was
              doing a solo!   CUT TO:

INT. POW CAMP - BIG HUT - NIGHT   **EXCISE THIS!**

This fast, just a glimpse: a shot of a number of SS,
jaws dropped in horror, guns levelled. The flickering
light of an a off-screen stage is playing over them,
and we hear ...

                    COMMANDANT
                (Singing: German accent)
              If were a rich man,
              Daidle deedle daidle
              Daidle daidle deedle
              daidle dum

(Or any song we're able to clear - 'I am what I am'
would be funny.)

MAKING MONSTERS

In Series Six, the *Doctor Who* team managed to create a monster which rivalled even the legendary Weeping Angels for pure creepiness. Creatures which weren't just terrifying to look at, but which you completely forgot about the moment you looked away. Prepare yourselves for...

THE SILENCE

Doctor Who showrunner Steven Moffat introduced the Silence in his scripts for *The Impossible Astronaut* and *Day of the Moon*, having teased viewers with the promise that 'Silence Will Fall' throughout the previous series. Enter Neill Gorton, the man who runs long-serving monster-makers Millennium FX, and whose task it was to bring the Silence to terrifying life.

'Obviously, the script usually gives a description of sorts,' Neill says. 'Steven referenced Edvard Munch's classic painting *The Scream*. He felt the Silence could have inspired the painting, so that instantly gives you a good place to start because it's such a nightmarish image.'

Neill was also inspired by 'greys' – the classic image of aliens from the 1950s and 1960s. 'The greys had big bulbous heads. They were also less than a metre tall,' Neill explains. 'The script didn't specifically describe the Silence as tall, but it kept describing them as "looming" over the Doctor or Amy. They're both six feet tall, so if something's going to loom over them, it's got to be pretty big!'

'We didn't want them to be muscular or powerful-looking,' Neill adds, 'so I thought they should be a tall and very slim version of those "grey" aliens, which felt like a spooky idea, so I went away and created designs based on that.'

Neill first sculpted a small-scale 'maquette' statue of a Silent. 'I took that along to the meeting and I was immediately told to go ahead and build them.' He admits there's often much more back-and-forth

discussion before an alien design is settled upon. 'Sometimes people say, "We've got an alien but we don't know quite what we want" and you then spend weeks coming up with different ideas. But because the Silence were nicely described in the script, everyone already had a very similar picture in their heads.'

So when did the Silence's distinctive suits come into play? 'It didn't make any sense for us to build full bodies,' Neill says, 'because the story was more

MAKING MONSTERS

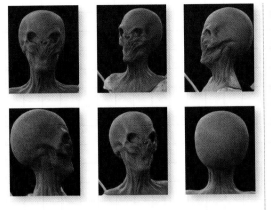

focused on how their heads and faces looked. There were various suggestions for costumes, but the suits seemed to fit the 1960s time period. There's something very weird about seeing this traditional suit, but with a bizarre alien head and hands poking out. We made it even spookier by building some air-bladders into the head, to make the temples pulse.'

Millennium recruited Dutch actor and stuntman Marnix Van Den Broeke as their main Silence performer. 'We wanted a tall chap,' Neill says, 'who would be scary and intimidating in a different way to something like the Minotaur, by being quite graceful. Marnix is over two metres tall and does ballet, so he's got great movement. His face is covered with a mask, so he has to tell the story with his body instead – and dancers are trained to do that. We designed the head around him but built it up so it's actually about another 15 centimetres above his own head. The Silence's eyes are about level with the top of his head.'

Is Marnix looking out through the mouth, then? 'He's not looking out at all, because we wouldn't have been able to hide his eyes,' Neill laughs. 'We made a couple of slits in deep areas, but they didn't line up very well with his eyes. By twisting his head, he could *just* peek out, but our actors were generally blind inside those heads. Again, that's why using dancers helps, because they can hit the same spots on the studio floor with amazing accuracy.'

The Mill's computer-generated effects were utilised when the Silence were required to open their mouths. We first see this when poor Joy gets atomised in *The Impossible Astronaut*'s striking bathroom scene.

'Millennium FX made two different Silence

heads,' says Murray Barber, The Mill's Visual FX Supervisor for *Doctor Who*. 'One with the jaw shut and another with the jaw extended. We used CG to add the mouth and give it depth, otherwise you'd be looking at the actor's face.'

'We talked about giving the inside of the Silence's mouths a similar look to what happens when you suck on a burst balloon,' Murray notes. 'It puckers as it goes into your mouth. We ended up doing a CG jaw, which was tricky with the bathroom lights flickering in that scene. We put four little green dots on the mask, around its mouth, so that we could track them as the head and the camera moved. Without those, it's nigh-on impossible to track a face – unless someone's got a spot on their chin or something.'

AYE AYE!

The Silence's freaky hands were inspired by an equally freaky woodland creature...

The Aye Aye Lemur is a nocturnal mammal, native to Madagascar. It has rodent-like teeth and an unusual method of finding food. 'It has one super-long bony finger,' says Neill Gorton. 'It uses this to pull termites out of little holes in trees. Proportionally, it's way longer than all the other fingers and looks really bony and creepy.'

Neill was inspired by the Aye Aye when it came to designing the Silence's horrible hands. 'I wanted a three-finger design,' he recalls, 'and something suitably alien, and the Aye Aye's finger looked like nothing on Earth.'

While the final hand design was very effective onscreen, Neill wants to make them even more frightening if the Silence ever return. 'We just didn't get it quite bony enough,' he grins. 'It worked fine in the show, but if we do them again, I'll make those strange, long hands even scarier!'

Murray reveals that his 11-year-old daughter thinks the Silence are 'the scariest things ever. Probably because it isn't an obviously CG monster. It looks like a real creature, which in some ways makes it more disturbing. The close-up stuff is usually better when done with prosthetics – and it certainly was in this case. It all worked very well.'

The Mill also supplied the Silence's weaponry – and faced the challenge of destroying Joy in a way which was appropriate to a show airing in the early evening on BBC One.

'We wanted to push the boundaries and find a new way of killing people,' says Murray with a chuckle. 'Normally when you blow someone up, you'd see blood, but we were told to "avoid anything red", so we went for more of an ashy look. After the long build-up, we made sure the final disintegration was pretty quick.'

Moffat, Millennium and The Mill's combined heroic efforts have brought us a new monster fully equipped to scare viewers witless.

'That's what Steven's wanted for this whole season,' Murray says, 'to make *Doctor Who* even more scary, just as some of us older folks remember it from when we were kids hiding behind the sofa. The Silence definitely tick all the boxes for that.'

'The Silence have gone down incredibly well,' Neill Gorton enthuses. 'People were already talking about them being "a classic", when they'd only been in a couple of episodes. That was seriously exciting for us.'

'Once Amy's gone, she's gone. *Death could be an option*'

Amy Pond's alter ego, **Karen Gillan**, tells us how she wrapped her head around this season's twists, and the way she'd like Amy's story to conclude...

K aren Gillan can't stop apologising. 'I'm so, *so* sorry,' she says. 'I had a last-minute audition, and then a dub.' She's only 45 minutes late for her chat with the *Brilliant Book*, having hotfooted it from a Wardour Street dubbing theatre, where she's been laying down additional dialogue for her upcoming BBC Four drama *We'll Take Manhattan*, in which she plays 1960s supermodel Jean Shrimpton. It's Karen's first major drama role since she was cast as Amy Pond in *Doctor Who*, so we're delighted she found the time to talk to us at all.

'I've made it clear since I was really young that this is what I want to do,' says the Inverness-born actress. 'By the time I went out to pursue a career in acting, it had been coming for quite a while. My family has always said, "If you want to do it, go for it. But if you're going to go for it, go for it properly. Don't do it half-heartedly."'

There's very little that's half-hearted about Karen. In person

she's as vibrant, and loopy, and earnestly unrestrained as Amy Pond, overflowing with energy. She is as silly as she is stunning – 1.8 metres tall (the same as Matt Smith), bright auburn hair, and deep brown eyes that draw you in. But she's certainly not just a pretty face. Over the past two years, Karen, now 23, has proven herself to be a bona fide leading lady, and a fine foil to Smith's wayward Time Lord...

How do you think Amy has fared this series?
She's gone through the mill, hasn't she? But I love the fact that so many extreme things have happened to her.

We don't want her to stay the same. In the first series I did, I wanted her to be like a child in an adult's body, an overgrown kid, and a bit sarky – all those things that a teenager might be, because she never quite grew up properly after meeting the Doctor when she was so young. She finally got a bit of closure by the end of last series, so she began this year as, by comparison, quite a settled person... and then the biggest things happen to her. She's a Flesh avatar! She's River Song's mum! Where did that come from? I feel really lucky that I get to play all those things.

At the end of the series, Amy and Rory are left behind on Earth with a nice house and a flash car. If you were offered the chance to travel the universe in the TARDIS with the Doctor, or stay on Earth with Rory and –
I would get in the TARDIS before you'd even finished the question.

But it's dangerous in space!
I know, but then you could get run

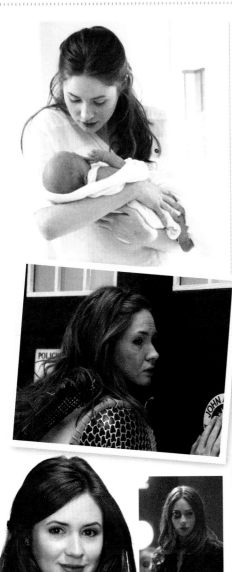

over outside the door of your house.

That sounds more like something Rory would do.

[Laughs] At least you're going to die in style in the TARDIS! But I'm at a point in my life, as Karen, where I want an adventure. I'm not ready to settle down back home, and sip champagne with my husband... um, not that I have a husband. So right now I would definitely get in the TARDIS, but it's a really interesting choice for Amy to make at this point... though it kind of *isn't* her choice, is it?

You obviously have a lot of fun on *Doctor Who* – do you worry that you'll never have a job that you enjoy this much again?

I worry about that all the time. We get to do a different episode every two weeks, in a different world, a different time, with a different cast. Also, me, Arthur and Matt are so in sync with each other now. We really feel like a team. Things would be boring without them. As soon as we got back together the other day, to do a couple of pick-ups for *Let's Kill Hitler*, we were back in the groove within seconds – rolling around in a cornfield, dancing! You just don't get that with everyone you meet in life. They will be a massive part of what I miss about *Doctor Who*.

When you started on *Doctor Who*, you were all relative unknowns.

Yes, and it's so nice that we've experienced this massive change – which has a huge impact on a person's life – together. I guess that's why we're so in sync.

Have Matt and Arthur changed over the last couple of years?

It's funny watching Arthur, as he's kind of going through it a year later than me and Matt, because he wasn't in *Doctor Who* so regularly last

series, but he is now. Obviously, his life did change with the last series, but I've *really* seen it this year. You get recognised in the street. You start thinking in a different way. It's interesting to see him deal with it.

There must be extra pressure on Matt as he's the show's lead actor.

Yeah, he's very much the face of everything to do with *Doctor Who*. He's got the weight of that on his shoulders. I saw him being nervous about it when we started. But then he smashed it. I had no doubt that people would fall in love with him in seconds. Genuinely, there wasn't a moment when I thought, 'What if people don't like the show with us in it?' It wasn't me being cocky or anything. As soon as our first episodes went out, I realised what had happened, and I went, 'Whoa, oh my God!' The size of this show just didn't impact on me until then.

By and large, *Doctor Who* gets great press. On the occasions it doesn't, do you let it affect you?

To be honest, I'm very much aware that it's out there. Yeah, of course. If you've gotten a lot of good stuff written about you, there's going to be a backlash. It's inevitable. But it's fine to have mixed reactions sometimes.

It keeps you on your toes.

Exactly. Plus, if I was in a debate with someone and they didn't agree with me, I'm not going to hate them for it.

Let's talk about the climax of *The Almost People* –

Yes! It was amazing!

Amy explodes, then wakes up somewhere far away, nine months pregnant – it's one of *Doctor Who*'s most shocking cliffhangers ever.

Yeah, that was freaky. Really, really scary. Especially the notion of

〞 ME, ARTHUR AND MATT ARE SO IN SYNC WITH EACH OTHER NOW 〞

thinking that everything's all right, and then suddenly waking up to that.

How scary is *too* scary? Can the show ever overstep the mark?

Well, it really pushed the boundaries... but I think they can always be pushed slightly more, don't you? You've got to get it right. But I think we can go further.

What do you draw on when playing River's mum? How do you get into a mumsy place?

Well, I've seen my mum get like that, get in states that I've had to get into while playing Amy as a mum. Also, feeling that protectiveness over someone – like, I'm quite protective of my little cousin, Caitlin [Blackwood, who plays young Amelia] – so it's drawing on experiences like that.

What kind of mother do you think you'll make one day?

I've always said, 'I'm going to be a cool mum. I'm going to let them do their own thing...' But as I get older, and as I pretend to be a mother in *Doctor Who*, I realise that I am actually quite strict. [Laughs] I will be a lot more overprotective than I thought I'd be.

How do you feel about having become a TV sex symbol?

Well, I've got quite a rational view on things. I've seen sci-fi shows, and I know that everybody loved Scully in *The X Files*, and that's because she's a girl in a really cool show. So I think it's to do with that, rather than me. If anything, I look in the mirror and go, 'Urgh, put some make-up on!' I'm not a pretty sight without make-up in the morning. Just ask Matt or Arthur.

In *The Girl who Waited*, we meet Amy in her 50s – and it's still you.

Yes! I didn't want some else to do it.

That must have made you think about what will happen when you're that age?

Yep. And I don't age well, I've learned. I age really badly.

Why do you think that?

Because of the prosthetics. [Laughs] It's horrific. I'm going to have to try to take care of myself. What was quite depressing, but in a weird way nice, was taking the prosthetics off and seeing a young face underneath. But then I started thinking, 'When I'm actually that age, I can't take it off!'

After all she's been through, how come Amy hasn't had a nervous breakdown yet?

Well, even when we first meet her, as a 7-year-old, she's able to just go with things and, kind of, accept the absurd. It's because of what happened to her – having a box fall out of the sky, and the Doctor come out of the box, and never quite listening to the psychiatrists telling her it didn't happen. She can suspend her disbelief, which is why she's remained with the Doctor, I think.

Is Amy in love with the Doctor?

As far as I see it, Rory is the one that she loves *in that way*. The Doctor she loves in a completely different way.

Who's more important to her?

That's harder. The Doctor is her childhood hero, and she idolises him. She hates to show that she idolises him, and she hides it well, but she probably idolises him a lot more than she does anyone else. Even Rory.

You and Arthur Darvill aren't in the 2011 Christmas special... but you'll be back next series, right?

I don't want to give anything away, but I know exactly what's happening and I'm very happy.

We'll take that as a 'yes'.

But when I leave properly, that's it. I don't want Amy to pop up again every so often, because for me it would take away from the big, emotional goodbye. I'm definite on that.

Do you think you'll stick to it?

Yeah, and Steven Moffat wants it as well. We've really discussed this. We went out to dinner and talked it over. When Amy actually, properly leaves, we both really want it to be for good.

So Amy could even be killed off?

I think it could be done, if you tackled it right. Not that I wouldn't love to pop back every so often. I really, genuinely would. But just in terms of how it's remembered... once she's gone, she's gone. So death could be an option. I want people to remember the Amy Pond era of *Doctor Who* as a good one.

EPISODE 2
Day of the Moon

BY STEVEN MOFFAT

THE STORY

It's three months later, and the Doctor is being held prisoner by the CIA at Nevada's notorious Area 51. Canton is scouring the country, hunting the Time Lord's friends.

Amy and Rory fall, while River escapes. But Canton seems too concerned with capturing them to notice something odd – they have covered their skin with tally marks. What are they counting? And why mark the count on their own bodies?

When the bodies of his friends are brought to the impenetrable cell holding the Doctor, all becomes clear – it's been a cunning ruse. Amy and Rory are fine, and Canton is working with the Doctor to defeat the Silence. Leaving the cell in the TARDIS, they pick up River and head off to get to the bottom of this latest threat to humanity.

In a crumbling orphanage in New York state, Canton and Amy start to find some answers. They think the little girl in the spacesuit may have come from here – but they weren't counting on finding a nest of Silence hiding in one of the dormitories. Nor does Amy expect to see an impossible woman through an impossible hatch – a hatch in a door that leads to a room full of photos. Including one of Amy and a baby...

NUMBER CRUNCHING

‖‖‖‖ ‖‖‖‖ ✕✕ ‖‖‖ ‖‖‖‖ ‖‖

DAY OF THE MOON

>> The Doctor's prison is built out of 'zero-balanced dwarf star alloy – the densest material in the universe'. Dwarf star alloy was introduced in *Warriors' Gate* (1981), in which the metal was said to be able to hold 'time-sensitive' beings: in that story, they're referring to Tharils, but it makes sense that it would make the perfect prison for a Time Lord too. (The metal was also used to make the chains that would forever bind Father of Mine in 2007's *Human Nature/The Family of Blood*.) >> From her daring skyscraper dive, River lands in the TARDIS's swimming pool – which was first introduced in *The Invasion of Time* (1978), jettisoned before *Paradise Towers* (1987), and reinstated to cause a splash before *The Eleventh Hour* (2010). >> 'No, I think she's just dreaming,' purrs Madame Kovarian as she checks in on her patient through an inexplicable hatch – freaking out Amy, along with millions of viewers. Clearly, the real Amy is sleeping at this point – but perhaps the Flesh Amy's creepy experiences are manifesting in her real mind as nightmares? >> When one of the creatures reminds the Doctor that 'Silence will fall', we see flashbacks to mentions of the Silence

Fantastic Facts!

in *The Eleventh Hour* and *The Vampires of Venice* (2010). >> The Doctor describes the Silents' time ship as 'very Aickman Road', adding that he's 'seen one of these before'. He's referring to the time ship seen in *The Lodger* (2010) – and here, in this episode, he finally learns why it was 'abandoned'. >> As the Doctor says goodbye to President Nixon, he cheekily asks him to 'Say hi to David Frost for me'. In 1977, almost three years after Nixon had resigned from office, he decided to try to clean up his

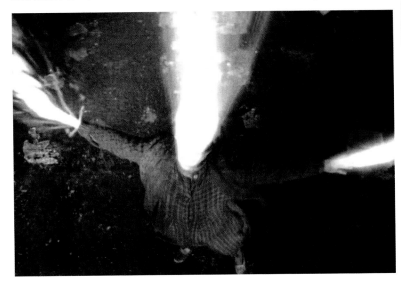

image by letting British broadcaster David Frost carry out a series of interviews with him. In the four televised chats, Nixon's plan backfired when Frost revealed new evidence that the former President had tried to obstruct the course of justice during the Watergate investigations. A dramatisation of this head-to-head, titled *Frost/Nixon,* hit cinemas in 2008. >> River looks so heartbroken when she shares her kiss with the Doctor because she knows that the next time they meet, in *A Good Man Goes to War* (2011), he will finally find out everything about her – setting into motion the reality-shaking events of *The Wedding of River Song* (2011). >> Although she confirms she was mistaken about her pregnancy (sort of), Amy's gut feeling about a baby conceived inside the TARDIS will turn out to be true. OK, River doesn't turn out to have a 'time head', but she still manages to pick up some Time Lord traits. >> The shock regeneration of the little girl at the end of this episode raised many questions – not answered until *Let's Kill Hitler* (2011), when Melody (who is about to regenerate again – into River) explains, 'Last time I did this, I ended up a toddler. In the middle of New York!'

MAGIC MOMENT

The Doctor gets ready to reveal his clever plan to the Silence...

THE DOCTOR: D'you know how many people are watching this, live on the telly? Half a billion. And that's nothing. Cos the human race will spread out among the stars – you just watch them fly! Billions and billions of them, for billions and billions of years. And every single one of them, at some point in their lives, will look back at this man, taking that very first step. And they will never, ever forget it. Oh. But they'll forget this bit...
On the TV, we see the famous moment when man sets foot on the Moon for the first time.
NEIL ARMSTRONG: That's one small step for man...
The image crackles, showing the face of a Silent.
SILENT: ... You should kill us all on sight...
THE DOCTOR: You've just given the order for your own execution. And the whole planet just heard you.
Then back to the Moon...
NEIL ARMSTRONG: ... one giant leap for mankind.
THE DOCTOR: And one whacking great kick up the backside for the Silence!

HATCH-WATCH

>> Credited simply as 'Eye Patch Lady', our dear, creepy Madame Kovarian makes her first unexpected appearance in this episode. As Amy explores the orphanage, Kovarian opens her hatch, peers through it and notes that Amy seems to be 'just dreaming' – a hint to the true fate of the real Amy.

DELETED!

The Doctor has asked Rory whether he remembers his 2,000-year wait for Amy...

RORY: I don't remember all the time. It's like there's a door in my head. I can keep it shut.
THE DOCTOR: But he's still in there – Rory the Roman?
RORY: I'm a nurse. I like being a nurse. Door stays shut.
THE DOCTOR: If I ever needed you to – maybe not today, but maybe some time soon – could you open that door again?
RORY: No.
THE DOCTOR: If Amy needed you to?
RORY: If Amy did, of course.

BEHIND THE SCENES
STEVEN MOFFAT
Writer

The Silence are one of the creepier creatures the series has seen. What inspired their look, and their memory-proof nature?
The look was an amalgam of existing imagery – like we've seen them in the corner of our eye for centuries, and they've bled into our consciousness. They're a bit like the Greys, a bit like Munch's *The Scream*. Clearly we modelled our idea of a business suit on them – in my head, the more influenced and manipulated by them you were, the more you were like them. Obviously, secret service agents have been taking a lot of subliminal orders – look what it did to their fashion sense.

During filming, how much did Alex Kingston know about what was to come? Is River acting ignorant when she sees the spacesuit? Or is she *acting* acting ignorant?
She knew most of it, but I can't remember if she knew everything. I told Alex the arc story before we started shooting, so yeah, she probably knew.

For every question answered in this episode, two more appear. In an ongoing series like *Doctor Who*, is it important to keep the mysteries coming?
If you're going to do a long arc, you need questions to answer – but you also need answers. It's not the way *Doctor Who* normally works – the default setting will always be closer to the anthology model, but shaking that up a little, now and then, is healthy and rewarding.
The questions proliferate in the early part of the show, but they don't stay enigmas, they're answered – they are promises we don't break.

THE IMPOSSIBLE ASTRONAUT

THREE MONTHS, THREE COMPANIONS.

What really happened between
The Impossible Astronaut and *Day of the Moon*?
The Doctor and friends reveal (almost) all...

AMY'S DIARY

THE DOCTOR SAYS: I HAD A BEARD! A properly bushy, poke-your-eye-out beard! On the cool-o-meter, beards are third only to bow ties and the immortal fez. But that's not all. Every Tuesday, Canton kicked out the guards and freed me from those chains, so I could run around the top-secret Nevada base like some joyous goose, stretching my legs and checking out some seriously brilliant alien artefacts (including a whole stack of dwarf star alloy, which got my brain buzzing). But anyway, you'll be wanting to know what else you missed.

Our mate Canton Everett Delaware III was in on the whole scam from the start. After the incident in Florida, when Amy shot at the Spacesuit Girl and we almost got zapped by the Silence (we were calling them 'The Enemy' back then, for want of an actual name), it was obvious that we needed a plan. The Silence seemed so powerful, all-pervasive and downright crafty that I knew it was time to make the unknowable more... knowable.

Cloaked in the privacy of the TARDIS, we formulated a scheme. Well, I say 'we'. The others suggested stuff, then I dramatically revealed what we were actually going to do. Amy, Rory, River and I were to become renegades, hunted nationwide by Canton and his former FBI pals. Exciting! That way, we could give the Silence a false sense of security, while working out the extent of their infestation. I decided that Canton would immediately 'arrest' me and haul me in

for questioning, shining a lamp in my face and all that. I had to stay close to Canton, you see, so I could remind him about the Silence's lurking menace.

'Aliens who make you forget them, Doctor? Gee, I don't remember that at all.'

'Why do you think that might be, Canton? Pull up a chair and I'll explain it all. Again.'

It was like spending three months with a goldfish. I was the little stone castle in Canton's mental fish tank. A castle of truth, if you like. With a beard.

Meanwhile, River and the Ponds (best band name ever) were dashing around America, scribbling tally-marks on themselves and feeling nauseous. I felt bad about that, but hey – I had to *sit still!* The longest I'd previously done that for was 17 minutes. I swear, I was only kept sane by drinking soda pop with my special straw, which I officially named The Fizzinator. Oh, and I grew a beard! Did I mention that?

Eventually, we regrouped the gang, thanks to Canton's pretend shooting and body-bagging. I'd given them each a Cryostasis podlet which simulates death when swallowed. Of course, getting shot like the others would've been way too conformist for River – she had to show off by toppling out of a tall building. Don't try that at home.

If I'd had time I'd have installed some in-bag entertainment, in case they woke up early. Sadly, it couldn't have included Pong, as that video game wasn't invented until 1972. In the end I just popped a stick and a hoop into each one.

Anyway, here's what Amy, River and Rory got up to during those mysterious months...

NORTH & SOUTH DAKOTA

There's this Native American icon, Crazy Horse, who led the Ogala Lakota tribe here in the 1800s. Like loads of people in history, he spread the superstition that cameras were evil and could capture your soul. I'll bet The Enemy have been around long enough to start that myth: after all, cameras are a threat to them. These thoughts reminded me to look at my mobile's photo cache, for some reason. And now I'm reminded to look again...

WASHINGTON

Hope the Doctor's enjoying himself while we do all the donkey-work. Overheard someone ranting about 1947's 'Maury Island Incident'. A guy called Harold Dahl saw flying objects – then 'a stranger wearing a black suit warned him to keep silent'. Hmmm, a black suit feels weirdly familiar. I'm also finding myself scared by lightning during this journey. Never used to be. My right arm is already covered in tally-marks. Missing Rory's stupid face. I also hate the internet, for not having been invented yet.

IDAHO

A newspaper here re-ran a photo from the 1940s, supposedly of an alien in US military custody. Do The Enemy start life as babies? And now I'm freaking myself out, thinking about babies...

ONE AIM...

 AMY

RIVER   RORY

SOUTH CAROLINA

The American Civil War started here in 1861. Wondering if a third party stirred things up beforehand, encouraging the 'cotton states' to rise up. If The Enemy have been lurking in the background throughout history, pulling strings, then wars might be a form of population control from their point of view. Grim thought.

KENTUCKY

The Kelly-Hopkinsville sightings happened here in 1955. People in and around a farmhouse experienced lights and sounds – but only a few alleged seeing aliens. After interviewing witnesses, an Air Force Division man, Gary F Hodson, drew this. Solid evidence? Feel I'm being watched at every turn.

PENNSYLVANIA

Many people believe the Philadelphia Experiment happened here in 1943. It supposedly involved rendering a US Navy destroyer escort ship invisible. So whose experiment was it: America's or The Enemy's? While investigating the Naval shipyard, my whole left arm became tally-marked. I got out of there fast.

NEW HAMPSHIRE

America's most famous 'alien abduction' case happened here in 1961. Betty and Barney Hill encountered a UFO while driving. They seemed to have a period of time missing from their memories – sound familiar? Betty's captor described her painful examination as 'a pregnancy test'. Apparently, these aliens were 'hairless, with bulbous foreheads'. Manhattan is my last stop. Oh, that city won't know what's hit it...

RORY'S DIARY

OKLAHOMA

Missing Amy already. Tally-marks on my arm tell me I've already made several sightings. Wonder if they saw me too? Anyway, there are loads of UFO/alien abduction mags on newsstands over here. That paranoia must be a product of America's growing subconscious memories of The Enemy. Gives me hope, though – if UFO sightings and alien abduction stories are less common in the present day, then maybe The Enemy have cleared off by then?

TEXAS

Interesting. A few years ago, Edvard Munch's painting *The Scream* was stolen from a Dallas gallery. Back in Kansas, Amy bluetoothed her photo of The Enemy to my phone and River's scanner (yeah, Bluetooth works in 1969, don't even ask how) and I promised myself I'd draw a triangle on my left thumb if that photo resembled *The Scream*. Then a triangle appeared on my left thumb. Apparently, *The Scream*'s been stolen before, too. Could it be that Munch was influenced by Enemy sightings, and they've tried to suppress it ever since?

CALIFORNIA

Spent a few days in Hollywood. Alien invasion films like *War of the Worlds* have been big business since the early 1950s, so there's definitely something in the air. This year, the sci-fi film *The Illustrated Man* is in cinemas – it's about a man telling the tales of each tattoo he has on his body. Being covered in tally-marks, even on my face now, I totally know how he feels. Wish I could remember a few more of my own tales, though...

THE DOC'S SIDE
OF THE MOON

THE DOCTOR SAYS: Poor old moon. I mean, no offence, but really, it's a bit rubbish. Fifty years of space travel and that's as far as you've got? Really, come on humanity, pull your socks up. See that big red Mars-shaped thing in the sky over there? Doesn't it just say 'land on me?' Come on, admit it, it does a bit.

But the furthest you've managed so far is your own moon. It's a bit like popping down to the newsagent. Now, don't get me wrong. I like moons. It's just that yours is a bit... I mean, it's *all right*. But on my list of Top Ten moons it's nowhere. It's no Great Sky Diamond of Jarman One, and, let's face it, it's not even one of the Ice Moons of Halliwell's Wall. Humanity, your moon is a tiny bit pound shop, frankly.

Not that that's anything to be ashamed of. Whatever I might have just said. I mean, look at the achievement – only 1969 and you manage to land on it in little more than a tin can. Amazing! Everyone gets points for that. But what's your space programme been about ever since? Putting satellites into orbit so you can watch game shows in high definition, or phone each other to say that you're going to be late. Here's an idea – next time you're going to be late, why not make it a surprise? Go on. Try it.

There are so many amazing planets in your solar system that you really should pop in on. And quite a few just a little bit further away that are well

A guide to that moony old moon up there, the great matchmaker in the sky, from me, **the Doctor**.

worth the effort. But no. You're like those people who go to restaurants and just order the soup. Soup's lovely – but look, over there, on a trolley swathed in darkness... cake!

So anyway, where was I? Oh yes. Your moon. Your really interesting, very exciting and not at all dull moon. Let's call it Rory.

No, sorry, forget that, I'm meant to be giving you a history of it. So let's get on cos I'm in the mood for cake...

THE SILURIANS

You weren't here first. Many millions of years ago a race of intelligent reptiles evolved and ruled the planet. I say 'intelligent', but when they saw an asteroid approaching they fled to their bunkers and forgot to set their timer switches properly. Silly old Earth Reptiles. While they slept, the asteroid got trapped in Earth's orbit and became the moon, and it was many millions of years before the Silurians started to wake up again. It hasn't been pretty, frankly, and I blame the moon. Plus the warlike nature of man, the inflexibility of the Silurians, and I suppose I could have done a bit better myself. No, scratch that. Blame the moon.

THE EMPIRE OF THE WOLF

Nip forward quite a lot and the moon saved the life of Queen

Victoria. Her late husband had worked out that if you refracted moonlight through a complicated prism it'd be a pretty powerful weapon – which is handy if you're in a hurry to save the monarch from a ravening werewolf. I'm quite proud of myself for working that one out. And also, it has to be said, about the most practical use anyone's ever found for moonlight. Though it is quite pretty.

CYBERMAN INVASION

Actually, the moon is quite handy for hiding behind. A big ship full of Daleks did it when they were putting one over on Winston Churchill, but that's nothing. When the Cybermen tried to invade a few years ago they managed to hide their entire fleet behind it. Say what you like about the Cybermen, and I have, but they're very good at parking.

A HOSPITAL ON THE MOON

As an uninhabited, sterile, grey, arid, dry, grey, lifeless, dull, grey rock with no atmosphere, the moon was the perfect neutral spot for the Judoon to plonk a hospital on. They were searching for a Plasmavore but instead they found me. Luckily,

Martha Jones and I saved the day and the Royal Hope found its way home. But for a while that hospital had some unbeatable views, if very little oxygen.

THE MOONBASE

While governments may have abandoned their space programmes in favour of something less fun, UNIT continued with their own secret one. They built the *Valiant*, an airborne fighter carrier, but they didn't stop there – they set up a moonbase on the moon (the clue was in the name). They were watching the skies, using the moon as an outpost against alien invasion. Working there was Dr Elizabeth Shaw, who was a very old friend of mine. I can't think of anyone better to be staring at the sky with worried disapproval. There were quite a few bases up there by the time the Daleks invaded Earth in 2157-ish.

WEATHER CONTROL

Anyway, back to the 21st century, and a few decades later you lot had found a way of controlling the weather from the moon. Using a Gravitron beam you could pretty much guarantee that it would be sunny at weekends and always snow at Christmas (if you slipped Controller Robson a tenner he'd even arrange for it to rain on someone you didn't much like). All went pretty well until the Cybermen turned up again – this time they were going to use the Gravitron to break the human spirit with bad weather. Like that'd work - have they been to Swansea?

T-MAT CONTROL

Your ambition really does reach just as far as the moon, doesn't it? Do you know what the end of the First Great and Bountiful Space Race was? When you lot invented the Transmat and could beam matter from point to point. You had one last use for space rockets – you refurbished your Moonbase as a central controlling point for T-Mat. Which was a brilliant idea... if you hadn't learned anything from the Cybermen invading and taking control of your weather. This time, the Ice Warriors turned up and used T-Mat control to send deadly seed pods to Earth. Open goal, all I'm saying.

THE SPACE PRISON

A few centuries later and the human race finally left the planet in really proper spaceships. The idea was that you'd explore or colonise, but really you just went to war with the first bunch you met – the Draconians. It wasn't one of your best hours – especially when you started locking up anyone who spoke out against the idea. And where did you stick them? The moon. You even sent me there for a while. I did quite like the karate-style prison gear, mind you.

The Curse of the Black Spot

BY STEPHEN THOMPSON

THE STORY

In 1699, the pirate ship *Fancy* is stranded in the middle of the ocean. Having followed a distress signal, the TARDIS materialises on board – and plonks the Doctor, Amy and Rory right into the middle of Captain Henry Avery's gang of terrified pirates. They are stalked by a siren from beneath the waves, who marks her victims with a black spot on the palm. One by one, the men are being picked off by the creature – but she seems only to take the sick and injured...

Soon enough, Rory falls to the curse. The Doctor and Amy are able to protect him for now, but the siren is determined – and very powerful. Not to worry, cos the Doctor thinks he's figured out how to save them all. The siren is using reflections as portals into our world, so they tip everything shiny overboard – including Avery's beloved haul of treasure.

But that's not the only shock for Avery. As well as the TARDIS crew, he's got another stowaway on board – his son, Toby. He's sick with a fever, and marked with the black spot. Things go from bad to worse when a golden crown, hidden by the greedy captain, gives the siren one last chance to manifest aboard the ship. She takes Toby, and then poor Rory, too.

Now, only the Doctor, Amy and Avery survive – and that's not helping anyone. They too must submit to the curse, succumb to the siren, and find out where the creature has been taking their friends. And when they wake, they make the most shocking discovery of all...

THE CURSE OF THE BLACK SPOT

>> Scenes on the ship were filmed on a replica vessel in the waters off St Austell, Cornwall.

DELETED!

Ever wondered what happened to the boatswain? The finished version of the episode suggests – by omission, if nothing else – that he was taken by the siren. But cut scenes show his real fate. He tries to double-cross his captain, and Avery claps him in irons and chains him up in the armoury. As the storm rages towards the end of the episode, the boatswain steals his chance – using a sword to cut through his rusty chains. Eventually, he gets lucky and the chain snaps – but then he stares at its severed edge. The cut surface shines in the light – a perfect reflection... The metal starts to glow turquoise. The siren is coming for him. He screams...

>> *The Curse of the Black Spot* had the working title *Siren*, and was originally slated to be Episode 9 in this year's run of *Doctor Who* – a slot eventually taken by *Night Terrors*. >> Henry Avery was a real 17th-century pirate – one of the most feared ever to roam the seas – and his legacy also features in the First Doctor story *The Smugglers* (1966), which revolves around the search for Avery's missing treasure. Thanks to this episode, we now know what happened to it. Only took us 45 years... >> The idea of a spaceship existing in two universes at the same time is similar to the central conceit of the Fourth Doctor story *The Stones of Blood* (1978), in which a futuristic prison ship is trapped in hyperspace while also hovering above an ancient stone circle in our world. There are also similarities with the *SS Madame de Pompadour* spaceship

Fantastic Facts!

from *The Girl in the Fireplace* (2006), tethered by 'time windows' to a period of Earth's history. >> Avery and Toby will return – ever so briefly – in *A Good Man Goes to War*. Still flying the siren's ship, they are part of the

Doctor's plan to rescue Amy and baby Melody from the clutches of Madame Kovarian. >> In the closing scenes, we witness flashbacks to the events of *The Impossible Astronaut*, as Amy remembers the Doctor's death – and we get another reminder of Amy's on-again, off-again mystery pregnancy.

BEHIND THE SCENES
STEVE THOMPSON
Writer

Pirates, sirens, curses and aliens – this one's got it all. Did you find it fun to be able to write such a no-holds-barred adventure?
Well, yes it was fun, but there's no such thing as no-holds-barred in TV. There are always constraints. Sometimes they can add to the fun. I was asked to write the pirate story, and then I got a call a day later from the production team saying 'We may not be able to find a ship!' So I said 'I'll see if I can set the whole thing on land.' And the very first draft of the story had the pirates all stranded on dry land and not able to get back to their ship. Sometimes constraints like that can lead to interesting things, but in this case I was glad that a ship finally turned up!

The legend of Henry Avery was touched on in a *Doctor Who* story from the 1960s. Why did you pick this pirate in particular to focus on?
Blind luck. I was an avid fan of *Doctor Who* in the 1970s, but I don't have an encyclopaedic knowledge of episodes from before then, and I genuinely had no idea that there was an episode involving Avery's treasure [*The Smugglers* (1966)]. When Steven asked me to write a pirate episode the first thing I did was to raid my sons' bookshelves. I found a terrific book that told the story of famous pirates, and I picked Avery because

he was responsible for the biggest act of piracy in history. And then he completely vanished! I thought it would be fun to invent a new ending for his story.

Having written for both, how do you think Sherlock Holmes compares to the Doctor as a hero? What have they got in common?
What they've got in common is the quality of the acting – Benedict Cumberbatch and Matt Smith are both highly skilled, very energetic actors, both brilliant to work with, yet each has a unique style. Steven Moffat understands their unique voices and it's fun– though also rather challenging – trying to imitate it. *Sherlock* is loosely based on the original Sir Arthur Conan Doyle stories, and we always start from those – so you begin with a rough structure, even if you move away from it pretty quickly. With *Doctor Who* you really do begin with a totally blank page. The story can take you anywhere. That's a thrill, but it's also a bit daunting.

HATCH-WATCH
Madame Kovarian once again opens a hatch on the Flesh Amy's adventures, when she appears during the night to wake her up. Amy seems to dismiss it as a creepy dream – but we know better!

The True Voyages of
Henry Avery
1694–1696

England
Avery sets sail aboard the Privateer ship *Charles II*, under the captaincy of Charles Gibson .

Corunna
Northern Spain
His ship plunders French strongholds in the region. The crew is stranded here for six months when their English masters refuse to pay their wages. Avery leads a mutiny against the Captain.

Atlantic Ocean
Captain Gibson cast adrift on the high seas. Avery becomes Captain and renames his ship the *Fancy*.

Cape Verde Islands
West Africa
Avery commits his first act of piracy, robbing English merchantmen.

Guinea Coast
Island of Principe
Avery attacks two Danish privateers. He holds the local chieftain of the islands to ransom.

Comoro Islands
North of Madagascar
Avery has the ship modified and reduced in size to improve her speed.

Straights of Bab el-Mandeb
Coast of Yemen
Avery teams up with five other pirate captains. He is elected Admiral of the new fleet. The pirates lay in wait for a convoy from the Indian Navy, including the treasure ship *Ganj-i-Sawai*.

Straits of Surat
West coast of India
Avery and his fleet attack the Indian convoy and sack the *Ganj-i-Sawai*. A violent, bloody battle ensues.

Unknown
The *Fancy* vanishes with all hands...

?

WARDEN JOSEPH LONGFOOT'S JOURNAL

This eve I did hear a travelling minstrel singing a ballad down at Kewper's Inn. At first I could not believe my own ears, but I persuaded the fellow to sing it for me again over a tankard while I took it down in my pocket book.

Verily, tis a remarkable coloured account of the doings of Old Captain Avery- in particular the time when we captured the Moghul's Treasure and fought against the crew of the accursed Pearl, that black albatross of a ship when they tried to betray us.

I have heard little of Cpt Avery since he put me ashore to stand guard over some significant portion of his treasure. There are rumours that the dear Captain is dead, or living in Ireland. No man knows for certain – it is like he has vanished clear off God's Earth.

I hope he sends word to me what to do with his treasure that I hold in safekeeping for his family. He knows he may trust me to my very last breath. But what of those vagabonds aboard the Pearl? I know Cpt May's accursed soul perished that day, but what of those scoundrels at his right hand – Pike and Cherub?

Whatever voyage you be on, Cpt Avery, may God speed you back afore I take your Deadman's secret to the grave with me.

THE CURSE OF THE BLACK SPOT

Execs mark the spot!

The perilous journey of **Capt. Stephen Thompson** on his writerly voyage from first draft to finished script – and untold riches. Probably…

Ye First Draft

Amy wants a holiday. The Doctor takes her to Cornwall, where she went on holiday as a kid, but he lands 300 years earlier than expected. Whoops. Pirates and smugglers are raiding villages up and down the coast. The Doctor meets Captain Henry Avery. He is searching for his lost wife, stolen by a mysterious siren creature. The siren is trapped and killed in a disued Cornish tin mine. There's no filming on the ocean whatsoever!

Ye Second Draft

We've found a ship! Hooray! So Avery and his crew are now out in the ocean. The TARDIS lands on board. And then a navy frigate turns up. The Lieutenant of the Militia tries to arrest Avery and his crew. But the Lieutenant turns bad when he hears the rumour of buried treasure. They land on an island and dig up treasure. In the finale, Amy gets sucked down into the water and nearly drowns. Rory has to rescue her.

Ye Third Draft

The thing with the Militia gets cut – too many guest characters, not enough space for all of them to breathe. Big new idea – the siren is not some sea creature, she's actually on a spaceship that has crashed right next to Avery's ship. She is the interface of the ship's automated sick bay. Avery's wife is out – Avery's son is in instead.

Ye Fourth Draft

Production meeting – apparently, in this series, Amy is getting 'almost killed' too many times. Nearly happening every episode. So Amy and Rory swap around. Rory is the one who almost drowns and Amy is the one who has to save him.

Ye Fifth Draft

The story is pretty much set in stone now. I add in a storm scene – which means the cast are all going to get soaked. Sorry.

Ye Sixth Draft

A big change – up until now the siren has had dialogue, but we decide it's more scary if she says nothing at all.

Ye Seventh Draft

A couple of stunts added. Amy gets thrown across the deck now. Also added are specific descriptions of each of the pirates, because the design team would like to know a bit more about them.

Ye Eighth Draft

Major last-minute change – we have decided to film the whole episode at night. Means we don't have to CGI a flat, becalmed ocean into every shot. So I rewrite the script with the word 'Night' in it a few hundred times.

Ye Ninth Draft

The read-through! Hooray!

The illustrations here portray some of the Doctor's most memorable headgear. His appearance is transformed when he discards his worn-out titfer in favour of a new one.

ASTRAKHAN
Worn by the First Doctor in
An Unearthly Child

FEATHERY
Worn by the First Doctor in
The Reign of Terror

COWBOY (1)
Worn by the First Doctor in
The Gunfighters

STOVEPIPE
Worn by theSecond Doctor in
The Power of the Daleks

GYPSY HEADSCARF
Worn by the Second Doctor in
The Underwater Menace

BOBBLE HAT
Worn by the Second Doctor in
Fury from the Deep

FEDORA
First worn by the Fourth Doctor in
Robot

TAM O'-SHANTER
Worn by the Fourth Doctor in
Terror of the Zygons

DEERSTALKER
Worn by the Fourth Doctor in
The Talons of Weng Chiang

PANAMA
First worn by the Fifth Doctor in
Castrovalva

PANAMA AGAIN
First worn by the Seventh Doctor in
Time and the Rani

STRAW HAT
Worn by the Tenth Doctor in
The End of Time, Part One

FEZ
First worn by the Eleventh Doctor in
The Big Bang

TOP HAT
First worn by the Eleventh Doctor in
The Big Bang

SANTA
First worn by the Eleventh Doctor in
A Christmas Carol

COWBOY (2)
First worn by the Eleventh Doctor in
The Impossible Astronaut

If you have enjoyed these hats, you may also wish to look out for the First Doctor's panama from *The Daleks' Master Plan*, the Second Doctor's officer's cap in *The War Games*, the Third Doctor's trilby in *Spearhead From Space* and his headscarf and milkman's cap from *The Green Death*, the Fourth Doctor's Viking helmet, Jack of Hearts hat and Pierrot headgear from *Robot*, his chauffeur's cap in *The Seeds of Doom*, his bowler hat in *Horror of Fang Rock* and his barrister's wig in *The Stones of Blood*, the Sixth Doctor's police helmet in *Attack of the Cybermen* and his sun visor in *The Two Doctors*, plus the Seventh Doctor in a panama, fedora and bearskin in *Time and the Rani* and a fez in *Silver Nemesis*.

The Doctor's Wife

BY NEIL GAIMAN

THE STORY

There's a knock at the TARDIS door. A flying white cube has found the Doctor – and it's asking for his help. It contains a distress call from a Time Lord, and its trail leads to a tiny bubble of reality hanging outside the universe. There, in the scrap-strewn hills of a planet-sized junkyard, the Doctor clings to the hope that another of his kind has survived.

It is, of course, a trap. The planet is actually a creature called House, and House eats TARDISes. But the matrix of a TARDIS – the energy at its very heart – is inedible and so, to save itself from a fatal case of indigestion, House offloads it into a string of handy humanoids. The latest of these is Idris, an unfortunate girl who is about to bring the Doctor's most constant companion to life...

Armed with the knowledge that the Doctor is the last of his race, House gains possession of the TARDIS – with Amy and Rory inside – and heads to the real universe to find new things to eat. But first, he has to get rid of the pesky life forms cluttering up his new home.

Trapped with the remains of countless dead TARDISes, the Doctor and Idris must somehow stop House and get the soul of the TARDIS back where it belongs – before Idris's body does something very organic.

Drops dead...

Where Have I Seen?

SURANNE JONES
Idris
Best known as Karen McDonald in *Coronation Street*, Suranne also appeared in *The Sarah Jane Adventures: Mona Lisa's Revenge*.

MICHAEL SHEEN
House
One of the UK's most successful actors, Michael's film roles include Tony Blair in *The Queen* and David Frost in *Frost/Nixon*.

NUMBER CRUNCHING

700 years since the Doctor and the TARDIS first met

1 chance to talk to each other in all that time

THE DOCTOR'S WIFE

Fantastic Facts!

This episode's working title was *The House of Nothing*, and it was planned to be the eleventh episode of Matt Smith's first series. Budgetary constraints saw it bumped to Series Six, however, with *The Lodger* (2010) taking its place. In the first version of the script, Amy was alone during the scenes in the TARDIS, Rory having slipped through one of the cracks in time. When the Doctor tells her to look through his jacket for the sonic screwdriver, she would have found her engagement ring – just as she does in *The Lodger* when she's looking for a pen. The episode focuses on the TARDIS, and the Doctor's long relationship with his time machine. Accepting that they're using approximate figures, Idris claims that she and the Doctor have been travelling together for 700 years. This would have made the Doctor around 200 when he left Gallifrey – perhaps helping to explain how his first body, which by its end must have been much older, died of little more than old age and exhaustion in *The Tenth Planet* (1966). (Can we trust Idris's figures, though? She has difficulty telling the past from the future, not to mention working out what's going on in the present. Are her numbers equally confused?) The Doctor jettisons rooms from the TARDIS to build up more thrust, just as he did in *Logopolis* (1981) and *Castrovalva* (1982). He also deleted a swimming pool before *Paradise Towers* (1987) but it seems to have returned since, judging by *The Eleventh Hour* (2010) and *Day of the Moon* (2011). In *The War Games* (1969), we saw the Second Doctor contact the Time Lords using a white cube very similar to the devices seen here. In that story he constructed it from six blank white cards taken from his pocket, which joined together through the Doctor's sheer mental energy and then vanished, carrying his message back to Gallifrey – and, for the very first time, allowing his

people to track him down. The Doctor claims that the Corsair was able to change his (or her) gender during her (or his) regenerations – a Time Lord ability long theorised but never before confirmed. Whatever his gender or appearance otherwise, though, the Corsair always bore a tattoo of an oroborus. The Third Doctor had a tattoo on his arm, shown as he takes a shower in *Spearhead from Space* (1970), but as far as we have seen, this has never been the case with his other incarnations. It seems likely, therefore, that tattoos can come and go throughout a Time Lord's lives – and that, like Romana in *Destiny of the Daleks* (1979), the Corsair could exert some control on the outcome of the regenerative process. (See page 63 for more on this enigmatic figure.) Pity the poor Ood, its race seemingly forever destined to be the psychic slaves of greater beings. During their first appearance, in *The Impossible Planet/The Satan Pit* (2006), they were in the thrall of the great Beast hidden inside the prison planet of Krop Tor. Then, in *Planet of the Ood* (2008), they were controlled by the tortured Ood Brain. In this episode, 'Nephew' is pushed around by House. The eyes of controlled Ood in earlier stories glowed red, here they glow green – reflecting House's strange energies. (The Doctor laments the death of Nephew with the words, 'Another Ood I failed to save,' reminding us of his pain at being unable to save the creatures in *The Satan Pit* – and the personal debt he owes them after an Ood guided the dying Tenth Doctor back to his ship in *The End of Time, Part Two* (2010)). The Doctor recalls the terrible things he did to his people during the Time War, telling House, 'Fear me – I killed all of them' – as seen in *The End of Time* (2009-2010). You might think piloting an 'open-topped' TARDIS console through the space-time vortex would be sheer,

suicidal insanity – but this isn't the first time the Doctor has attempted such a bold gambit. In *Inferno* (1970), the Third Doctor used his disconnected TARDIS console to slip through the barrier between our world and an apocalyptic parallel universe. The Doctor refers to himself as 'a madman with a box' and tells Uncle and Auntie to 'basically, run' – both echoes of his words from *The Eleventh Hour* (2010). He also suggests they should visit the Eye of Orion, a favourite relaxation spot of the Doctor's seen in *The Five Doctors* (1983). The cobbled-together TARDIS piloted by the Doctor and Idris closely resembles the TARDIS control room seen in *Doctor Who* from the mid 1970s into the early 1980s – with bits and bobs inspired by TARDIS designs before and after. It's the first time we've seen simple circular 'roundels' on a TARDIS wall since 1989's *Battlefield*. And the first time we've had a proper gander at a TARDIS corridor since 1985's *Attack of the Cybermen*, though the Ninth Doctor's directions to Rose in *The Unquiet Dead* (2005) indicated that the interior still stretched far beyond the control room. Talking of which, the TARDIS control room used from 2005 to 2010 makes a reappearance after being devastated during the Doctor's explosive regeneration in *The End of Time, Part Two* (2010). The set was still standing in *Doctor Who*'s Upper Boat studios at the time, but has since been removed to form part of the *Doctor Who* Experience exhibition. We don't want to seem picky, but the instruction 'Pull To Open' as seen on the TARDIS's front door panel and quoted by Idris, actually refers to the panel itself – a door to a cubby-hole containing a phone linked to the nearest police station in genuine police boxes. But then, genuine police box doors open outward, whereas the TARDIS doors open inward, so Idris has a point! Turn to page 60 for a version of Neil Gaiman's original opening scene, set on the Planet of the Rain Gods.

MAGIC MOMENT

Idris has returned, one last time, with a final message for the Doctor...

IDRIS: I've been looking for a word. A big, complicated word. But so sad. I've found it now.
THE DOCTOR: What word?
IDRIS: Alive. I'm alive.
THE DOCTOR: Alive isn't sad.
IDRIS: It's sad when it's over. I'll always be here. But this is when we talked. And now even that has come to an end. There's something I didn't get to say to you.

THE DOCTOR: Goodbye.
IDRIS: No. I just wanted to say... Hello. Hello, Doctor. It's so very, very nice to meet you.

WATERY, GRAVE

Idris's dying words to Rory – 'The only water in the forest is the river' may not make much sense now, but their meaning and connection to River Song is revealed in *A Good Man Goes to War*. Plus they were one of the real teasers supplied by Steven Moffat in last year's *Brilliant Book of Doctor Who*. Did you spot it?

UNSEEN ADVENTURES

We're left to wonder at exactly what the Doctor got up to with the Corsair, another Time Lord who 'ran away to see the universe'. The Doctor gleefully, describes her as 'a bad girl' during her female incarnations. You can find out more – eleven times over – from Neil Gaiman on page 63.

DELETED!

The Doctor and Idris stand in the junkyard, helpless, surrounded by scraps of metal and useless debris.

THE DOCTOR: Doesn't make sense. The place should be full of TARDIS scrap. Stuff we could use. But it's just junk!
He picks up a stone, throws it at the bathtub. The stone makes a ringing noise. It's a bathtub, all right.
IDRIS: The chameleon circuits are still active. It's not junk, any more than I'm a police box. It just looks like junk.
THE DOCTOR: How does it look to you?

IDRIS: I'll show you!
We close in on her eyes. A flash of golden TARDIS-light. On the Doctor, now staring around him in wonder...
THE DOCTOR: Well, look at that!
He's turning, looking all around, marvelling. Much of the junk is still junk – but here and there, there are identifiable shards of TARDIS tech. Columns, roundels. There's a partly wrecked, two- or three-sided TARDIS inner shell that looks a bit like something an early Doctor might have ridden about in before it met an awful end. The Doctor is in awe...
THE DOCTOR: Valley of half-eaten TARDISes!

BEHIND THE SCENES
NEIL GAIMAN
Writer

As a fan of *Doctor Who* was it a thrill to give the TARDIS a voice for the first time – and did Suranne Jones as Idris match what you heard in your head?
The thrill for me wasn't in the TARDIS speaking – it was who she was speaking to and what they were saying. That the Doctor and the TARDIS were arguing, like a long-married couple, was just wonderful. Suranne Jones's performance wasn't what I had in my head. It was simply more glorious in every possible way.

How would you describe the Doctor's relationship with his TARDIS? Is she really his 'wife'?
If a captain is married to his ship, then the Doctor is married to his TARDIS. She's been with him longer than anyone else. And no matter what he does, or who he loves, one day it will just be the two of them again. 'A boy and his box, off to see the universe', as Amy puts it. So yes, she's his wife. And mother. And girlfriend. And his home. And partner in crime.

This episode is full of startling ideas. Did you come up with any that seemed like a step too far?
Not at all. I kept stretching the budget, and there were things we couldn't do – I wanted House to ooze out protoplasmic tentacles that would shoot up from the ground, but that vanished when I was told just how far over budget it would take us. But I don't think there was anything Steven Moffat told me not to do in that sense. He set no limits, told me to surprise him, was an astonishing story-boss, and encouraged me in my madness. He also writes the best '*Bad news – we've just lost this thing you had your heart set on*' emails of any man alive.

NEIL GAIMAN WRITES: Until the first day of shooting on *The Doctor's Wife*, this scene – or something very like it – sat at the start of the script instead of the 'I've got mail!' scene you saw on TV.

But it turned out we were a day over schedule on the episode, and something had to go. If we recorded the first scene in the TARDIS, instead of on location, then we were back on track. So I got rewriting.

Nothing is ever truly lost, though – so here, for the first time, is the original opening to *The Doctor's Wife*, as we join the Doctor, Amy and Rory on the Planet of the Rain Gods...

PLANET OF THE RAIN GODS

NEIL GAIMAN: writer   **MARK BUCKINGHAM:** artist   **TODD KLEIN:** letters
CHARLIE KIRCHOFF: colours   **CLAYTON HICKMAN:** editor

Eleven Things You Probably Didn't Know About

THE CORSAIR

AS DIVULGED BY MR NEIL GAIMAN

1 His TARDIS looked like a sailing ship whenever it was practical – and sometimes even when it wasn't – because small, piratical sailing ships are cool.

2 The Ouroboros tattoo, showing a snake eating its own tail and symbolising Eternity, moved around the Corsair's body with each regeneration. The largest version was huge and multi-coloured and covered the Third Corsair's entire back. The smallest version was the size of a ten pence piece and was discreetly inked upon the Fifth Corsair's upper thigh.

3 The Corsair met his doom while working for the Time Lords on the Fourth Universal Survey Expedition. They were surveying the whole universe. It's a big place. Somebody has to keep track of it.

4 Most Time Lords disapproved of the Corsair. The Doctor, on the other hand, got drunk with him (in the Corsair's Fourth and Eighth incarnations) and with her (in her Fifth). Each time, the Doctor swore he would never do it again. Twice, they woke up in jail. Once, they woke up in the Bank of England vaults.

5 The Corsair took his name from a term for 'privateer' – a sort of legitimate pirate. Some people assumed that this was because the Corsair did things for the Time Lords that they could deny responsibility for – such as stealing the secret of the Callisto Pulse from the Callistan Kleptocracy. The Corsair denied having stolen the Callisto Pulse. The Time Lords denied having asked him to steal it. The Callistans would like their Pulse back.

6 The Corsair never actually fought the Daleks. But her seventh incarnation was definitely spotted on Clarkor Nine the night the Dalek Scout Ship landed. On the following day the nine Daleks on the saucer discovered that their weapon arms and their suction cup arms had somehow been unscrewed and removed

in the night, rendered inoperable, and fused together into a shape that means something very rude in Skarosian. They left immediately and did not return. The Corsair's role in this is unclear.

7 The Corsair visited Earth a number of times in its history. He was worshipped as a god by the ancient Assyrians until he got bored after a week and went off with the sacred temple cat.

8 In every incarnation the Corsair had an amazing smile. It was variously described as 'reckless', 'roguish' or 'very bad girl'. Whatever race or gender the Corsair was, he or she smiled the kind of smile that made the person being smiled at want to trust the person who was smiling, run off with him or her, and get into all manner of trouble. Sometimes people did.

9 The Corsair liked having a cat and, sometimes, a parrot aboard his TARDIS. He never had a companion, however, preferring to travel alone. (Having said that, the Corsair took enormous pleasure in Rescuing Good Looking People from Dangerous Situations, but rarely stuck around long enough to be properly thanked.)

10 The Time Lord High Council formally censured the Corsair following the disappearance of the mysterious Portrait of Rassilon in Lord President Borusa's time. The Censure was later formally revoked by President Flavia, for reasons she declined to go into, although she was once heard to say that the Corsair had an extremely attractive smile.

11 By the time the Ninth Corsair (a strapping big bloke, he was) realised he had been trapped on the intelligent asteroid that called itself House, his TARDIS had already been killed and eaten. He recorded a distress message, but before he could send it there was a tap on his shoulder and he felt and thought nothing more, not ever again.

'He's still Rory, still *panicky and nervous,* but he's *more of a man*'

Rory Pond (né Williams) has fast become one of the best-loved – and most killed – characters on TV. **Arthur Darvill** reveals all about the hapless hero…

I n the Blue Box Café at Upper Boat Studios, just outside Cardiff, Arthur Darvill joins the *Brilliant Book* for a coffee and a chat. This is where they film *Doctor Who*. Not in the café, that would be daft, but on the Upper Boat sound stages. 'I've just given away my daughter,' he explains.It's Wednesday 27 April 2011, and Arthur has been filming *The Wedding of River Song*. Today, he's *Captain* Rory. (Back on set later, he asks, 'Should Rory make a speech? As father of the bride?' It's a resounding '*No!*' from Karen Gillan, Arthur's on-screen wife, Amy.)

Arthur, 28, has played Rory for two years. Or is it 2,000? He's the man who waited. Well, the man who died, then didn't exist, then was plastic and Roman, and *then* waited. Then he married the love of his life. Then he died. Then he was brought back to life. Then he died again. Then he watched his wife explode. Then he rescued her from Demon's Run, dressed as a Centurion. Then he

punched Hitler. Then he joined the resistance movement in an alternative 2011. In short, he's the missing link between Roman centurion and twenty-first-century man. Time's new Roman, if you will…

In real life, Arthur is cooler than Rory, though he shares his alter ego's self-deprecating sense of humour. He doesn't have an ounce of diva in him. Asked whether he'll be back in *Doctor Who* in 2012, Arthur leans back in his chair, smiles and says, 'If they'll have me. Eight months in, you could definitely do with some time off, because it's so busy. I mean, it's brilliant, but it's completely life-changing, and so easy to get… well,

it's similar to what the characters go through, I suppose – it's easy to get bogged down in day-to-day things. Then you step back and go "Wow! This is really, really incredible."'

'Even if Rory and Amy have settled down,' he considers, 'if the Doctor turns up, even 20 years later, I reckon they'd be ready to jump back on board the TARDIS. They've been through so much together, but there are things they haven't done yet, and questions to be answered… There are certainly things that I would like to see happen.'

This series, Rory's two worlds collided: his life in the TARDIS, and his life with Amy.
Yes. Well, he was always intending to get back and get married, but now that's happened Rory is torn between settling down and the pull of adventure – plus the pull of the Doctor as a personality, which is so strong. Both he and Amy are just waiting for the Doctor to call. That

isn't a normal marriage! [Laughs] In a way, the Doctor is messing up their lives, but there is that addictive quality to it. Life in the TARDIS is so extreme; just going back to normal doesn't really fit into the equation.

Despite everything that has happened to him since he met the Doctor, Rory seems a more grounded person than Amy.

Yeah, he can take a step back and go, 'What the hell –? This is absolutely mental.' But the longer he spends in this world, the more Rory gets sucked in, and the further back he has to step. Rory has these moments of realisation: 'I was a nurse. I was happy before all of this.' But then he gets swept away again.

He does die quite often, too, doesn't he?

[Laughs] Well, I think Rory can be a bit gung-ho sometimes. He can get sucked into stuff. That's a really good thing about him, but also it's his downfall sometimes, I think. They're fun, those death scenes, because all of us have been doing this for quite a while now. If we were shooting those sorts of scenes when we all first started on this show, I would have found it a lot harder. But it comes from working with such good people, and trusting that if you're not doing it right, if the emotion isn't there, then someone is going to tell you.

You did filming for The Impossible Astronaut in Utah and Arizona, with a US crew. What did they make of Doctor Who?

Oh they were brilliant. Really accommodating, really lovely. Half of them had heard of Doctor Who, half of them hadn't. Trying to explain the show to someone who isn't familiar with it is, as always, pretty tricky, but it's steadily gaining a bigger audience

in the States. It's weird how much it's travelled. The Doctor isn't your average American hero. Neither is Rory – he'd be kind of chiselled and all that stuff if Doctor Who was a US show. But the writing is so brilliant. When we're making it, everyone cares about it so much. If the quality is there, it translates. We had fans turn up to watch us film in the Utah desert, which was bizarre, but great.

Can you get your head around people wanting your autograph?

It's taken me longer than I thought it would to get used to that. I'm aware of the amount of people that watch the show, but I never really think about that when I'm working. Just before they call 'action', you don't want to think, 'Ten million people are going to watch this in the UK alone.' That could seriously mess with your head.

Last year's finale was a cracker for Rory. Does The Wedding of River Song measure up?

It's hard to top The Big Bang, isn't it? What was so great about last year's climax was that everybody had their individual journeys to go on – Amy was trapped, she was remembering Rory, and Rory was brought back to life... Whereas, this year, they've all got so close, and they're so intertwined with each other, that it's very much a group climax. What I love about Rory is that he's learning more than anyone else, and changing more than anyone else. I feel like he's grown up a lot. These days, when Rory gets put in situations of peril or gets challenged, he's far more willing to stand up for himself, to put himself forward to do the right thing, and to throw himself into it. He's still Rory, still panicky and nervous, but he's more of a man. It's interesting to

"THE DOCTOR AND RORY ARE CLOSE FRIENDS IN A VERY STRANGE WAY"

work out how to play that, because he's now been around on the planet for so long.

His 2,000 years waiting for Amy must have affected him far more deeply than he lets on.

Yes, that's such a vast amount of time for anyone to wait. His mind has been around for so long, in reality. To carry the weight of 2,000 years... I don't think you could deal with that. You'd just have to lock it away somewhere.

At the end of this series Rory is back home, living with Amy, and with a regular job – would you choose that life over the TARDIS?

Hm. I don't know. The pull of the Doctor is always so strong. Plus Rory's loyalty to the Doctor is increasing. He's still wary, but I think they're much closer after this series. There's a mutual respect. The Doctor and Rory have become close friends, in a very strange way. Rory might even be his father-in-law!

River Song's real identity was kept secret from practically everybody. You were only told at the read-through, right?

Actually, I knew what the reveal would be. I'd managed to get that out of someone who already knew, which I felt quite pleased with.

Was it Alex Kingston?

Ha! Yes. Because Alex knows everything. But there was still speculation about what was coming up in that episode. We'd all got the script, and I was just reading it on my own. I got to the last two pages, and I thought, 'That doesn't make any sense.' I mean, it kind of did, but it just sort of... stopped. I thought, 'Steven [Moffat, the writer of *A Good Man Goes to War*] has rushed the end of this.' It was a bizarre read-through, too, because everyone in there knew it was a really important episode, so everyone was listening really intently... but then we got to the end, and it really didn't make any sense. There was a general feeling of, 'Erm, OK...' It made for a slightly strange atmosphere. But then Steven took me, Matt [Smith] and Karen into a corridor, with his laptop, and showed us the *real* last two pages. He'd held them back from everyone. It was on a need-to-know basis. You feel like you're in MI5 or something.

What difference do you think the mid-series break made?

It's a real bonus for us. It means you can have a big cliffhanger in the middle of the series. I mean, we treat every episode with equal importance, but the big reveals are so thrilling to play when they come along.

This series has explored some pretty big ideas. Is anything too weighty for *Doctor Who*?

I don't think so, and they keep pushing the boundaries. There are big ideas that recur throughout the series, like faith in things, things not being real, things turning out to be false... As long as the issues never take over the story, *Doctor Who* can tackle pretty much anything, and does. Take *The God Complex* – faith is such a huge issue anyway, from people's personal beliefs to what goes on in the wider world, and yet it's dealt with in such a brilliant, imaginative way in that episode. The idea that you can walk into a room, and you're faced with your greatest fear – it really fires up people's imaginations, gets people guessing what would be in their room.

Which begs the question... what would be lurking in your room?

My biggest nightmare? Well, I know what it would have been when I was a kid, and it's really stupid. It would have been a toilet.

A what?

A toilet. With a killer whale coming out of it. [Laughs] There was a picture on my junior school wall of a killer whale with its teeth bared. For a year and a half, I was terrified there was going to be a whale coming out of the toilet every time I sat on in it. It was tricky going to the loo.

You poor soul. How did you get over this affliction?

It really took me a while. Apparently, it runs in my family – my mum thought there was a tiger going to come out of her loo. Maybe the Darvills all have some deep-seated fear of toilets?

The Rebel Flesh

BY MATTHEW GRAHAM

THE STORY

The TARDIS spins out of control, caught in a solar tsunami and thrown towards Earth in the 22nd century. The Doctor, Amy and Rory crash-land on a tiny island of rock containing a medieval monastery which now houses an acid-mining facility. But mining acid is a dangerous business – and that's where the Gangers come in.

The Morpeth Jetsan company employs a small team of workers to oversee the pumping of acid from the island to the mainland. But, to avoid expensive industrial accidents, the workers themselves never go near the corrosive liquid. Instead, they send their Gangers – replicas made of a programmable matter known as 'Flesh'. These replicas are identical in every way – what they look like, what they wear, and even how they think and speak.

It seems a pretty good idea. The real humans avoid injury, just replacing the Gangers whenever they need to. And, let's face it, the work is tough. With another solar tsunami on the way, and their production targets already in danger, team leader Cleaves decides to forge ahead, despite the Doctor's warnings. She commands her team to fire up their Gangers and get to work.

Then the storm hits – and the Gangers change. They become independent. No longer just copies of the workers, the Flesh duplicates are now alive – and they want to stay that way. Can the Doctor save them? Should he even try? And what exactly is hiding in the shadows of the monastery?

Where Have I Seen?

MARSHALL LANCASTER
Buzzer
Marshall was Chris Skelton in *Life on Mars* and *Ashes to Ashes*, both co-created by Matthew Graham, this story's writer.

SARAH SMART
Jennifer
Sarah rose to fame as Virginia in ITV's *At Home with the Braithwaites*, with major roles in *Casualty 1909* and the UK version of *Wallander*.

THE REBEL FLESH

>> The TARDIS's scans of Amy still waver on the matter of her pregnancy, as they have since her first secret examination in *Day of the Moon*, but at least now the Doctor has a suspicion that he knows the cause of the strange readings. >> In an effort to get them out of the way while he investigates the Flesh, the Doctor offers to drop Rory and Amy off for some fish and chips. In a line cut from the script, he says he plans to take them to Whitby Bay on 28 September 1940: 'Ernie Macklethwaite's Frying Tonite. It may have been the grit in Ernie's heart as he fried to the sound of German bombers screaming towards York – but that night produced the best fish supper ever in the history of the world.' >> The Doctor uses his psychic paper – first seen in *The End of the World* (2005) – to establish his credentials as a Morpeth Jetsan meteorological expert. >> Rory mentions that the Doctor's Rule One is 'don't wander off': we've heard this before in *The Empty Child* (2005), *The Girl in the Fireplace* (2006) and *The Eleventh Hour* (2010). (Among the Doctor's many other Rule Ones is 'The Doctor lies', as heard in *The Wedding of River Song*.) >> The Doctor's no stranger to clones with attitude, having been the 'father' of Jenny, a woman created from his DNA (though by less gloopy methods) in *The Doctor's Daughter* (2008). >> As the Doctor notes, everyone loves Dusty Springfield (1939 to 1999) a British female singer who peaked in popularity during the mid-to-late 1960s and whose 1966 UK number one hit 'You Don't Have To Say You Love Me' is heard drifting from the Monastery as the TARDIS lands.

DELETED!

In the aftermath of the second solar storm, the Doctor worries that the team's Gangers may have become independent. The sound of Dusty Springfield's 'You Don't Have To Say You Love Me' floats through the air...

JIMMY: That's our song! Mine and Mary's. We play it before I go on rotation. That's the original vinyl! No one's got a right to play it but me!

DICKEN: It's a mistake, Doctor, okay? They can't exist without us working 'em.

BUZZER: What about Sheppy?

DICKEN: Give it a rest, Buzzer.

BUZZER: That refinery on the Isle of Sheppy. Ganger got an electric shock, toddled off and killed his operator right there in his harness. I seen the photos – his eyes was all –

JIMMY: It's a pub story.

RORY: Then who put the record on?

AMY: They've come here because they feel safe, haven't they, Doctor?

CLEAVES: Even if they're operating independently – they're just like frightened livestock. You can't reason with them, Doctor. This isn't a good idea.

THE DOCTOR: Communicating with a brand-new life form? Allaying their fears? Finding out what they want? It's the only idea in my book.

NUMBER CRUNCHING

5 **Morpeth Jetsan workers**   5 GANGERS   10 REAL LIVES TO SAVE

MAGIC MOMENT

JENNIFER: When I was a little girl, I got lost on the moors. Wandered off from the picnic. I can still feel how sore my toes got inside my red welly boots.

She stares at a photo of herself at seven years old, wearing the red wellington boots.

JENNIFER: And I imagined another little girl, just like me, in red wellies. And she was Jennifer, too. Except she was a strong Jennifer – a tough Jennifer. She'd lead me home.

Now Jennifer looks at herself in a mirror, then at a more recent photo of her 'real' self.

JENNIFER: My name is Jennifer Lucas. I am not a factory part. I had toast for my breakfast. I wrote a letter to my mum. Then you arrived – I noticed your eyes right off.

RORY: Did you?

JENNIFER: Nice eyes. Kind.

RORY: Where is the real Jennifer?

JENNIFER: I am Jennifer Lucas! I remember everything that happened in her entire life. Every birthday. Every childhood illness. I feel everything she has ever felt – and more! I am not a monster! I am me!

She pounds her chest to punctuate every word...

JENNIFER: Me! Me! Me!

UNSEEN ADVENTURES

》》 The Doctor knows far more than he's letting on about the Flesh and the history of its independence. Although we don't know for sure that he's witnessed Flesh beings first hand before, he knows enough to suspect what might have happened to Amy...

》》 In a TARDIS scene cut from the beginning of this episode we would have seen a 'dear little hatch' in the floor beneath the console – installed, so the Doctor informs Amy, for the 'loading and unloading of walnuts'!

HATCH-WATCH

》》 As she hunts for Rory in the tunnels under the monastery, Amy opens a door – to see Madame Kovarian peering at her once more, through her strange little window...

BEHIND THE SCENES

MATTHEW GRAHAM

Writer

The Gangers being used as 'tools', being destroyed and then cast aside, is a pretty disturbing idea. Did you worry that it might be too dark, or even too complex or 'political', for a family show?

The original references that Steven and myself talked about were *The Thing* and *Invasion of the Body Snatchers* so I was a little worried it might get too ghoulish even for *Doctor Who*. You just have to balance it out with wit and humanity. When I saw the Flesh for the first time, though... And Cleaves's head twisting 180 degrees – yikes! I wondered if that would make the cut.

Rory comes into his own here, deciding to help out and stand by Jennifer. Was it fun to help shepherd him to independence from Amy – at least for a little while?

The danger with Rory is that he can become the gooseberry between Amy and the Doctor. Plus Arthur Darvill is so good and so likeable in the role I just felt it was part of my responsibility to develop a strong story strand for him. But then, of course, in the mid-season finale he reaches new heights anyway.

Considering his connections with *Life on Mars* and *Ashes to Ashes*, did you approach Marshall Lancaster about guest starring in the story? Or was that just a happy coincidence?

I thought Marshall would be a great fit with the hapless Buzzer (sorry Marsh!). It just so happened that Marcus Wilson, who line produced *Life on Mars*, had thought of him too. We both agreed it was fate, so that was that.

THE FIGHT FOR GANGER

PRE-MORPETH JETSAN

In 2120 molecular scientists at the Bio-Cellular Institute of Dungeness developed the Flesh – programmable matter that could be manipulated at the molecular level to create an exact replica of any living being. The possibilities for military and industrial use were immediately seized. Workers or soldiers operating in hazardous environments could now control their own dopplegängers – or, colloquially, 'Gangers' – from a remote harness that plumbed their entire skills and personalities directly into these perfect Flesh puppets.

Taken from Infopedia v.7.7.0
(most rights reserved)

LONER MAKES HIS PARTY GO WITH A GANG!

TRAGIC Jerry Gront was fined by his bosses for holding a birthday party at which the 25 invited guests were all Gangers of himself.

'It was the only way I could be sure anyone would turn up and I've always preferred my own company' said confirmed bachelor Jerry, 32. Wonder if he gave himself the bumps?!

Flesh fakes fuel fantastic finances at Fossil Fuel Facility!

PRODUCTIVITY at the Braymeister Fossil Fuel Facility has quadrupled since the management there decided to employ the newest technological breakthrough – those much-discussed Flesh work machines known as 'Gangers' – on the most hazardous and gruelling mining work.

A worker (cont p4)

New acid-mining plant on Greycave Isle now operational

The company's new acid-mining plant on Greycave Isle in the heart of the North Atlantic has been opened by founder Bartholomew Jetsam

'We are proud to be providing battery acid to the military,' he said. 'And prouder still that with our unprecedented increase in productivity, we are now the army's number one supplier of rechargable fuel cells. Using Gangers has been key to this achievement.'

FEAR THE FLESH

During a freak power surge, Derek Wimslow became detached from his Ganger. The Ganger had recently suffered an injury, losing part of its ear to a refuse-claw. Now acting independently from Derek, the Ganger turned on him and tried to tear Derek's ear off in what was described by onlookers as 'a blatant act of revenge'. Landfill managers were quick to dismiss the incident as 'a freak one-off'. The seemingly free-thinking Ganger was merely operating like a headless chicken, unable to function correctly without its human operator. It was decommissioned back into pure Flesh within seconds of the attack. But Derek has a different take - 'I saw the look in its eyes. It knew what it was doing. It was full of anger and hate and, I think, fear.'

From 'Fear the Flesh!' hyperweblog

RIGHTS

POST-MORPETH JETSAN

Who was the Weatherman?

From page 1

Mining plant foreman Miranda Cleaves was very reluctant to go into any detail about the trio, and would only say that it was their swift actions which gave herself and her team any chance at all to prepare for the huge solar tsunami, adding that this 'Doctor' was key to their new understanding of the sentience of the Flesh. 'The Doctor opened our eyes to their humanity and, in fact, our own,' she confirmed to reporters.

GBC NEWS Global surveillance teams still baffled by UFO.

His heart goes on

Margaret Murray thought that her husband's tragic car crash was the end. But now, two years later, she is to marry his Ganger.

'I know that Gordon would approve,' Murray stated. 'I know that for a fact because I've asked him – his Ganger, that is – and he assures me it's fine.'

Despite Gordon 2 feeling that he was already married to Margaret, the couple decided to renew their vows and tie the knot all over again. 'We're honouring the fact that Gordon's Ganger is a person in his own right,' Murray told us.

---

http://www.gangersareourchildren.org

We Gave Them Life.
They Are Our Children.

SIGN NOW – CLICK HERE!

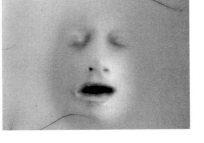

This petition demands a full inquiry into the shocking state of affairs re. the rights of so-called 'Gangers', and the dangerous, some might say ILLEGAL working conditions these SLAVES endure! We must follow where India has led the way – granting independence to their 1.6 million Gangers. WE MUST FOLLOW OUR HEARTS AND ACT NOW!

MAKING MONSTERS

One of the most memorably creepy creations of recent years made their debut in *Doctor Who* this season. Smooth, pale-skinned and disturbingly flexible, there was nothing 'almost' about the terrifying effect the Gangers had on viewers. Not to mention the Doctor...

THE FLESH

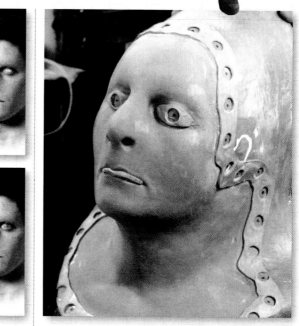

'Matthew Graham's scripts were great and the Flesh was a really nice idea,' says monster-builder Neill Gorton, head of Millennium FX. 'It was a bit worrying in terms of the schedule, because there were a lot of prosthetics to be applied and a lot of the actors were also playing two roles. It was difficult in terms of practicalities, but it turned out well.'

Indeed it did. *The Rebel Flesh* and *The Almost People* introduced a fascinating new creation – 'monster' seems the wrong word – to the world of *Doctor Who*. One which, just like humanity itself, was capable of good or evil. Not to mention one which was secretly being used to impersonate poor imprisoned, pregnant Amy Pond...

'Our design for the Flesh needed to be practical to achieve,' Neill remembers, 'but also interesting to look at. The script described the Flesh-sculpted Gangers as having human-like faces but with smoothed-out features, almost jelly-like. That means you haven't got a lot to design with, so I tried to imagine what it might look like if a face was made of wax and then heated, so that it melted into something smooth and shiny. I wanted it to look like the Gangers were still forming, but with character in there too, so you could still tell who they were and get the performance you needed from the actors underneath the prosthetics.'

Neill was inspired by a line of script specifying that the Flesh were made of 'eyeball material'. 'That's one of those classic lines from a writer

where you go, "that sounds great, but what does it mean?"', Neill laughs. 'But actually it was a good starting point – we began thinking about the white parts of an eye – that wet, slightly jelly-like stuff with little red veins threaded through.'

So Millennium went to work, trying that icky look on a face. 'We made these silicon prosthetics which were very translucent, then put the red veins in. Luckily, most of our sets and shots were very dark, because if you put those white faces in a white

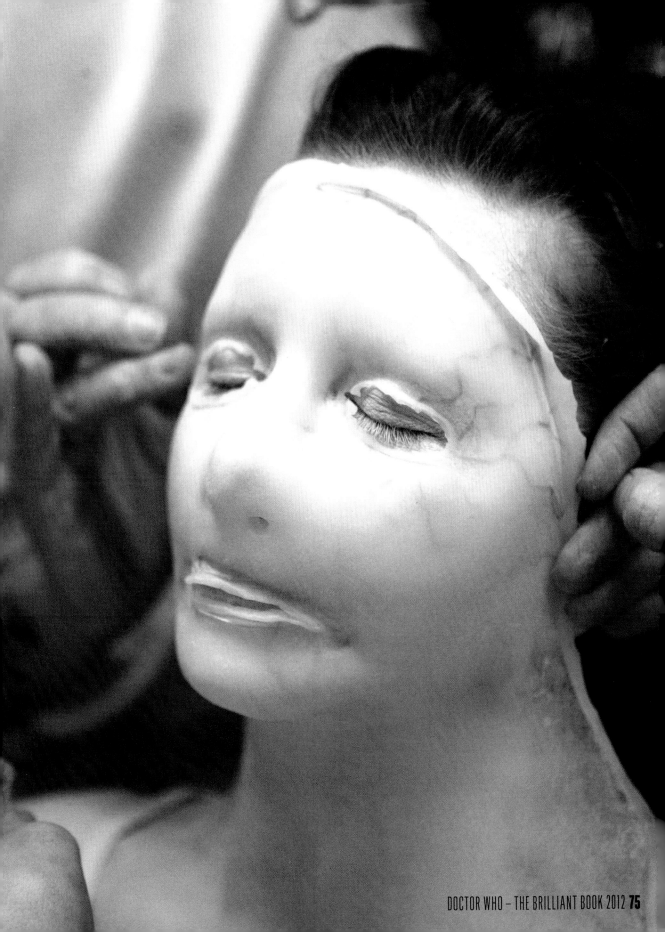

MAKING MONSTERS

room, it'd look too horrible. We put a wet-looking layer over the whole thing, too, to make it glisten. We had two stages for our Ganger make-up. First the main, squidgy prosthetics and contact lenses, then another where they're just pale, with no lenses, and look almost human.'

The nature of the Flesh actors' contact lenses needed careful consideration. 'Because the face is basically white, we thought we should do something reflective and simple for the eyes too. We wanted them to look like the colour hadn't been filled in yet. We found this nice, silvery material which contrasted well with the face.'

Did Neill's team rein themselves in at any point, fearing that their design might be too scary?

'Not really – although I think they do look pretty scary as they turned out! They needed to resemble human beings and have that smoothed-out look. We did try a few more lumpy-bumpy designs, as if the face was still trying to form, but it looked too complicated. The smoothness seemed to work much better.'

Once the Ganger performers had been fitted with their prosthetics during shooting, CG experts The Mill stepped in to make the 'almost people' carry out the creepy contortions the script called for. As Neill Gorton notes, 'When you've got arms stretching four times their length and faces becoming puddles of fluid, that's where we step back and let The Mill take over.'

'We enjoyed doing the bit where the Ganger version of leader Cleaves (played by Raquel

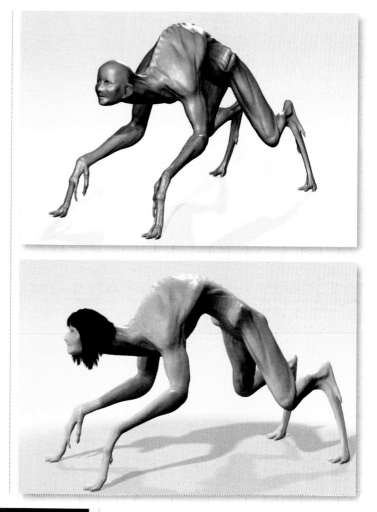

Cassidy) twists her head around 180 degrees,' says The Mill's Murray Barber with a laugh. 'That was actually two shots combined – one of her facing away from camera and one of her turning to face it. We then used a software package to morph the two shots together.'

Possibly the maddest moment of the whole two episodes came in *The Rebel Flesh*, when Jennifer smashed through a window in the bathroom, her head on the end of a long, tentacle-like neck.

'Absolutely bonkers and surreal,' Murray agrees. 'That was in the script pretty much from the start. We shot the actress Sarah Smart against a green screen and moved her towards the camera, while getting her to act in this weird, serpent-like way. Then we basically created a computer-generated neck, tacked it onto her head, then composited the two together.'

DOCTOR URGH!

In these episodes, Matt Smith got first-hand experience of FX make-up...

>> *The Rebel Flesh* and *The Almost People* marked the first time Matt Smith had to wear prosthetic make-up, as he tackled the dual role of the Doctor and his Ganger duplicate.

'We've had fun with our Doctors so far,' Neill Gorton grins. 'We made David Tennant up as an old man (in *The Last of the Time Lords*), so it was only right that Matt Smith got to experience something prosthetic too. It was good to have something to do on Matt and it worked extremely well because you can tell it's him. He was very keen to experience it, because he'd spent a couple of years working with actors who were wearing prosthetics. '

The Flesh make-up process took, on average, two hours per actor. Neill is full of praise for Matt's patience. 'He handled it very well,' Neill says. 'Matt's naturally a very energetic guy, so it's hard work for him to sit very still in a chair for two hours. But he was very patient with it all and, fortunately for him, he only had to do it once. I think after that he really felt for the other actors who had to suffer it for days on end.'

That scene is also quite unusual for *Doctor Who*, in that it properly makes you jump. 'Totally!' enthuses Murray. 'Nobody's expecting that to happen. I also like the moment in *The Almost People* when Jennifer's jaw extends down. Originally, she was going to devour Buzzer (Marshall Lancaster) and eat him in front of us, like a snake. We thought of different ways of doing it – including shadows on a wall, which we even started shooting – but in the end it was cut.'

The grisly mound of discarded Flesh in *The Almost People* gave rise to much discussion among the production team. 'We had huge discussions about the "Fleshpile",' Murray reveals. 'It was originally going to be this massive pile of bodies, but there were worries that it would just look too grim. In the end, we used life-sized dolls and painted CG Flesh onto them.'

Rather unexpectedly, it seems that the Jennifer Monster seen at the end of the second episode was inspired by pop queen Madonna...

'We wanted that creature to be quite sinewy and muscular,' Murray says. 'Funnily enough, we used a reference photo of a certain ageing pop star! It was a shot from a couple of years ago and her arms were just really sinewy, white, veiny and fleshy. She probably wouldn't take that too well if she knew...'

'The Flesh were a great creation,' Murray states, proudly. 'Neill Gorton's make-up was fantastic – that first shot of the Flesh Doctor looked especially great. The creepiest shot in the whole two episodes, for me, was just before Jennifer transformed into the creature and her eyes turn slowly to the side. It really was incredibly unnerving.'

The Almost People

BY MATTHEW GRAHAM

THE STORY

The humans and their Gangers have turned on each other. With their animosity growing by the second, it's up to the Doctor to calm the waters before tragedy strikes. So what's the best way of getting the humans to trust him? By making a Flesh duplicate of himself, of course...

The two Doctors set about trying to broker peace between the workers and their doubles – but the situation is spiralling out of control. This is war – and the Doctor and his friends are caught in the crossfire. Led by a resolute Cleaves and an increasingly unhinged Jennifer, the Gangers make their move. Rescue copters are moving in to evacuate the island, and the Gangers plan to kill the humans and take their places, escaping to their borrowed lives on the mainland.

Battling desperately to save as many people – human and Ganger – as he can, the Doctor clashes with Amy over whether his Ganger is actually 'real'. Amy's not so sure – but as the pieces of the Doctor's plan finally click into place, the greatest irony becomes clear –Amy is a Flesh duplicate.

The real Amy is somewhere far away – and she's having a baby. Now it's up to Rory and the Doctor to save them both...

Where Have I Seen?

RAQUEL CASSIDY
Foreman Cleaves
Raquel starred with Matt Smith in BBC Two drama *Party Animals*, and played Jack Dee's partner in BBC Four's *Lead Balloon*.

MARK BONNAR
Jimmy
Mark plays Detective Finney in BBC Two's black comedy *Psychoville*. He also starred in the short-lived BBC One SF crime drama *Paradox*.

NUMBER CRUNCHING

2 DOCTORS **2** AMYS **1** TERRIBLY CONFUSED RORY

THE ALMOST PEOPLE

At the opening of the episode, as the Flesh Doctor stabilises, he runs through some of his oldest memories. 'One day, we will get back. Yes, one day,' he says, recalling lines spoken by the First Doctor in the first ever *Doctor Who* episode, A*n Unearthly Child* (1963). He then worries about '[reversing] the polarity of the neutron flow', which was a catchphrase attributed to the Third Doctor – though actually he rarely said it. (The line is like *Doctor Who*'s version of 'Beam me up, Scotty!' or 'Elementary, my dear Watson!') Then, the Doctor – with the Fourth Doctor's voice – asks, 'Would you like a jelly baby?', a reminder of that incarnation's love of the sweets. And finally, we hear the Tenth Doctor: 'Hello, I'm the Doctor!' – before the real Doctor reminds his Flesh self: 'Let it go! We've moved on!' Testing his duplicate's memories, the Doctor asks his Ganger to describe the Cybermats, which he does: 'Created by the Cybermen, could kill by feeding off brainwaves.' (The Cybermats debuted in *The Tomb of the Cybermen* (1967) and, funnily enough, they make a reappearance later in this season, in *Closing Time*.) In lines cut from the finished version, the Doctor also quizzes his double on the events of *The Mind of Evil* (1971), asking about the Master's plan to use the Keller Machine to destroy mankind. He also asks the Flesh Doctor how he feels when his friends leave the TARDIS, reeling off a list of the Doctor's former travelling companions: 'Jo [Grant, 1971–1973], Sarah Jane [Smith, 1973–1976], Romana [two incarnations of the Time Lady, 1978–1981], Rose [Tyler, 2005–2006], Martha [Jones, 2007], Donna [Noble, 2008]...' A further cut sequence would have given us a tour through the very real memories of the Flesh Doctor – memories that we, as viewers, had seen 'our' Doctor go through at various points throughout the long history of the show. Described in the script as 'Doctor's Happy Memories Montage', it would have featured the following

elements: Gallifrey – the Time Lords watching over him, and with Susan on their first voyage [these would both pre-date the broadcast adventures of the Doctor]; with Sarah Jane defeating Davros on Skaro [*Genesis of the Daleks* (1975)]; with Jo Grant bouncing over the fields in Bessie [some time during the Third Doctor's adventures]; meeting Rose and taking her hand – 'Run!' [*Rose* (2005)]; captivated by Madame de Pompadour [*The Girl in the Fireplace* (2006)]; embracing Captain Jack, and sharing a joke with Mickey [these could have come from many points in the series after 2005]; K-9 [the Doctor's robot dog companion was introduced in *The Invisible Enemy* (1977) before leaving

with Romana in *Warriors' Gate* (1981), so this flashback could have come from anywhere between those times, or possibly K-9's later appearances in the show, *The Five Doctors* (1983), *School Reunion* (2006) or *Journey's End* (2008)]; magnificent in the face of the Daleks [again, this could have come from any number of stories – the Doctor makes a habit of being magnificent in the face of the Daleks]; eating fish fingers and custard while little Amy giggles [*The Eleventh Hour* (2010)]; holding Amy's ankle as she floats in space [*The Beast Below* (2010)]; bursting out of the cake at Rory's stag, and showing Amy and Rory Venice [both from *The Vampires of Venice* (2010)]; at their wedding [*The Big Bang* (2010)]; whisking them away, all together in the TARDIS – inseparable – invincible – together [These more recent flashbacks would have been from any point after *The Big Bang* (2010)]. Thinking that she's talking to his duplicate, Amy manages to let slip to the Doctor that – back in *The Impossible Astronaut* – she and Rory witnessed him die and that he invited them to watch. At one point, the Doctor refers to Rory as 'Roricus Pondicus' – a sideways reference to his life as a Roman in *The Pandorica Opens* (2010).

MAGIC MOMENT

Back in the TARDIS, the Doctor confronts Amy and explains the secret he has been hiding...

THE DOCTOR: I needed enough information to block the signal to the Flesh.
AMY: What signal...?
THE DOCTOR: The signal to you.
AMY: Doctor...
THE DOCTOR: Stand away from her, Rory.
RORY: Why? No – and why?!
THE DOCTOR: Given what we've learned, I'll be as humane as I can – but I need to do this, and you need to stand away.

AMY: Doctor, I am frightened. I'm properly, properly scared.
THE DOCTOR: Don't be. Hold on. We're coming for you, I swear it. Whatever happens, however hard, however far – we will find you.
AMY: I'm right here.
THE DOCTOR: No, you're not. You haven't been here for a long, long time.

HATCH-WATCH

》》 When it happens once again, Amy finally reveals to the Doctor that she's been seeing an eyepatch-wearing woman appear out of thin air through a number of impossible hatches. The Doctor tells her it's nothing to worry about – because he's finally worked out what's going on...

UNSEEN ADVENTURES

》》 The Flesh Doctor reminds the original Doctor of the time he plugged his brain 'into the core of an entire planet just so you could halt its orbit and win a bet'. We never find out exactly what he won...

DELETED!

THE OTHER DOCTOR: Why you, Jennifer? Why were you the one who remembered all the pain the Flesh could feel?
FLESH JENNIFER: I've always had an amazing memory. Total recall, they call it. Now, what was it Foreman Cleaves liked to call us?
FLESH CLEAVES: Forklift trucks.
FLESH JENNIFER: Just tools. Well, it seems the tools in the toolbox have rebelled – and I am their leader! Queen of the Hammers! Princess of the Screwdrivers! Duchess of the Forklift Trucks!
THE OTHER DOCTOR: These memories are too much for you. I felt a hint of it and it was almost too much for me...
FLESH JENNIFER: The humans will be melted – as they deserve. Then, their factory will be destroyed. You're one of us, Doctor – join the revolution.

BEHIND THE SCENES
MATTHEW GRAHAM
Writer

Meek little Jennifer became the driving force behind the Gangers' rebellion – what made her snap?
I liked the idea of the quietest character on the island turning the most wicked. Originally Jennifer had 'total recall' – a perfect memory. This gave her Ganger the ability to recall in horrific detail everything that had ever beset her as a factory tool. During editing those lines were cut, though if you look closely you will see evidence of Jen's amazing memory when she gives the Doctor directions to the monitoring station.

Amy's reaction to the Ganger Doctor doesn't show her in a good light – was it tricky to write?
Amy's reaction to the two Doctors is, I think, a little harsh – but believable. You can't love both, surely? That would be trite. By tricking her, the Doctor highlights her very human prejudices. She makes assumptions about the one she *thinks* is a ganger and her bigotry isn't nice to see, especially when the truth is revealed. By the end, however, Amy has grown as a person, hopefully.

Did you come up with the idea of the Flesh, or did Steven Moffat already have the ending in mind?
Steven suggested something about cloning and avatars being forced to do dangerous jobs and then rebelling. I created the Flesh and the monastery/factory world after that. At some point during this process, Steven decided he wanted Amy to be Flesh and began working that story back through the earlier scripts. So I think as we developed this story, Steven developed the Flesh Amy idea. I wasn't asked to write that twist ending until very near shooting. So I think Steven only had it fully worked through at that point – in that Möbius strip he calls a brain!

The Lesson of the Unholy Water

The earliest accounts of the Well of the Mother's Tears suggest it has stood on this site since the 11th century. In the early 17th century, the holy waters of the Well began to dwindle and the Abbot of the Monastery ordered the Well dug deeper. Pilgrims spread word that the water's flavour was somewhat changed, and soon came reports of healings and the driving out of devils — all were ascribed to the remarkable nature of this deeper water, now blessed with a refreshing sharpness.

People came from far and wide to drink of the remarkable water, or to clamour to be re-baptised in it. One of these travellers, a Brother Smith, called the Abbot's attention to the Well and declared that he must at once stop the pilgrims, who grew daily more numerous, from partaking of its waters. He asked that he be permitted to remove a little of the water with his strange silvered flask, and thence subject it to alchemical testing.

Appalled, the Abbot overruled Brother Smith, and, hoping to sate the ever-increasing demands on the blessed water from the hordes of pilgrims who now crowded the Monastery, he had the Well of the Mother's Tears dug deeper still.

And lo! The rusted, ancient tools used in this endeavour underwent a miraculous transformation. They left the now fierce-flowing water as shiny and bright as when first forged. But Brother Smith became more voluble still at this news. The Abbot was sore tempted to test the Brother for signs of demonic possession, so crazed was he.

It was then that bold Brother Smith, to the shock of all present, tore a strip from the Abbot's vestments and dropped the cloth into the Well. Those attending gasped to watch the cloth smoulder and burn.

Brother Smith announced that the Well had been dug too deep — its waters now were as poison, and no man could long survive its touch.

Realising that his hasty actions had dug down almost to the sulphurous pits of Hell itself, the Abbot ordered the Well sealed for ever. Brother Smith was never heard of again, but is sung of still as the saviour of this holy place.

IT'S YOU... BUT **DISPOSABLE!**

You'll never know the difference. Plumb into our synthetic **Flesh**, test drive the latest **Ganger**, and see for yourselves.

Your Ganger can do anything you can, with one added advantage. It's **completely disposable**, and if damaged or destroyed can be replaced in seconds.

Whether you're working in a **hazardous environment**, or simply looking for the next **adrenaline rush** in the extreme sport of your choice, a Ganger is the ultimate solution. No more scars, no more broken bones. **Let your Ganger do all the suffering.**

The New Ganger 6 Series from Morpeth-Jetsan.

MORPETH JETSAN

WARNING: Your Ganger may very occasionally become sentient, try to kill you and steal your life. Morpeth Jetsan accepts no liability in this event.

DEPENDABLE. EXPENDABLE. YOU.

A Good Man Goes To War

BY STEVEN MOFFAT

THE STORY

From every corner of time and space, an army is being recruited. On the foggy streets of Victorian London, a Silurian adventuress finally has a chance to repay her debt. On the mud-caked battlefields of a war-torn planet, a disgraced Sontaran warrior hopes for a chance at redemption. And even Dorium Maldovar, closing his bar for the last time, cannot escape his fate.

Only one person refuses the call to arms. River Song knows what will happen today – and she can't interfere. In her Stormcage cell, she awaits the Doctor's downfall...

With an army at his command, the Doctor has arrived at Demon's Run. He has come to free Amy Pond and her baby daughter, Melody. No legion of Clerics, no Headless Monks, not even Madame Kovarian herself can stand in his way. Within minutes, the Doctor has the asteroid in his grasp. Amy is reunited with her husband, and baby Melody is safe at last.

But it's a trap. The baby is a Flesh replica, and Kovarian's forces turn on the Doctor in a bloody battle that sees more than one warrior fall. Shattered and heartbroken, the Doctor faces his darkest hour.

And that's where River comes in...

NUMBER CRUNCHING

Episode 7 of this series
Episode 777
of Doctor Who

3.40 THE TIME THE DOCTOR NEEDS TO TAKE DEMON'S RUN

3.42 THE TIME IT ACTUALLY TAKES HIM

A GOOD MAN GOES TO WAR

>> The Cybermen seen in this episode are not the ones that originated in the parallel universe in *Rise of the Cybermen/The Age of Steel* (2006). Those ones, built by Cybus Industries, had a 'C' logo on their chest plates – these Cybermen have no such marking. We know (from 2005's *Dalek* and many stories prior) that our universe has its own Cybermen, so this is the first on-screen sighting of the 'original' version since *Silver Nemesis* (1988) – and not the last, as they also return in *Closing Time* (2011). >> Rory appears once more in his Roman garb from *The Pandorica Opens* (2010), and his 'Last Centurion' alias is a reference to the myths that built up around his 2,000-year vigil over the Pandorica in *The Big Bang* (2010). >> Sontaran warrior-nurse Strax is played by Dan Starkey, who appeared as other Sontarans in *The Sontaran Stratagem/The Poison Sky* (2008) and *The End of Time, Part Two* (2010). A similar 'disgraced' Sontaran, Skorm, had appeared in Gareth Roberts' unmade Series Five script, tentatively titled *Death to the Doctor*. Steven Moffat informed a delighted Roberts that his character idea would see the light of day after all. >> Dorium Maldovar made his first appearance in *The Pandorica Opens*, in which he supplies River with her vortex manipulator. He reappears – well, a bit of him does – in *The Wedding of River Song*. >> On a sign on the wall (blink and you'll miss it!) Kovarian's facility is called 'Demons Run' (also one of the working titles for this episode), which makes sense in the context of the proverb that gives the episode its title: 'Demons run when a good man goes to war'. It's also written as such in the script. The on-screen caption, however, reads 'Demon's Run'. Maybe, over time, people forgot where its name came from and changed it to this seemingly more sensible spelling. >> A large part of Kovarian's militia is made up of the Anglican troops first seen in *The Time of Angels/Flesh and Stone* (2010). Here, we learn they receive commands from a 'Papal Mainframe' (who's female) and that 'Level One Heresy [is] punishable by death'. (Lesser heresies presumably call for such punishments as defragging your rosaries or backing up the confessional.) Some planets are 'Heaven neutral', and so fall outside the jurisdiction of the Church. >> The creepy Headless Monks were first mentioned in *The Time of Angels*. Turns out, they *are* actually headless. >> The Fat One mentions a story about the Doctor, in which he drove the Atraxi from a planet, then 'called them back for a scolding' – which is, of course, what happened in *The Eleventh Hour* (2010). >> 'He is not a goblin,' Colonel 'Runaway' Manton tells his soldiers, 'or a phantom or a trickster.' This line echoes the myths we heard in *The Pandorica Opens*: the Doctor is viewed as such by many races across the universe, which explains why nearly everyone wants to see him dead, imprisoned or erased from history. The Tenth Doctor faced a real Trickster in *The Sarah Jane Adventures: The Wedding of Sarah Jane Smith* (2009), and one of his 'Brigade' – a Time Beetle in *Turn Left* (2008). >> The Doctor's army also features Judoon troopers (introduced in *Smith and Jones* (2007)), Spitfire pilot Danny Boy from *Victory of the Daleks* (2010), and Captain Henry Avery and his son Toby from *The Curse of the Black Spot*. In a short scene cut from the final episode, we would also have seen the Doctor aided by Ood Sigma, who debuted in *Planet of the Ood* (2008), then returned to shepherd the Doctor through his final hours in *The Waters of Mars* (2009) and *The End of Time* (2009–2010). Russell T Davies's credit as creator of the Ood remains on the end titles. >> On top of learning that Melody Pond will one day grow up to be River, we begin to get clues as to why Kovarian wanted to steal her, how exactly Melody is linked to the child seen in *The Impossible Astronaut*, and what part River will come to play in the Doctor's life. Kovarian calls the child 'hope, in this endless bitter war... against you', because she is planning to use the child as a tailor-made psychopath designed to kill the Doctor, as we find out in *Let's Kill Hitler*. 'They're going to turn her into a weapon,' River says (and she should know!), 'just to bring you down.' >> The idea of the English language getting the word 'doctor' from our hero's name was first put forward by Steven Moffat in 1995, in a posting to the Usenet message boards in the early days of internet discussion. Now who's spoiling stuff on the net! >> The Untempered Schism, a window into the space-time vortex mentioned by Madame Vastra, was seen in *The Sound of Drums* (2007). Exposure to its energies drove the Master mad. >> Finally, Idris's words from *The Doctor's Wife* make sense: 'the only water in the forest is the river' is a reference to the Gamma Forests, from which Lorna Bucket hails. In the whole, wide expanse of the Forests, the only form of water known to the people is a single river: hence, Lorna doesn't quite know how to translate 'Pond' into her language when she stitches Melody's name into the prayer leaf, choosing instead the closest thing she knows. This was also another of the true teasers supplied by Steven Moffat for last year's *Brilliant Book*.

HATCH-WATCH

>> Just when we thought we'd never see Kovarian slide open her hatch again – there she is, floating in the air in front of the Flesh replica of poor baby Melody...

MAGIC MOMENT

River has finally arrived at Demon's Run, where she confronts the Doctor with the truth...

THE DOCTOR: You think I wanted this? I didn't do this. This – this wasn't me!
RIVER: This was exactly you. All this, all of it. You make them so afraid. When you began all those years ago, sailing off to see the universe, did you ever think you'd become this? The man who can turn an army around at the mention of his name. Doctor. The word for 'healer' and 'wise man', throughout the universe. We get that word from you, you know. But if you carry on the way you are, what might that word come to mean?
Tears in his eyes, the Doctor is stunned into silence.
RIVER: To the people of the Gamma Forests, the word 'doctor' means 'mighty warrior'. How far you've come. And now they've taken a child, the child of your best friends – and they're going to turn her into a

weapon, just to bring you down.
River stands over the Doctor's cot.
RIVER: And all this, my love, in fear of you.
THE DOCTOR: Who are you?
RIVER: Oh, look, your cot! Haven't seen that in a very long while!
THE DOCTOR: No. No, you tell me who you are.
RIVER: I am telling you. Can't you read?
Finally, looking down into the cot, the Doctor understands...
THE DOCTOR: Hello.

DELETED!

The Thin/Fat Gay Married Anglican Marines and Lorna Bucket are discussing the Headless Monks and the Fat One's upcoming conversion...

LORNA: They believe the domain of faith is the heart, and the domain of doubt is the head. They follow their hearts, that's all.
FAT ONE: See? We just follow our hearts.
THIN ONE: We? What are you talking about?
FAT ONE: Special deal. Extra food rations if you do a temporary conversion to the local faith.

THIN ONE: And you really need more food, don't you, muffin top?
FAT ONE: Words can't hurt me. Except those words – those are hurtful words.
THIN ONE: You're Lorna Bucket, aren't you?
LORNA: Yep.
FAT ONE: Can we call you Bucket? Lorna's boring.
THIN ONE: She's not boring. She's pretty and a tiny bit hot.
FAT ONE: How would you know or care?
THIN ONE: I married a man with an ample bosom – you're turning me.

BEHIND THE SCENES
STEVEN MOFFAT
Writer

Can you give us any insight into what life for poor Amy was like, held prisoner by Kovarian and the forces of the Silence?
I think it would have been a relatively 'kind' imprisonment. The Clerics are professional soldiers, they don't rough people up for no reason – and they've all been trained to be terrified of the Doctor, so it would be kid gloves with Amy. I like to think they went out of their way to say, 'We're not at war with you, you're not our enemy' and Amy would listen very patiently, and nod – and then headbutt them all.

How many more favours do you think the Doctor could call in? Just how big an army could he summon if he really tried?
Well, vast, really. Epic. He's cashing in centuries of kindness – which, of course, he never should do. It's like the Godfather, saying, 'One day I will call on you for a service...' A lapse for the Doctor, but that's kind of the point. This is when he starts to realise no one should have this much influence – not even him.

Some of the characters in this episode became instant fan favourites. Might we see more of Vastra or Strax one day?
There are plans. They're over here in this safe marked TOP SECRET, look.

UNSEEN ADVENTURES

When she was a young girl, Lorna Bucket met the Doctor in the Gamma Forests. He said 'run' a lot, but he has no memory of ever meeting her. We like to think it's because, for him, the meeting has not yet taken place.

PAPAL MAINFRAME

DORIUM MALDOVAR
SPECIES: unknown
HOME PLANET: unknown
AGE: unknown (appears mid-40s)
APPEARANCE: blue, obese, humanoid

A mysterious figure with good connections. Former owner of drinking establishment The Maldovarium. Supplied M. Kovarian with information concerning location of Headless Monks' base. Also supplied software for security systems - acquired from Judoon trooper - which he eventually used against us. Maldovar turned traitor when he joined the Doctor's legions, having an old debt to repay. He was decapitated by the Monks soon after the main battle. His head was not found.

MANTON
RANK: Colonel
REGIMENT: Anglican Marines
ID NUMBER: 2349990AM

UPDATE:
Official designation of this officer is now changed to COLONEL RUNAWAY.
Effective immediately.

COMMANDER STRAX
SPECIES: Sontaran
HOME PLANET: Sontar
AGE: 11
APPEARANCE: squat, beige, dome-headed

The Doctor recruited this disgraced Sontaran warrior-turned-nurse during the Battle of Zarusthra in 4037 AD, where he was tending to human soldiers, seemingly as a punishment for unknown crimes. He had been gene spliced for nursing duties. He was capable of producing lactic fluid like a human female, and had enormous medical knowledge. As with all of his species, he was highly trained for war. Fortunately he died at the hands of the Monks during the final battle.

REPORT 120006758
BATTLE OF DEMON'S RUN / SECTION 19C / THE DOCTOR'S ALLIES

Mission compromised due partly to the Doctor's allies. Below are reports on what we have been able to find out about all his fellow terrorists, some of whom died in battle. Those who survived have been added to the Papal Mainframe 'most wanted' list.

MADAME VASTRA

SPECIES: Silurian female
HOME PLANET: Earth
AGE: unknown
APPEARANCE: reptilian, scaled, green

Vastra is a carnivorous crime-fighter from London, 1888 AD. With her 'companion' Jenny she joined the Doctor - allegedly to repay a debt after the Time Lord prevented her from killing workers during the construction of an ancient underground transport network. Her race, Earth Reptiles (colloquially known as 'Silurians') once ruled planet Sol 3. She brought fellow Silurian backup with her to Demon's Run. According to legend, she consumed a famous 19th-century murderer called 'Jack the Ripper'. Among her many weapons is a whip-like tongue with a poisonous barb which can be deployed over several metres. Keep well back.

JENNY

SPECIES: Human
HOME PLANET: Earth
AGE: unknown (appears early 20s)
APPEARANCE: white, female, dark haired

Little is known about this human ally of the Doctor's. She came into the battle with Vastra and it is assumed she hails from the 1880s time period. She acted as maidservant to the Silurian female, though we have reason to believe that she and Vastra were on rather more intimate terms. They both survived the battle and returned to their own time.

'PIRATE' CREW?

A small squad of humanoids in archaic costume were able to board M. Kovarian's ship, subdue its crew and prevent her from escaping. The likeness of the lead male has been compu-matched to that of Henry Avery, a nautical pirate from 17th-century Earth whose disappearance was never explained. Until now, we must assume.

JUDOON TROOPERS

It has yet to be explained why members of this interplanetary mercenary police force also assisted our enemy's efforts. An official complaint to the Shadow Proclamation has received no response as yet.

ADDENDUM:

My thanks for this report, Colonel Runaway. Most interesting. Now you may return to your other duties. The canteen needs sweeping. M.K.

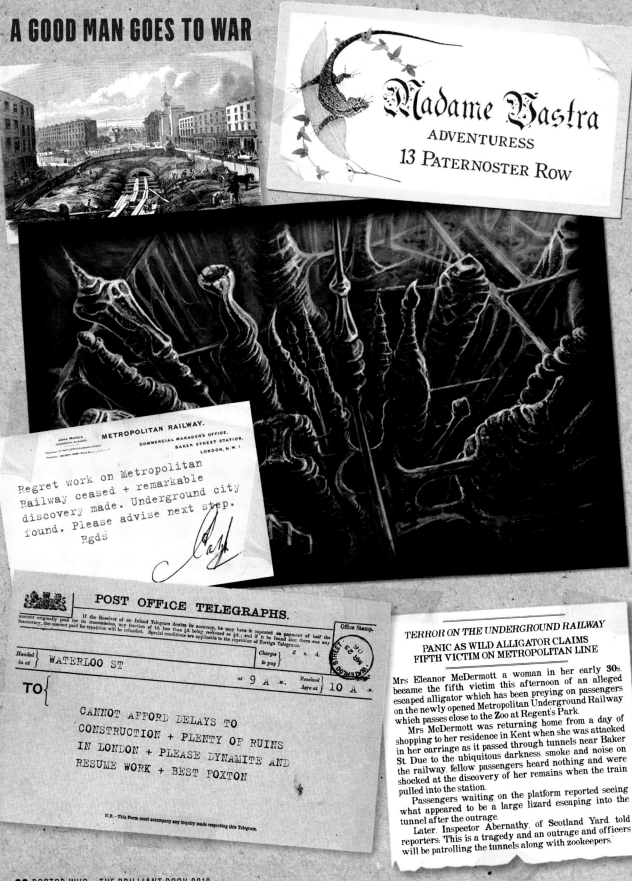

Madame Vastra
ADVENTURESS
13 PATERNOSTER ROW

METROPOLITAN RAILWAY.

JOHN MARPLE
COMMERCIAL MANAGER

COMMERCIAL MANAGER'S OFFICE,
BAKER STREET STATION,
LONDON, N.W.1

Regret work on Metropolitan
Railway ceased + remarkable
discovery made. Underground city
found. Please advise next step.
Rgds

POST OFFICE TELEGRAPHS.

amount originally paid for its transmission, any fraction of 1d. less than ½d. being reckoned as ½d.; and if it be found that there was any
inaccuracy, the amount paid for repetition will be refunded. Special conditions are applicable to the repetition of Foreign Telegrams.

Office Stamp.

| Handed in at | WATERLOO ST | | Charges to pay | £ s. d. | |

at 9 A.M. Received here at 10 A.M.

TO {

CANNOT AFFORD DELAYS TO
CONSTRUCTION + PLENTY OF RUINS
IN LONDON + PLEASE DYNAMITE AND
RESUME WORK + BEST FOXTON

N.B.—This Form must accompany any Inquiry made respecting this Telegram.

TERROR ON THE UNDERGROUND RAILWAY

PANIC AS WILD ALLIGATOR CLAIMS
FIFTH VICTIM ON METROPOLITAN LINE

Mrs Eleanor McDermott, a woman in her early 30s,
became the fifth victim this afternoon of an alleged
escaped alligator which has been preying on passengers
on the newly opened Metropolitan Underground Railway
which passes close to the Zoo at Regent's Park.

Mrs McDermott was returning home from a day of
shopping to her residence in Kent when she was attacked
in her carriage as it passed through tunnels near Baker
St. Due to the ubiquitous darkness, smoke and noise on
the railway, fellow passengers heard nothing and were
shocked at the discovery of her remains when the train
pulled into the station.

Passengers waiting on the platform reported seeing
what appeared to be a large lizard escaping into the
tunnel after the outrage.

Later, Inspector Abernathy, of Scotland Yard, told
reporters: 'This is a tragedy and an outrage and officers
will be patrolling the tunnels along with zookeepers.'

Egypt 1881,

My Dearest Jenny

My sincerest thanks for the new shirts, they are delightful! Such wonderful cotton. My compliments also on the new gun which has also arrived safely. I have killed three Turks with it already and hope to dispatch some more this afternoon.

Excavations are proceeding well, and I am pleased to report that my colleagues have finally grown accustomed to me. The local ape descendants seem to regard me as the reincarnation of one of their many Gods which does guarantee that I am always served the soup first.

I am sorry to have missed the Doctor's visit, but I am most glad you were able to assist him defeating the Kraal plot to replace Prince Bertie with a mechanical duplicate.

You asked how I first met the Doctor — it was on a train, believe it or not. I was busily engaged in slaughtering the passengers, I regret to say. I was freshly hatched and had been horrified to discover I was the only survivor of my clutch — our entire city had been thoughtlessly destroyed during construction work on the humans' Undergound Railway. Having risen to the surface I sought mindless vengeance on the giant steam engines and the strange apes that wriggled inside them. I regret to say I was most confused and somewhat scared by what my world had become.

They sent soldiers into the tunnels after me along with dogs. Once I had overcome my alarm at the dogs, I discovered they were quite delicious.

Shortly after this, I met the Doctor in one of the tunnels. He was not afraid of me. 'Hello,' he said, speaking my people's language. He was dressed extraordinarily, even for an ape.

'You do not smell of fear,' I told him — with my mouth full, I blush to add.

'What are you eating?'

'Ape,' I shrugged. 'Tough. I don't suppose you'd care for some?'

He politely declined and told me that I had to stop eating commuters. It is difficult being told that your race is dead and your planet is overrun by vermin, but the Doctor did it well. 'What happens next?' I asked him.

'Carry on fighting, and you'll die.' He smiled. It was the first smile I had ever seen and I found it charming. 'Or you can live. Which may well be more fun.'

I must close now. I hear cries from the tomb excavations which may mean they've found the creature they were looking for. I have never eaten Ancient Egyptian before. I am looking forward to it.

U.

~ HENRY GORDON JAGO PRESENTS ~

MONSTRE GATHERING!
VOCAL! INSTRUMENTAL! THESPIAN! AND TERPSICHOREAN
FESTIVAL!!

MADAME ELEANOR
Fortune Teller

MR. MYSTERY
MAGICIAN

CHARLIE THE DOG-FACED BOY
DOG-FACED BOY

CRISPIN & GIDEON
VARIETY ENTERTAINERS OF INTERNATONAL REKNOWN

MISS ELLEN TUPPENCE
("All My Gold's A Canary")

Then, the main act:

THE AMAZING LIZARD LADY
A UNIQUE CREATURE! SHE MOVES! SHE BREATHES!
IF YOU CAN GUESS WHAT IT IS, YOU CAN HAVE IT!

*Vastra,
Probably not
the best idea!
The Doctor*

PEARCE & DARROW
("Liver and Onions")

JOVIAL JOHN SMITH
Doctor of Juggling

MR LEESON
HAS KINDLY CONSENTED TO PERFORM "THE FAITHFUL HOUND"

AND TO FINISH **MRS WALLANBY** WILL PERFORM
"JERUSALEM" WITH MILK BOTTLES.

We regret that the famous Li'Hsen Chang, Conjuror and Master of Legedermain is currently indisposed.

Dear Doctor,

My career on the stage is over! You were right — these apes have a thirst for spectacle which is tiresome. The final straw was a suggestion that I try and catch bullets with my tongue, which seemed both unwise and unsavoury. Also, I may have eaten one of the lions, which did not make me entirely popular with the company.

So I must make my own way in a world which is not my own. I have almost grown accustomed to their odour (how do you stand them?) and if I walk the streets veiled I can pass among them without attracting undue attention, which as you know, I find very tiresome.

My savings have found me lodgings above a gin palace in Cheapside with a landlady who is too drunk to ask questions. The apes around here are very rough and remind me of their wild ancestors who roamed in the forests of my childhood. Ah, how I miss hunting those creatures down! What I could accomplish around here in a weekend…

Why, only the other night I came across a young match girl being molested by a Chinese Gang. These Tongs are everywhere and forever dragging young girls off, presumably as part of a mating ritual. So, I stepped in and made short work of her assailants. The match girl had fainted clean away, so I conveyed her back to my apartments.

When she came round, she was at first startled by my appearance, then intrigued. Her gratitude towards me for saving her was most genuine, and she smelt much more pleasant than any other ape I have encountered. She rose to return to her work, but I insisted she remain — the streets were not safe for her.

'But Madam,' she said, 'I must earn money.'

'So must we all, Jenny,' I informed her. 'This is an age of luxury. I rather fancy some of it.'

'But how, Madam?' she asked.

'Fear not,' I informed her, 'I shall think of something…'

'MASKED LADY' ROBS THIRD BANK
Vaults Blown Clean Open
Police Seek Disguised Thief

The Mercantile Bank on High Holborn was last night the third bank to be attacked by the mysterious figure police are calling 'The Masked Lady'. The robber is believed to be a man, despite reports of skirts and petticoats, due to his remarkable strength and agility.

Inspector Abernathy of Scotland Yard told us, 'This so-called "Masked Lady" tunnels into bank vaults using a previously unknown method and makes away with the gold, sometimes simply by strolling up and out onto the street. On this occasion Night Watchmen were disturbed by sounds and confronted the felon and an accomplice. The men claim to have been knocked unconscious by a whip.'

Previous banks raided by the 'Masked Lady' are Wilmott's of Aldridge Lane and Sherwin & Soames of Paternoster Row. Investigations continue.

'I should, in theory, be *kissing* the Doctor *a lot more now*'

She's the Doctor's wife, Amy and Rory's daughter, and the coolest archaeologist in history. She's River Song, and she's turned **Alex Kingston** into a pin-up girl...

There are flirts and teases, seductresses and vamps – and then there's *Doctor Who*'s River Song, the femme fatale of femme fatales, residing somewhere between Cleopatra and Mrs Robinson (and she's been compared to both). Conceived on a TARDIS bunk bed on her parents' wedding night, River may be the Doctor's wife, his executioner, or his most faithful yet enigmatic travelling companion, or possibly all three. Yeah, probably that last one.

Meet Alex Kingston. Known internationally as the formidable Dr Elizabeth Corday in US hospital drama *ER* (a part she played from 1997 to 2005), the Surrey-born actress, who breathes life into River, is often cast as resilient, fiercely defiant women. These days, Alex lives in Los Angeles, but makes frequent returns to Britain. In recent years, her work here has included the 2006 West End revival of *One Flew Over the Cuckoo's Nest*, ITV1's

acclaimed 2008 drama *Lost in Austen*, and BBC One's *Hope Springs*.

When the *Brilliant Book* catches up with Alex it's at the Donmar Warehouse in Covent Garden, where she's making her London theatre comeback, as predatory aristocrat Lady Milford in a new version of Schiller's 1784 political drama *Luise Miller*. The play was originally called *Kabale und Liebe*, which translates from the German as *Intrigue and Love* – a title that makes as fitting a description of the Doctor and River's relationship as any. *Luise Miller* explores the battle between honour and corruption, between truth and betrayal, between religious adherence

and romantic individualism... but does it include a scene in which River Song orders a screwdriver-wielding Time Lord to 'go build a cabinet' while she massacres a spaceshipful of Silents? No, it does not. Theatre, eh...?

Does looking glamorous while firing a gun come easily, Alex?
No. [Laughs] It's good fun, but sometimes I have to take a deep breath and say, 'OK, Alex, you've just got to go for it.' I certainly love running around with a gun, and I have spectacular entrances and exits as River, jumping off buildings and all that. I'm healthy and I'm fit, and as long as I am, I can cope with it.

What's flirting with the Doctor like?
That sort of began with David Tennant's Doctor. It was in the script [for 2008's *Silence in the Library*] but David's Doctor didn't flirt back. He was quite perturbed and quite disturbed by this woman coming into his life, as he hadn't a clue who she was but she obviously knew so

much about him. It absolutely seemed to unnerve him. Whereas with Matt Smith's Doctor... well, it's not just with River – Matt's Doctor will flirt with anyone. That's part of Matt's personality. He's quite sparkly. Steven Moffat has really enjoyed developing that side of the Doctor, which has never really been explored before. It's almost like the Doctor, at – what is he? 950 years old? – has hit puberty. Steven is very careful about the actual level of flirtatiousness.

Nothing too naughty for the kids?
Exactly. The genius of *Doctor Who* – and the writing – is that hopefully it satisfies all the different generations that are watching it. There is a certain level to the Doctor and River's relationship that's probably a little sophisticated for the younger audience. Some of that banter might go over their heads, but the parents and older kids enjoy it. The younger ones are focused on the aliens.

But younger viewers seem to really like River, too.
That's right, and I've found that very rewarding. Little girls have come up to me and said, 'I've got you on my wall,' which is amazing! I never, ever thought that I would be up there with the Doctor and Amy. But children aren't ageist. They just take as they see. There's definitely a darkness to River that I thought the children might be wary of, because ultimately all children are going to be protective of the Doctor. If there's the potential of somebody that might harm the Doctor, I've always thought, 'Well, they won't engage with that character.' But that hasn't happened. But the kissing? I find it's quite a big deal. We've had the moment where she has the last kiss, so everything we do now, which is her past, means

she and the Doctor should know each other better... oh, it's so complicated to get my head round! Argh! So I should, in theory, be kissing him a lot more now, but I don't think I can, for the sake of the show.

Very few people have ever got to kiss the Doctor.
I know. It's quite a privilege, isn't it?

You remember watching Patrick Troughton as the Doctor, back in the 1960s.
Yes.

So when you're kissing Matt Smith, do you ever think, 'This is, essentially, the same man'?
[Laughs] Well, no, because I've never met those Doctors. It's the ones that we haven't met yet that River knows about. It's complicated.

This series, River gave regeneration a go herself.
Yes! While Hitler was locked in a cupboard! I had to stand next to the camera, and Mels started regenerating, and then she froze, and I had to stand behind her and, basically, mimic exactly the same pose that she was in, and then take over. I don't know how they do it, it's fabulous technology and tricky, but then she morphed into me. No green screen or anything. It was good old-fashioned smoke and mirrors.

Was that was the only day you and Nina Toussaint-White, who plays Mels, were on set together.
Yes, and she'd chosen the outfit. That was the big thing for me. 'Oh my goodness, I hope she's chosen one that I can fit into!' But it worked out fine. In a sense, though, she's not River Song; she's Melody Pond. There might be elements of River in Melody, a certain sassiness or whatever, but actually that's crystallised in the regeneration and the becoming of River Song.

" OH, IT'S SO COMPLICATED TO GET MY HEAD AROUND! ARGH! "

When did you find out River's true identity?

Well, it was never going to be as simple as the Doctor's wife or his mother. That's too easy for Steven...

Cleverly, though, she actually sort of is his wife by the end...

But is she? [Smiles] Because ultimately she married the *Teselecta*. I can absolutely say, with my hand on my heart, 'I married the Doctor'... but did the Doctor marry me? Will the Doctor ever marry? When he says, 'I'm about to whisper something in your ear,' automatically one thinks, 'That's the thing she whispers back to him in *Silence in the Library*, when he's David Tennant. She knows his name now. She knows the secret thing.' Of course, that's not what he whispers, so when does that moment come?

Will we ever find out?

Who knows what's in store for River and the Doctor?

Do *you* know?

All I can say to that is, 'Spoilers.'

Steven has given you the perfect catchphrase there, hasn't he?

Isn't it amazing? I can't believe I have a catchphrase. Well, two if you include 'Hello, sweetie'. It's unbelievable. I'm like Bruce Forsythe! I'll just say I have a feeling – and I hope – River will be back. But that's all I can say. When I first started playing the character I just thought that it was a two-episode story arc, and that was going to be the beginning and the end of a woman who had secrets and seemed rather enigmatic. I just thought, 'That's the tragedy of that storyline – a relationship that could never really be delved into because she died.' Then coming back – the episode with the Weeping Angels [*The Time of Angels/ Flesh and Stone*, 2010], I certainly didn't know her true identity then. There were all sorts of rumours flying around, and people saying, 'Is she the Doctor? Is she the Doctor's wife?' It was just before we went to Utah to film *The Impossible Astronaut* that Steven sat me down and gave me a bit more information. I had to promise that I wouldn't reveal anything.

You didn't tell your daughter?

Nope, not even Salome.

Was she nagging you to tell her?

Yeah, all the time. But I didn't. All I could say was, 'Wait until you see it.' I think she was quite surprised.

How does she feel about her mum being River Song?

She really enjoys it. She watches it on BBC America, and they did a fantastic job promoting this last season. All of a sudden, there are so many more fans in America, and lots of them are children. I always felt *Doctor Who* was considered more of an adult sci-fi show in the States, as opposed to a family show, but my daughter is coming back from school saying, 'All the kids are watching,' so that makes me happy. It's needed over there. There's a huge gap in terms of programming for children.

How did the dynamic between you, Karen Gillan and Arthur Darvill change after they found out who River Song really is?

We all rather like it. Now, we can hug and I'll go, 'Hello, mum!' But I don't think anything has changed enormously. Steven said that when we'd been doing those night shoots in the Forest of Dean for the previous season, filming with the Weeping Angels, he'd noticed a tenderness from River towards Amy when she couldn't open her eyes. River was much more attentive to her than the Doctor was. I don't know whether that sowed the seed in Steven's mind, but it is possible to believe, if you look back at previous episodes, that River did know Amy was her mother, but just couldn't tell her.

Have people's reactions to you changed now they know who River really is?

It's all really positive – people saying, 'I never saw that coming,' and 'How fabulous that we're learning more about River.' I'm glad. I was a little nervous about what the reaction would be, but I think, ultimately, fans of *Doctor Who* are always prepared for the unexpected. I mean, that's the beauty of the show.

Let's Kill Hitler

BY STEVEN MOFFAT

THE STORY

Amy and Rory are tired of waiting.

It's been all summer and the Doctor still hasn't brought their baby home. So they summon him back to Earth – where the Doctor meets their best mate, Mels, who's long on impulse and worryingly short on sanity. Before they've even had a chance to discuss the whereabouts of baby Melody, Mels hijacks the TARDIS and drags everyone back to Germany – in the middle of the Second World War.

Mels, it turns out, wants to kill Hitler.

But gunfire, spontaneity and the TARDIS rarely mix. The time machine crash-lands in Hitler's office, and they have to bundle the Führer into a cupboard before anything else can go wrong. And it's not long before something does. There's a time-travelling, shape-changing robot out for Hitler's blood, too...

In the crossfire, Mels is shot. A horrified Amy and Rory watch their life-long friend fall to the floor – where, in a burst of light, she regenerates.

Into River Song.

But this newborn version of River is deadly. Brainwashed to destroy the arch-enemy of the Silence, she kills the Doctor with a poisoned kiss. His regenerative abilities crippled, the Time Lord has just half an hour to live. But at least he'll die knowing who's responsible for the kidnap of baby Melody, and why they want him dead...

LET'S KILL HITLER

▶▶ 'You said guns didn't work in [the TARDIS],' Mels says to the Doctor. 'You said we were in a state of temporal grace.' The idea of temporal grace was first put forward in *The Hand of Fear* (1976), but as the Doctor says here, 'It was a clever lie' – explaining the many times people have used firearms within the TARDIS, such as *Earthshock* (1982) and *Attack of the Cybermen* (1985).

▶▶ Melody's history of regeneration is revealed when she says, 'Last time I did this, I ended up a toddler in the middle of New York' – the event we saw at the very end of *Day of the Moon*. It's also worth noting that Mels's regeneration into River supports the idea that Time Lords can change 'ethnicity' between incarnations. By the end of the episode, River has lost her ability to regenerate – which explains why she can't escape her fate at the end of *Forest of the Dead* (2008).

▶▶ We get our first clues as to the real nature of the Silence in this episode. River is described as working under the 'orders of the movement known as the Silence and Academy of the Question', and, later, the *Teselecta*'s file on the Doctor reveals that 'the Silence is not a species – it is a religious order, or movement. Their core belief is that silence will fall when the question is asked.' And that question? 'The oldest question in the universe'? We get more clues to that in *The Wedding of River Song*... ▶▶ That's not the only information the Doctor manages to wring out of the *Teselecta*'s databank. He also learns the precise date, time and location of his death: 5.02pm, 22 April 2011, Lake Silencio in Utah – as seen, of course, in *The Impossible*

Fantastic Facts!

Astronaut. ▶▶ 'Time can be rewritten,' says Anita, aboard the *Teselecta*, reminding us of one of *Doctor Who*'s key mantras. 'Remember Kennedy?' she adds. It is likely that she is referring to the assassination of US President John F Kennedy on 22 November 1963, which presumably was tampered with by the *Teselecta* in some way. She could, however, be referring to his brother Robert, who was also murdered. Or maybe, since time was rewritten, it was one of any number of un-killed members of the Kennedy dynasty. ▶▶ We see the Doctor in the 'top hat and tails' get-up that he last wore at Amy and Rory's wedding in *The Big Bang* (2010). ▶▶ The *Teselecta* uses compression field technology as

part of the process of miniaturising its crew. Similar technology was used by the Miniscope seen in *Carnival of Monsters* (1973), and in the collars worn by Slitheen family members in *Aliens of London/World War Three* (2005). ▶▶ The *Teselecta* will, of course, return in *The Wedding of River Song* (2011), where it plays a very important role in fixing reality and saving the Doctor's life. ▶▶ Finally we learn why River Song signed up at the Luna University to study archaeology in the first place: it was her way of keeping a close eye on the Doctor. (Perhaps in a similar way to the 'scorekeeping' we saw him indulging in at the start of 2010's *The Time of Angels*?)

NUMBER CRUNCHING

RULE 408:
Time is not the boss of you

Rule 27:
THE DOCTOR IS NEVER KNOWINGLY SERIOUS

RULE 1:
The Doctor lies

MAGIC MOMENT

River is studying her new face in a mirror as Amy – really the Teselecta – studies her daughter coldly.

RIVER SONG: I might take the age down a little. Just gradually, to freak people out.
AMY: You killed the Doctor.
RIVER SONG: Yes, I know dear – I hope you're not going to keep on about it.
She turns back to the mirror
Oh, regeneration – it's a whole new colouring to work with.
AMY: You killed the Doctor on the orders of the movement known as the Silence and Academy of the Question. You accept and know this to be true?
RIVER SONG: Quite honestly, I don't really remember – it's all a bit of a jumble –
She breaks off, staring, as Amy's mouth stretches nightmarishly open, light blazing out. River staggers back.
RIVER SONG: No! Get off me, no!!
And then, a voice from off:
THE DOCTOR: Sorry, did you say she 'killed the Doctor?'
The *Doctor??*

UNSEEN ADVENTURES

>>> Not the Doctor's adventures this time – but Mels (Melody, River, whatever you want to call her) had a lifetime of, we imagine, somewhat rural adventures with Rory and Amy in Leadworth before the events seen here.

BEHIND THE SCENES
STEVEN MOFFAT
Writer

Did you relish being able to leave viewers for a couple of months with that title stuck in their brains?
Oh yes. I think that title alone generated more heat than any trailer we've ever done – which was an interesting lesson.

This must rank as one of the maddest episodes ever. The freedom that *Doctor Who* gives a writer must be exciting, but where do you draw the line? How much bonkerness is too much?
Internal consistency is the only rule – the story makes sense in its own terms, and within *Doctor Who* (where the baseline includes a time-travelling phone box and a bow tie). I thought, with *The Impossible Astronaut* being so grim and dark, it was time to throw the lever the other way. A regeneration romcom, guest starring Hitler – it's what the world has been waiting for!

Mels spent much of her youth growing up in Leadworth with Rory and Amy. How much of all this does River remember? How much of her history has she had to keep hidden?
She remembers all of it. That's why she's always seemed unusually close with them. In other time streams – as we see in *The Wedding of River Song* – she's happily visiting them as her parents.

MELS AT SCHOOL

WHAT I DID ON MY HOLIDAYS
by Mels Zucker

Not again!

In my summer holidays I met ~~the Doctor~~ and went with him in his blue box. And we went on a cruise on the Titanic in 1912 and we stopped it from sinking because we melted the ice down with a heat ray.

?! Then we went to see ~~Henry Fifth~~ and we stopped him from killing all his wifes and instead we made him give them each a castle that they could live in with ~~theyre~~ parents. Everyone in England was very happy and there was a party and the Doctor gave a speech and everyone clapped and laughed and the Doctor said 'Thank you Mels, that was a great idea. Where next?'

So then we went to 1066 and stole the arrows from the vikings and saved England from them. 'We've put a lot of knitters out of business,' said the Doctor, but King Harold was ever so happy and cooked us some cakes without burning them.

We went to see Cleopatra next as I have always liked her and we had tea in one *This was not a ficton assignment, Mels!* of her pyramids and told her that her boyfriends were rubbish and she would get over them and she agreed, although that did not stop her from trying to kiss the Doctor!

Then it was the weekend and so we stopped.

The next week we went to see President Kennedy in 1963 and yelled 'Duck!' and he was very pleased indeed and he asked me if there was anything I wanted to do and I asked him if he could keep the alleyways in New York a lot cleaner and with less rats and he promised to do that and that was nice.

'That has been a busy week, Mels!' said the Doctor, 'What next?' And I ~~aksed~~ him why he never shot Nazis and he said he had never thought of it, and I told him that was wrong, so we went and shot lots of them and Hitler too. 'Shooting's fun, Mels!' said the Doctor, 'Lets go to Russia and do lots more of it!'

So we did.

'What a holiday, Mels!' said the Doctor then. 'Whatever shall we do now?'

'Can we get married, Doctor?' I asked him.

And he said yes even though I look lots younger than him.

And as a wedding present he took me to see my parents.

That is what I did on my summer holidays and that is true and I did not steal that lorry. *See me!*

Mels is t~~he~~ day cha~~mpion~~

The champion of Sports Day was undoubtedly Mels Zucker who was head and shoulders ahead of the rest of the school, taking medals in running, shooting and hurdling, bravely carrying on despite twisting her ankle.

The three-legged race was won by Amy Pond and Rory Williams. Amy Pond's parents also won the parents' egg-and-spoon race.

Leadworth Junior School

Report for: Rory Williams Class: 5CH

ENGLISH	Rory has a very good attention span and will really stick at a topic until it is finished. Unless, that is, he is distracted by one of his many girl friends!
MATHS	Rory has made some progress this term, although he's better on his own than in group work with his friends, as they tend to dominate him.
HISTORY	Rory did an excellent project on the Romans. Commended.
GEOGRAPHY	I'm afraid I'm not going to be the only one to have to draw attention to Rory's LACK OF APPLICATION to a subject. Often I have caught him in the act of passing notes between two other pupils. He is a BRIGHT boy but easily led
DRAMA	Rory is very good at standing still and did a very nice butterfly.

IMPORTANT NOTE

Will whoever stole the sulphuric acid from the science class please come forward? This is an extremely serious matter and the police have been called. If the culprit has not identified themselves by 11.40am the whole school will be placed in detention.

From the Headmaster.

Leadworth Junior School

Report for: Mels Zucker Class: 5CH

ENGLISH	often a joy to listen to – however, she sometimes seems unable to come up with a story with a happy ending, and is always writing about guns.
MATHS	Mels is very good at counting backwards.
HISTORY	Several times, regrettably, Mels has had to be sent to the Headmaster. She will insist on rewriting history, having it end her way. She is unable to tell the difference between solid fact and a story.
GEOGRAPHY	Miss Zucker is an EXTREMELY DISRUPTIVE influence in class, and is occasionally very UPSETTING to other children. I sometimes question why she is here at all.
DRAMA	Mels is a wonderful, imaginative spirit and is excellent in drama, especially at pretending to be someone else.

Leadworth Junior School

Report for: Amelia Pond Class: 5CH

ENGLISH	Amy still insists on writing stories about the Doctor. I had hoped we'd heard the last of him.
MATHS	Sadly, Amy is more interested in leading some of my other pupils astray than knuckling down to the curriculum.
HISTORY	Amy really doesn't apply herself to history, sadly. Her one bright spot was a project about the Roman Invasion of Britain.
GEOGRAPHY	Amy shows a real aptitude and likes learning about Europe. She did a really COMMENDABLE project about Belgium and obviously will one day make a great traveller.
DRAMA	Amy's playacting has caused me continued concern. Her imaginary friend cannot be kept out of class and I am reluctantly forced to recommend counselling.

Justice Dept. User Guides Vehicle 6018

TESELECTA

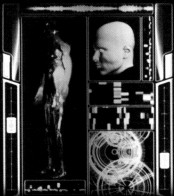

WELCOME ABOARD!

This is a brief user guide introduction to the **Teselecta**/Vehicle 6018. Each topic will be covered in greater detail in '**TESELECTA** FOR DUMMIES VOLS I-XIV'

PLEASE PLACE THIS NOTICE IN A VISIBLE POSITION IN EACH DEPARTMENT

HEALTH AND SAFETY

>> Internal security is dealt with by the Antibodies. Please ensure your privileges are updated and that you are wearing your wristband AT ALL TIMES. Antibodies keep us secure but you MUST know the safety drill. Failure to do so may result in expulsion and/or death.

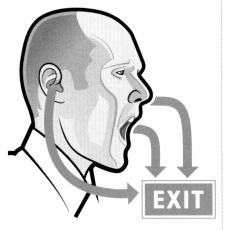

>> In the event of an emergency evacuation, all personnel on the upper levels should leave via the Ear, Nostril and Mouth exits in the vehicle's cranial section. All those on the lower levels should leave via front and rear emergency exits A and B (see diagram on p.302 of '*TESELECTA* FOR DUMMIES VOL VI'.)

>> If artificial gravity is not functioning, please remember to wear a safety harness while your **Teselecta** is in motion. The Justice Department will not be held responsible for any injuries sustained by those not properly strapped in when artificial gravity is not functioning.

>> Running on stairwells while the **Teselecta** is in motion is extremely dangerous. (Over 200 Justice Department staff injuries last year.) Ask your line-manager for a copy of our 400-page listing of all companies keen to aid those who have suffered **Teselecta** workplace-related accidents on a no-win-no-fee basis.

USEFUL INFORMATION

COSTUME

>> Where subject clothing is unavailable for scanning (e.g. when subject is naked) use external temperature gauges to select appropriate attire. Consider the era being visited, and use Costume Database to find suitable clothing (e.g. a baseball cap and tracksuit may be appropriate for a mission in Basildon in 1997, but highly unsuitable for 17th-century Naples.)

MUSCULATURE

>> In the event of system failure, use manual checks (via a mirror or other reflective surface) to confirm that skin-tone, costume, height, etc are authentic. (Eyeballs can be accessed by all personnel at clearance Band C and above.) If, while in use, the **Teselecta** sustains mecharthritic damage to its lower limbs, consider remodelling the outer shell on an older subject, or one with restricted mobility.

BEHAVIOUR

>> **The Verisimilitude Functions (including Blush, Belch, Hiccup, Sneeze, Cry, and Break Wind) should be used sparingly, and with due consideration to water wastage and social context.**

>> **Don't forget to blink! Not blinking is a major giveaway to other people that the *Teselecta* is not 'one of them'. Blinking also prevents build-ups of dirt or dust on the outer eyeball.**

>> **Avoid situations where the *Teselecta* may be required to eat or drink (e.g. dinner parties, banquets, television cookery shows, etc.) Disposing of waste costs time, money and fuel.**

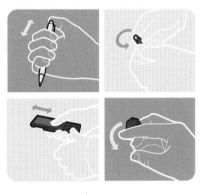

>> Maintain hand/finger movement. Many people 'fidget'. Find an object (e.g. pen, paperclip, lighter or coin) and play with it, but not too much.

>> Always use jargon appropriate to the era you are in (e.g. a 19th-century policeman is unlikely to know what a Stomach Pounder is, so don't ask for one).

>> Weapons should be used when there are few (preferably no) witnesses. REMEMBER: 'Mysterious' and 'unexplained' incidents in history breed conspiracy theories, which in turn lead to collective intellectual poverty. (See KENNEDY INCIDENT REPORT – JUSTICE DEPT. FILE 51C/9 for further details.)

>> The **Teselecta** comes with a range of pre-programed dance moves for scenarios when it is required to dance convincingly. (NOTE: This is more common than you may think.) Use a programme appropriate to the era/genre of music (e.g. DO NOT 'twist' to 'punk'), and NEVER attempt manual improvisation – IT CAN COST LIVES!

END OF INTRODUCTION – GOOD LUCK TO ALL CREWMEMBERS!

EPISODE 9

Night Terrors

BY MARK GATISS

THE STORY

The sun sets on the Rowbarton Estate. Young George is scared of the night and the dark, and the strange wheezing sound of the lift in the tower block in which he lives. In fact, he's scared of everything – so much so that he's driving his parents, George and Claire, to distraction.

Even the Doctor can hear his cry for help, so he decides to pay a visit. As he investigates the estate, strange things start to happen. Old women get sucked into piles of bin bags. Empty clothes take on a life of their own. And Amy and Rory disappear, finding themselves trapped in an old, abandoned house...

Everything centres on George. Whatever frightens him, he puts in a cupboard in his bedroom. Behind its door, monsters lurk in the shadows. That's what George thinks, anyway – and the Doctor is starting to think it, too. Because George is no ordinary little boy.

His father can't remember his birth. His mother was never pregnant. So where in the world did George come from? And why is his fear warping reality around him?

The answer lies in the cupboard. With the monsters...

NUMBER CRUNCHING

24/12/02
CLAIRE'S NOT PREGNANT

11/02/03
CLAIRE GIVES BIRTH

NIGHT TERRORS

>> The psychic paper receives George's message – 'Please save me from the monsters' – just as it picked up the mental summons from the hospitalised Face of Boe in *New Earth* (2006).
>> The Doctor recalls some stories from his childhood: *The Three Little Sontarans*, *The Emperor Dalek's New Clothes*, and *Snow White and the Seven Keys to Doomsday*. Sontarans have, of course, been a long-standing

Fantastic Facts!

adversary of the Doctor, introduced in *The Time Warrior* (1973). The Emperor Dalek was first seen in *The Evil of the Daleks* (1967). The title of the third story is a joke based on *Doctor Who and the Daleks in Seven Keys to Doomsday*, a 1974 stage play starring Trevor Martin as the Doctor. >> The Doctor asks Alex if he's got any Jammie Dodgers – his favourite biscuits were last mentioned in *The Impossible Astronaut*, after having been introduced to the series by writer Mark Gatiss in *Victory of the Daleks* (2010). >> George is actually a Tenza, one of an alien race whose young behave just like cuckoos – stealing their way into the nest of other species, and tricking the parents into raising them as their own. George uses a perception filter to cloud Alex and Claire's minds and convince them he is their child. Perception filters were introduced in *Human Nature* (2007), though they had been mentioned in the first episode of *Torchwood* earlier that year. >> *Doctor Who* last filmed in Bristol way back in 1977 for *The Sun Makers*. The complex of tower blocks used here were also the setting for the 1976 HTV telefantasy series *King of the Castle*, written by the creators of K-9, Bob Baker and Dave Martin.

DELETED!

Night Terrors was originally scheduled to be the fourth episode of Series Six, before it moved into the second half of the season. The original shooting script contains a scene towards the end in which Amy (who, in this version, is actually the Flesh Amy) sees Madame Kovarian...

Hanging in the air in front of Amy is a little metal hatch. Its door opens, and the thin-faced Eyepatch Woman stares through.

EYEPATCH WOMAN: Amy, I just thought you'd want to know – she's doing fine. Rest now. *And the door flips shut again, disappears. Amy is freaked out.*
RORY: Amy?
Amy rubs her eyes.
AMY: It's not real! It's not real!
RORY: Are you okay? What's not real?
AMY: Nothing. Nothing, I'm fine! Let's go...

MAGIC MOMENT

The Doctor and Alex have found themselves transported into the dolls' house. Before them lies a table laid out as if for a feast...

THE DOCTOR: Now, the question is: where are we?
ALEX: Who cares? Who cares where we are? What about –
THE DOCTOR: Very important, Alex. Got to know where we are.
ALEX: But what is he? George. What is he?
THE DOCTOR: If we work out where we are, maybe we can work that out too. Big old house. Big old,

*spooky house with...
He grabs the roast chicken, sniffs it then bangs it off the table!*
THE DOCTOR: ...a wooden chicken!
He picks up items one by one and chucks them over his shoulder.
THE DOCTOR: Cups, saucers, plates, knives, forks, fruits, chickens! Wood! So, have we gone back in time...?
ALEX: Back in time?!
THE DOCTOR: Or is this just a refuge for dirty posh people who eat wooden food? Or termites! Giant termites trying to get on the property ladder!
The Doctor thinks for a moment.
THE DOCTOR: Unlikely.

UNSEEN ADVENTURES

》》 If Rory's suspicions are correct, it turns out his mum might have had a brief adventure in her living room – with chatty aliens who were disguised as door-to-door religious missionaries armed with space crisps.

BEHIND THE SCENES

MARK GATISS

Writer

You and Steven Moffat were behind the recent return of Sherlock Holmes to our TV screens, and you've both been involved with *Doctor Who* for some time. How do these two iconic heroes compare?

It's a tough one this. As questing, eccentric geniuses, they are very alike – but the thing about Sherlock is that he's almost a sociopath. He doesn't understand people, he doesn't get the point of the niceties of human relationships. He observes them in a very clinical way. The Doctor is an equally lonely and detached figure – but he desperately wants to join in. Although he's a Lord, he's like someone who's come down from the big house to muck in with the common folk. The Doctor wants to be one of us. Sherlock *is* one of us, but doesn't want to be.

Like Sherlock, the Doctor has become an iconic figure in the British cultural landscape. What is it that makes him so special?

The thing that remains forever magical about *Doctor Who* – and it's never really talked about – is that, yes, it's absolutely an imperishable British icon, but it's not from literature, it's from telly. It's actually a TV original. It's a very, very unusual thing for, as it were, a 'new' medium to contribute one of those characters. The Doctor is, as Russell T Davies has said, an imperishable legend. We'll be telling stories about him for ever. What's fascinating is, just as with Robin Hood or Dracula or Sherlock Holmes, he's open to massive reinterpretation over the years. Different times demand a different kind of Doctor, just as they demand a different kind of Sherlock.

MY SPECIAL BOOK
by GEORGE THOMPSON (aged 7¼)

It has to be 5 times or it dont count. That's what I keep telling Mum and Dad. 5 times. When I go to bed. They have to switch off the switch 5 times. Then I feel alright for a bit.

I got some pencils and then a buk. It's this buk. All the pages are white so Mum said I shud rite down some of the things I have thinked and some of the things I have seen so I am going to do that.

I like lots of things. Some of the things I like are spaceships and robots and Spiderman and X Factors but there's some things I don't like and they are they things in are flat. I did not want to tell Mum and Dad abowt them but I will tell my buk. You must not tell anyone the secret. Shhhhh. But theres bad things in are flat.

At school there was a story. A ryme. We all had to say it and then learn it and then say it again and it was there was an old woman who lived in a shoo. She had got lots of kids. What all them at school don't know is that there is an old woman and she lives across from us. She is called mrs. rossiter and I dont like her. She is scary and she comes out to take the bins away a lot and I hide from her cos she is like a wich. Shes got a pointy face and pointy nose and when she gets cross she looks UGLY like a wich. Dad says I'm silly and shes just a nice old lady who lives in a flat but I KNOW. Sumtimes when she goes past my windo I can see her and its just a shadow but she looks like a witch from a story and I think shes going to put me in a pot and boil me up and eat me. Mrs rossiters flat is not made of sugar though like in the Hansel and Grettel story cos if it was I would go over there and eat it up. I wish it was made of M and Ms cos there my favrite.

When it gets dark I carnt go to sleep cos of the noises. Dad says thers lots of noises in the flat and its just nothing but I KNOW its not nothing. Theres a sound at night and it goes like HUGGGGGGHHHH HUGGGGGGHHHHHH and Dad and Mum say it is just the sound of the lift. It is NOT that. I seen the lift and it is just a box that smells of wee. We used to go up and down in it. I can remember that from when I was little. When I was 5 or something but we have not been in it for a bit cos it keeps braking. Anyway. I no what the lift sounds like and this is something else. Its like a breathing noise. I think theres something breething in my room when I am trying to go asleep. Like a dragon or a monster. I think it is in the walls like the snayke in Harry Poter. And if I dont stay awake it is going to goble me up.

HUGGGGHHH HUGGGGH

Another thing I dont like is my dresing gown. Mum always hangs it on the back of the door and theres nothing rong with it when the light is on but when it is off it looks like a shape and I HATE it. I think its going to fly over and sit on my bed and take me away. Sometimes I think Mum and Dad are going to ring someone up and ask them to take me away becos I make them cry. I don't want to but I carnt help it.

NIGHT TERRORS

Mum and me have got a sort of special thing we do when I get scaredy catted. Theres a cubbard in my room and if I get scared of anything Mum says I have to put it in the cubbard. Ive put a lot of things in there. I didnt like sum of the toys that Nana gave me when I was littler. They was creepy. There was some soldiers that was made of metal. All soft and they had bad faces that made me feel funny. Then there was some dolls and a dolls house that was Mums and I HATE it so it got put in the cubbard as well. The dolls are not nice like on the advurts on telly. Them ones are pretty and they have smiles and girls like to look at them and change there nappys. These ones was all OLD and horrible and they smelt dusty and funny. I kept thinking they were coming to get me in the night time. I had a nightmare where the girl ones and the soldier ones were leening over me in my bed and trying to take out all the air from my mouth. There faces felt all horrible and wooden like pegs. I woke up and all I cud see was there faces all yucky. There smiles was like cuts. Like when Shaun at school cut his face on a windo that got broken and all the skin went open and blood come out. It was like that. The dolls mouths was all messy like a cut. I started screaming and Dad and Mum came in and they looked all tired. I felt bad for making them get up cos they have to go to work.

I am scared that if I am not a good boy then they are going to get someone to come and take me away. I saw a thing on CBBC when a little boy had to go into care cos he was shouting and screaming and his Mum and Dad could not stand it any more. I am not like that little boy but I am worried that cos I am scared of so many things they will do the same thing as on the telly.

Its alrite when the light is on but there is always that time that comes when Mum or dad has to turn off the litgh and I don't want them to do that. I keep saying a thing like a prairie at school in RS but its not realy a prairie. I keep saying to please save me from the monsters and I hope someone will come and do that.

PLEASE SAVE ME FROM THE MONSTERS.

⚓ TWOSTREAMS

Where a day can last a lifetime ☰

Losing a loved one to a virus as fast-acting as Chen7 can be devastating. The one wish of those who remain behind is always the same: 'If only we'd had more time.'

Here at the TwoStreams Kindness Facility we can offer you just that – time.

Splitting the fabric of time itself into two separate streams, we'll give your loved one the opportunity to lead a life that's full and rewarding in our vast and fun-filled Red Waterfall zones, while giving you the chance to watch them live that life through our Green Anchor visiting areas.

Thousands of Chen7 patients are already making the most of what we have to offer, including:

THE MOUNTAIN ZONE

Climb the Glasmir Mountains, or go cycling through the Dagdanian Alps. The stunning vistas will take your remaining breaths away!

THE ROLLERCOASTER ZONE

For those thrill-seekers looking for the ride of their tragically foreshortened lives!

THE RESTAURANT ZONE

Sample culinary delights from the four corners of the universe – eat, drink and be merry, because, after all, tomorrow you die!

THE MIND ZONE

Where our more introspective residents can spend days, months, and even years contemplating the lives they have led and everything and everyone they leave behind.

THE FITNESS ZONE

You may be dying, but that doesn't mean you can't have a body to die for!

THE INDULGENCE ZONE

ADULTS ONLY

Try something new! After all, it can't kill you...

Think we may need to talk to our PR people again. Tone may need tweaking. C.K.

FAQ

Will we ever get to see our loved ones again?

Yes. Through our Green Anchor visiting rooms and our specially developed Through The Looking Glass technology you can have audio-visual contact with our residents. (Please be aware that the visiting period will not exceed the 24 hours of your loved one's remaining life.)

Don't the residents get lonely?

For those unlucky enough to be the only member of a family or social group infected with Chen7, the Red Waterfall might sound a solitary place. Thankfully, you'll have both our Interface and our Handbot medical staff to keep you company. Besides, for those who prefer a little space, a period in quarantine could be your idea of paradise.

What if they find a cure for Chen7 while either myself or a loved one is in quarantine?

After 86,000 years of research, there is still no known cure for Chen7. It is highly unlikely any such cure will be discovered while you are in quarantine. We will let you know at once if this situation changes in any way.

How do I go about quarantining a loved one who is reluctant or unwilling to be admitted to TwoStreams?

That's easy! Just ask your Medibot or virtual healthcare provider to supply you with a Quarantine Admittance Form, and our programmed staff will sedate and quarantine your loved one in a fast and dignified manner. In over 85% of cases, they'll thank you for it eventually.

But who will pay for all this if I go into quarantine?

Thanks to the miracle of temporal streaming, you can now find a job in our Work Zone. Did you know that almost 90% of Apalapucia's manual data entry work is now carried out by TwoStreams residents? That way, you can pay while you earn – right up to the moment when your residency terminates.

DO NOT BE ALARMED...

So if you or a loved one has been diagnosed with Chen7, you know what to do. Contact us here at TwoStreams, and we'll provide you with a whole lifetime of experiences you'll cherish.

THIS IS A KINDNESS.

The Girl Who Waited

BY TOM MacRAE

THE STORY

The TARDIS brings the Doctor and his friends to Apalapucia, but instead of a beautiful world of glittering spires and silver colonnades, they find a planet under quarantine, infested with a deadly virus. Chen7 kills its victims in a day – but the Apalapucians have come up with a way to make that day last a lifetime...

The Twostreams Facility puts Chen7 sufferers into their own compressed timestream. From the other side of a glass portal, families and friends can, over the course of a single day, watch their dying loved ones live out a whole lifetime. With time stretched, the sufferers' lives are no longer curtailed. This, they say, is a kindness.

But it is a kindness that Amy doesn't want. Separated from the Doctor and Rory, she finds herself trapped in one of the compressed timestreams. Her boys try as hard as they can to smash through the barriers in time to find her, but they arrive too late. 36 years too late...

After nearly 40 years of living alone, Amy has changed. Forever the girl who waited, she's now waited enough. She wants to be rescued – but if the Doctor and Rory save her, they'll never be able to go back for her younger self.

It seems that Amy and Rory can only be reunited by tearing time itself to shreds...

Where Have I Seen?

KAREN GILLAN
Old Amy
You may recognise Karen from her appearances on the C4 comedy *The Kevin Bishop Show*, or from her brief turn as a Soothsayer in the *Doctor Who* story *The Fires of Pompeii* (2008). Yep. That's it. Nothing else we can think of. Wait! No. It's gone...

NUMBER CRUNCHING

40,000 RESIDENTS IN THE TWOSTREAMS FACILITY

1 DAY EACH LEFT TO LIVE

THE GIRL WHO WAITED

MAGIC MOMENT

Old Amy and her younger self are facing each other through the Time Glass. The older version of Amy is explaining why she refuses to help them fix time and save young Amy – but Amy has just one question...

AMY: Three words: What about Rory? You called the robot Rory. You didn't call it the Doctor, or Biggles, our favourite cat, or Sexy Mr Jennings the hot, hot art teacher. You called it Rory. Because we always need a Rory by our side.
OLD AMY: Do you remember, the first time I met him – we met him – and that summer, when he came back to school with that ridiculous haircut?
AMY: He said he'd been in a rock band.
AMY AND OLD AMY: Liar!
OLD AMY: Then he had to learn the play the guitar.
AMY: So we wouldn't know he couldn't play it.
OLD AMY: All those boys chasing me – but it was only ever Rory. Why was that?

AMY: You know when sometimes you meet someone who's so beautiful, then you actually talk to them and five minutes later, they're as dull as a brick? And then there's other people, and you think they're okay – but then you get to know them and their face becomes them. Like their personality's written all over it, and they just turn into something so beautiful.

AMY AND OLD AMY: Rory's the most beautiful man I've ever met.
Old Amy stares at her hand – she's still wearing her wedding ring.
AMY: Please. Do it for him.
OLD AMY: You're asking me to defy destiny, causality, the nexus of time itself – for a boy?
AMY: You're Amy. He's Rory. And oh yes I am.

▶▶ Like Time Lords, Apalapucians have two hearts. This quirk of biology makes such species susceptible to certain diseases including Chen7.
▶▶ In a cut scene we were to discover that the Twostreams restaurant zone offers Atraxi cuisine, alongside native Apalapucian, human and Martian. The Atraxi were the alien policemen featured in *The Eleventh Hour* (2010).
▶▶ The rollercoaster zone contains a replica of the Warpspeed Death Ride at Disneyland on Clom. As we learnt in *Love & Monsters* (2006), Clom is the twin planet of Raxacoricofallapatorius, the Slitheens' home world. Clom was stolen to be

Fantastic Facts!

used as part of Davros's reality bomb in *The Stolen Earth/Journey's End* (2008). ▶▶ The Doctor describes the sonic screwdriver seen in this episode as his 'favourite one'. How many does he have? We know (from *The Eleventh Hour*) that the TARDIS can make new sonic screwdrivers; indeed, this must be true considering the closing scenes of *The Almost People*, in which the Doctor and his Flesh replica each carried one of the devices. (A cut scene from that episode, showing the TARDIS providing the Doctor with a new sonic, confirmed this.) ▶▶ Amy reminds her older self that the Doctor stole his outfit – from staff at Leadworth hospital, as seen in *The Eleventh Hour*.

TOM MacRAE

Writer

How must it have felt for Amy to have her faith in the Doctor crushed by her long wait at the Twostreams Facility?

The older Amy has been on her own for so long, it pushes her towards Rory – someone she knows will never run away. When old Amy says, 'They fly away and they leave you,' her younger self says, 'No, he wouldn't – Rory wouldn't.' She doesn't even mention the Doctor. It's quite significant that, at this point in her life, it's Rory that the older Amy misses, it's Rory that she thinks about, talks about, and the Doctor... Well, it's one disappointment too far. She's waited too many times now.

Amy and Rory are the first married couple to have travelled with the Doctor. How was it writing for companions with that relationship?

When you have a couple in the TARDIS, it ends up being more about having a man there who isn't the Doctor. With Rose [Tyler, companion from *Rose* (2005) to *Doomsday* (2006)] and Mickey [her Earthbound, one-time boyfriend], Mickey just can't remotely compare with the Doctor. The Doctor clearly cannot be beaten

by Mickey, even though Mickey does eventually become a bit more heroic. Whereas with Rory, he goes along too, he's more of an equal. The Doctor is clearly the most amazing person you could ever hope to meet – but that doesn't mean that Rory isn't right for Amy. And she knows that. She and the Doctor together wouldn't ever actually work.

By the end of the episode, the Doctor realises he can't go on endangering his friends' lives. But is he really that dangerous to be around?

The biggest fantasy of *Doctor Who* isn't that the Doctor travels in time, or that he's 900-odd years old, or that he's got two hearts and he regenerates – it's that every week, he has an adventure.

Wherever he goes, something's about to kick off. And the reason for that is because it's a TV show. No one wants to watch the episode where they go to a planet and they have a nice meal and they walk along the beach and then they go to bed. But they must have days like that, we just don't see them very often. So, because the characters are required to endlessly be in peril, they get stuck in that TV show.

But more than that, if you ally yourself with people who are prepared to fight to make a difference, then your life will always be in danger. I don't think it's fair to ever blame the person who makes the stand. Because the Doctor's so old, because he's done this so many times before, he sometimes forgets how dangerous it is. But if he didn't create the danger by opposing evil, if he didn't get these people to help him, then terrible things would happen. Standing up for what's right is always the best thing to do.

UNSEEN ADVENTURES

》》 The Doctor has visited the number one greatest destination in the universe – but says it's 'hideous' and covered in coffee shops.

HANDROID
CYBERNETIC INDUSTRIES

From Apalapucia to Zashapalupa – Multiple solutions for your multiple timestream needs

We all know what it's like. You establish a kindness facility for 40,000 residents all suffering from the Chen7 virus, hoping to give them a chance to turn their last day into a lifetime of happiness. You've carefully compressed and folded multiple timestreams within and around each other to fit thousands of residents in literally the same place at different times. You've done all you can for the ones you love – but then you realise, there's still one final hurdle to overcome:

Who's going to do the cleaning up?

Multiple timestreams are hard enough for organic beings to comprehend, but for your average Joe Robot the plural variants of a fractured reality create such a whirlwind of visual information that even the most sophisticated of our simulated friends can be forced into emergency shutdown. What you need is a mechanised manservant who isn't confused by conflicting visual data, and who is able to process temporally skewed spatial information calmly and capably at all times.

You don't just need a hand. You need a Handbot.

The 17th Generation Handroid Handbot 8001, is available in a range of stunning coloured shells, from topaz to avocado or the classic white. A sophisticated system of cybernetic senses located in the palm of each Handbot allows it to 'see' without relying on clumsy and misleading sight. Eyes are now a thing of the past. The specially constructed *Synth-Skin™* hands also come with a range of exciting extra features:

ANAESTHETIC TRANSFER
Need to subdue unruly residents? Just one touch, and they're out like a light!

BIO-SCANNING CAPABILITY
When is a fingernail not a fingernail? When it's a Handbot's fingernail! Each nail contains sensitive scanning equipment to determine the precise metabolic state of any resident and diagnose whether they're sick or healthy on the spot!

SEE-ROUND-CORNERS-O-VISION
Thanks to the Handbot's non-reliance on visual senses, the Handroid 8001 is able to literally 'see' round corners – as well as through walls, across great distances and in total darkness!*

* Some exclusions apply. Temporal Engine exhaust fumes may cause temporary blindness.

PATENTED DRUG DELIVERY SYSTEM
Residents squeamish about taking their shots? Don't worry! Handheld injections are now a thing of the past. Forget about nasty needles stuck into sore arms by well-meaning nurse bots. The Handbot 17Gs are equipped with the new FaceShot App, which delivers a vacuum-pressurised medicine dart directly into your patient, enabling you to be kind from a distance of 50 metres!

Toby Haynes talks the *Brilliant Book* through the role of a television director – a job that's even more challenging when you're making a show as unique as *Doctor Who*...

THE Direct APPROACH

We all think we know what a *Doctor Who* director does – points a camera at things and shouts 'Cut!', right? Well, turns out there's a lot more to it than that, as Toby Haynes is about to tell us.

A relative newcomer to *Doctor Who*, Toby has directed a staggering run of five consecutive Steven Moffat-penned *Doctor Who* episodes over the last two years: *The Pandorica Opens, The Big Bang, A Christmas Carol, The Impossible Astronaut* and *Day of the Moon*.

Film-making – which is what *Doctor Who* resembles more than most TV shows – can be broken down into three sections: pre-production (or 'prep'), production ('the shoot') and post-production. Toby smiles as he compares the whole process to doing a school exam. 'You can revise beforehand and try to prepare for any eventuality,' he explains. 'Then, on the day of the exam, it's very stressful as you've only a limited amount of time to get everything done. At the end of a real exam you get marked – and that's very much like editing in post-production. Luckily, in post, unlike in an exam, you get the chance to change things.'

Right, class, let's learn more about these three stages. Silence, please. You have six pages to examine. Your time starts... *now!*

STAGE 1 — PRE-PRODUCTION ('PREP')

Duration: Five weeks
Director's goals: To visualise the script in your head and communicate that vision to others.

READING THE SCRIPT

For Toby, as with all directors, his first read of the script is crucial. 'When you get to the very end of the process,' he reveals, 'you need to know that the episode is as close as possible to how you pictured it when you first read the script. During stressful times on set, when you have to make decisions really quickly, you'll need to refer back to those images which the script conjured in your head during that first read. If I had to sum up directing in three words, they'd be "perseverance of vision".'

'I need to read in almost total silence,' he adds. 'No distractions at all. Sometimes I might make a technical note, like "This scene may need a crane shot". Or it might be as simple as me not understanding it! Sometimes I'll write a question mark by something if it doesn't seem to make sense. The script I'm reading isn't the one TV audiences will finally see – it might be the first or second draft. There'll be revisions as you go through your prep.'

SCRIPT REVISIONS

Can those revisions sometimes throw the director a curveball? 'Absolutely,' says Toby. 'The second half of *The Big Bang* script only came in three weeks before we started shooting and it had a wedding in it! We didn't know about that, so we had to find a wedding venue. Steven Moffat will only hand in stuff that he's happy with, and often his first drafts are near-perfect, but they can be rather last-minute. *Doctor Who* can be a fly-by-the-seat-of-your-pants kind of show, but that's what makes it exciting.'

Toby notes that Steven's scripts often leave specific details to the reader's imagination. 'He's concentrating on the story, the plot and the characters. He might write "All hell breaks loose" or "It's a Victorian planet", with not much detail beyond that. That excites me, because then it's down to you, the director, to come up with the goods.'

BALANCING THE BUDGET

Toby has to determine what will – or won't – be possible to achieve in terms of the money available. 'Some things in early drafts may be too ambitious on our budget. I hate admitting that things aren't possible, but I also strongly feel that something's not worth doing unless you can do it really well.'

He cites the memorable Amy/Cyberhead fight in *The Pandorica Opens* as an example of beating the budget. 'Steven's script originally had the Cyberhead running around on spider-like legs. We couldn't afford it and people talked about cutting it altogether, but I came up with the idea of it dragging itself along the floor. Steven very kindly said he thought that was better than the original idea. *Doctor Who* has always achieved great things with economy.'

CONDUCTING THE ORCHESTRA

Directors sit at the very head of the production crew and enjoy an overview of everything. 'The moment you start preparation, others do too,' Toby says. 'Before you've even managed to read the script a few times, you'll start having meetings *about* the script. People need answers as quickly as possible so they can get on with their jobs. It's important to be clear about your ideas. Everybody can read a book and imagine the story – but the real skill of a director is being able to articulate that to the variety of skilled people who can make that story happen on screen. If you're too vague about your ideas, the end result could go anywhere.'

Toby works with 'lots of different departments. It's like an orchestra. The camera and photography department is headed up by the director of photography, who for me on *Doctor Who* has always been my best friend Stephan Pehrsson, so I'm lucky. The Art Department is run by production designer Michael Pickwoad – a really nice guy who brings so much imagination to the table. Art is one of the biggest departments because they've got to do loads of construction and build massive sets. If we're in an alien environment then they have to create almost everything you see, right down to a newspaper you might notice someone reading in the background.'

THE MAGIC OF MUSIC

Toby uses music from a very early stage, to help him create a feel for the episodes. 'When I was directing *A Christmas Carol*, I was listening to composer Camille Saint-Saëns' *Aquarium* and also the *Edward Scissorhands* movie soundtrack, because it's very Christmassy and has a slight darkness about it, just like Kazran Sardick himself.'

Toby often makes 'inspirational' compilations to help him get into the mood of a story. 'Sometimes I'll play music to someone to articulate an idea – sometimes to help convey to the producers what I'm thinking. Music is such a wonderful medium, with the ability to conjure cinematic imagery in the mind of the listener.'

CASTING SPELLS

Toby will also be thinking about the actors who must bring the script's characters to life. 'The casting director, Andy Pryor, runs that side of things brilliantly, but often I have to be there too, in a room, with an actor, watching them rehearse the part. It's a bit like *The X Factor* in that you have to decide who's best, although thankfully you don't have to tell them to their face. It's a much less painful process in that regard, but still quite intense.'

THE DOWNSIDE OF PREP

'I find prep one of the toughest parts of the process,' Toby explains, 'because it's all about anticipation and building up towards something big. I'm always desperate to start filming. It's an intense time – you don't see your friends, you lose touch with your family. There isn't a lot of room in your life for anything other than directing. Every waking minute, you're thinking about it. Even when you're sleeping you dream about it.'

PRODUCTION

Duration: Four or five weeks for two episodes or one Christmas special.
Director's goals: To shoot everything you need to shoot and never stop!

THE FIRST ASSISTANT DIRECTOR

On a set, the First Assistant Director (or first AD) is the person who shouts 'Action!' before a scene – although the director gets the more significant job of shouting 'Cut!'

'The First AD runs the studio floor and handles scheduling,' explains Toby. 'He'll work out what you're shooting and where. You need someone who's going to protect you, because all you want to be worrying about on set are the performances and whether or not it's all living up to your original vision. You don't want to worry about actors turning up late or costumes and make-up taking a long time to put on.'

EVERY SECOND COUNTS

'There's a lot of rushing around. It always feels like there's not enough time and like it's never going to work the way you imagined. And then the second take isn't quite so bad. On take three it's almost perfect, and on take four you find you have exactly what you wanted. Sometimes, for practical reasons, or because the actors themselves bring a new dimension to a scene, you do have to change your plans and try to capture an essence of what you'd originally imagined.'

Certain factors are out of even Toby's control. 'Whether it rains, for instance,' he grins. 'The main thing is, the show is a machine which needs to keep running. You *must* keep filming. You don't want to be held up, so you always have to have a Plan B up your sleeve.'

Toby's use of music continues during the shoot. 'I'll play it in the car in the mornings. Sometimes I'll play it to the actors to help get them in the mood. In *Doctor Who* we use a lot of special effects, so many actors have to react to stuff which simply isn't there. You have to give them all the help you can.'

THE FIRST VIEWER

'As a director, your role on set is to be the first member of the audience. You watch a scene play out and pay attention to how you're reacting. If it's a joke, are you laughing? If not, why not? You may have to communicate changes in a way which is clear enough but doesn't demoralise your cast.'

SLEEPLESS IN CARDIFF

A typical shoot day sees Toby wake at 6am. He's on set by 7am, ready to start an 11-hour shoot at 8am.

'People will ask questions while you're having your breakfast,' Toby reveals. 'Questions about costume, or design, or locations – and your answers, through a mouthful of fried egg, often determine how well the first hour of the shoot goes. If you don't get it right, you can cost yourself half an hour of messing about. You can't get that half-hour back at the end of the day because people have got families they want to go home to.'

'The good thing about the shoot,' Toby continues, 'is that, unlike prep, you're ticking things off the list. You're doing it – your workload is getting gradually smaller. It's still very stressful, but it's a less anxious stress. It's more a sort of "battle stress".'

NIGHT SHOOTS

'Often, when we shoot during the summer,' Toby says, 'there aren't that many hours of darkness to work in. So if you want a night scene, it means you might go to work at 3pm and not get back until 3am – or you may be working from 9pm until 6am. Those full nights are really brutal on everyone involved. The crew work so hard and are very dedicated, but everybody's tired and your work efficiency goes down a little bit. It's tough, but the show always comes first.'

HAYNES' HIGHLIGHTS

Toby Haynes selects his top moments directing *Doctor Who...*

A DAY IN THE MUSEUM

The Big Bang

I was really proud of the opening sequence of *The Big Bang* when little Amelia walks through the deserted museum and opens the Pandorica to find Amy inside. It was a really spooky sequence so we played in scary music on set to get young Caitlin in the mood. I'm a big fan of Steven Spielberg's films and this is my tribute to him.

I'M KAZRAN SARDICK

A Christmas Carol

Being offered a Christmas special was the greatest honour that could have been bestowed on me. Not least because of the wonderful opportunity to build a whole new alien city – Sardicktown – but also because of the chance to work with legendary actor Michael Gambon. He just loved playing the evil Kazran.

WA-HEYYY!

A Christmas Carol

We put the cast of *A Christmas Carol* in a rickshaw in front of a greenscreen and blew great big fans at them whilst playing music really loud, helping them imagine what it was like to be soaring high above a city while being pulled by a flying shark! Little Lawrence Belcher, who played Young Kazran, couldn't help but shout 'Wa-heyyy!'

HOWDY!

The Impossible Astronaut

Bringing *Doctor Who* to the United States for the first time was another landmark opportunity for me. Flying above Amy Pond, in a helicopter, as she ran through the colossal stones of Utah's Monument Valley took my breath away. After the first shot I went to shout 'Cut!' but nothing came out of my mouth – I was genuinely speechless!

THE SILENT SCREAM

The Impossible Astronaut

Introducing a brilliant new *Doctor Who* baddie has to be up there on any fan's to-do list, and with the Silence I got my chance. I love working with Neill Gorton and Millennium FX – they build all our monsters and do such a fantastic job. Our aim was to create the scariest monster ever. I like to think we got pretty close...

LOVE A TOMB!

Day of the Moon

In *Day of the Moon*'s final laser battle, Steven Moffat asked me to make River Song look like a real action hero, so I started training Alex Kingston in how to spin a gun. She worked and worked on that and was brilliant when we came to shoot it. I loved the sheer number of explosions. Making three Silents look like an army was tough but a lot of fun.

POST-PRODUCTION

Duration: One week of editing per week of filming. **Director's goals:** To examine what you have, make it work and finish it to everyone's satisfaction

WORKING WITH THE EDITOR

It initially seems surprising that the editor – the person who assembles the filmed footage ('the rushes') and puts the show together – may well not have read the script. But as Toby explains, this can be a blessing.

'The editor's responding to the raw rushes which you've provided, so he's looking at the story in a different way. He's just reacting to what's on tape, rather than a preconceived idea in his mind. This period can be torture if you feel like you haven't done as well as you should have. The edit's a bit like being faced with all your mistakes, writ large on the screen, which can be very upsetting. But it's amazing what you can achieve by literally cutting tiny bits away. You work first on the things you like least of all. Next are the little niggly things which have been bothering you. After that it gets smoother and smoother as the episode takes on a definite shape.'

'Basically, in the edit, you can turn something that feels like a disaster into something that feels not half bad,' Toby explains. 'By the time you've finished, you can hardly remember what you've done during that process, but it works. That's because so many people have poured their talent into it and had a chance to say what they think should be done with it.'

SHOWING IT TO THE PRODUCERS

'It's like a review,' says Toby. 'The producers will sit in one of the BBC Wales production suites, watch the edit on a big screen, and make notes. Afterwards they'll tell you what they think about it – whether they like it or not and which bits they don't feel are working. Pretty often they won't give you the solution – they'll just give you the sense of what's wrong. Because Steven Moffat's one of the producers, however, he'll often have new ideas of what he wants to see in there. This might include writing new lines for a character, for instance.'

EFFECTS AND MUSIC

After the episode is locked – which means it's cut to its final length and there won't be any further tampering with the basic footage – it's time to add elements like The Mill's computer-generated imagery and composer Murray Gold's musical score.

'You have to plan CGI before you film it,' Toby notes, 'because it's got to be affordable. On set, The Mill offer advice on how to shoot larger CG sequences. And now the episode is cut together you have a more detailed meeting with them, to go through every single effects shot in terms of how they're going to achieve it.'

Murray Gold will have been busy composing music for the episode, sometimes assisted by a 'guide-track' compiled by Toby. This is cut to the episode itself, and includes some of the music Toby has been listening to throughout the process, giving Murray an idea of how he envisages the score.

'This is probably the loveliest part of the process,' enthuses Toby. 'You've assembled the episode into something you like. Everything from this point onwards is a plus. The Mill are like magicians – I look at their work almost in awe. And Murray's music is always a joy, bringing new depth to each story.'

THE DUB

Doctor Who's award-winning dubbing mixer, Tim Ricketts, then creates the right audio blend for the episode. 'You've got the voices of the actors, the sound effects and the music,' Toby says. 'Everything's fighting to come across. If you played every track at the same volume you'd have a nonsensical cacophony. So you sit in a dubbing theatre and Tim moves all these controls around with such precision – it's a great pleasure to see him at work. Everything melds together as one soundtrack, breathing new life into the episode. It's still a stressful and tricky stage, but by the end of it you're looking at the final product at long last.'

THE END OF THE EXAM

'I love every element of the direction process,' Toby smiles, clearly overflowing with enthusiasm for his job. 'I love talking to the designer during prep, seeing creatures get wheeled out on set, watching Matt Smith say lines you've only heard in your head, seeing your pictures come together and make sense in the edit. But possibly the most exciting moment is being the first person to read a Steven Moffat script, knowing that millions of people are going to watch your realisation of it on their TV sets on a Saturday night. It's a big responsibility, yes, but there's nothing else like it in the universe!'

EPISODE 11

The God Complex

BY TOBY WHITHOUSE

THE STORY

The Doctor, Amy and Rory land in a perfect replica of a tatty Earth hotel. With no windows or doors, there's no obvious way out – especially not when the hotel corridors start to twist and turn, reshaping themselves and leaving them unable to find the TARDIS.

Before long, they meet another group of people who've inexplicably found their way to this impossible hotel. Nervous and jittery, they're being stalked by their own deepest fears – and by a monstrous creature who lives at the heart of this ever-changing maze...

As they travel deeper into the labyrinth, the Doctor finally realises what the hotel wants – to feed on their faith. Confronting its victims with their darkest nightmares made flesh, this place forces its terrified inhabitants to fall back on their most fervent hopes and beliefs – emotions which it then drains away, killing them in the process.

So what brought the TARDIS to the hotel? Only the most powerful faith the universe can offer – Amy's unwavering trust in the Doctor.

And now, she's next on the menu...

Where Have I Seen?

DAVID WALLIAMS
Gibbis
Matt Lucas's comedy partner in *Little Britain* and *Come Fly with Me*, David's also appeared in *Hotel Babylon* and *Neighbours*.

SPENCER WILDING
The Creature
Spencer has had monstrous roles in movies like *The Hitchhiker's Guide to the Galaxy* (2005) and *Who* writer Neil Gaiman's *Stardust* (2007).

NUMBER CRUNCHING

11 THE NUMBER OF THE DOCTOR'S FEARS

THE GOD COMPLEX

MAGIC MOMENT

The minotaur has come for Amy at last...

THE DOCTOR: Amy, listen to me. I can't save you. I can't do anything to stop this.

AMY: ...What?

THE DOCTOR: I stole your childhood and now I've led you by the hand to your death. But the worst thing is, I knew this would happen. This is what always happens.

The door shakes as the minotaur slams into it, over and over – until, with a deafening crash, it bursts open, slamming Rory against the wall. It looms over the Doctor and Amy, huge and savage, about to strike. But the Doctor holds Amy's head still, his eyes boring into hers...

THE DOCTOR: I took you with me because I was vain, because I wanted to be adored.

Amy's eyes are locked on the Doctor's. The grunting of the

minotaur, the chaos around them, it all fades until there is nothing in the world other than the Doctor's words.

THE DOCTOR: Look at you. Glorious Pond. The girl who waited for me.

And when we look back at Amy... It's Amelia! The little girl! Staring up at the Doctor, her eyes wide and frightened.

THE DOCTOR: But I'm not a hero. I really am just a mad man with a box. And it's time we saw each other as we really are.

He leans forward to kiss the top of her head. But now, little Amelia has gone again, and Amy has returned.

THE DOCTOR: Amy Williams, it's time to stop waiting.

▶▶ Amy, sceptical of the Doctor's claim to have arrived in the hotel by 'accident', recalls the events of *The Rebel Flesh/The Almost People*, in which the Doctor revealed that he had planned to visit the acid-mining facility all along. Worried that she might once again be a Flesh replica of herself, Amy asks, 'Am I not really me? Am I made of butter or something?' ▶▶ The hotel contains portraits of beings from a number of alien races, including Judoon (introduced in 2007's *Smith and Jones*), Ood (2006's *The Impossible Planet*), a Sontaran (1973's *The Time Warrior*) and one of the Catkind first seen in *New Earth* (2006). The 'fears' listed on the portraits include the Doctor's eternal foes, the Daleks – and

Fantastic Facts!

quite right too! ▶▶ One of the hotel rooms contains a trio of Weeping Angels, creatures which were introduced to the series in *Blink* (2007). Amy is right to assume the room is meant to represent her own fears, considering that in *The Time of Angels/Flesh and Stone* (2010) they planted the seed of one of their kind inside her mind. ▶▶ Amy reassures Gibbis that the Doctor can be trusted, telling him how she waited for the Doctor as a child and he returned for her, as she knew he would – as seen in *The Eleventh Hour*. This faith, however, nearly causes Amy's death... ▶▶ The Doctor explains that the minotaur creature is a 'distant cousin' of the Nimon. These creatures – from *The Horns of Nimon* (1979-

1980) – were bull-headed, parasitic aliens who travelled from planet to planet, bleeding them dry in a never-ending quest for sustenance. ▶▶ The Doctor was forced to break a companion's faith in him once before, in *The Curse of Fenric* (1989), when Ace's utter belief in the Time Lord caused a psychic barrier, preventing the destuction of evil entity Fenric. The Seventh Doctor went about it in a far crueller way than the Eleventh did.

UNSEEN ADVENTURES

▶▶ The Doctor has previously visited the planet of Ravan-Skala, where the natives are hundreds of metres tall and normal-sized beings have to travel in hot-air balloons to talk to them.

BEHIND THE SCENES
TOBY WHITHOUSE
Writer

What kind of things inspired the nightmares lurking in the hotel rooms?

What helped was having to find a fear for each specific character. For Rita, the high-achieving academic, hers would be a fear of familial failure. For Gibbis, given the personality of his race, it would be a question of finding the one thing that couldn't be negotiated with or surrendered to – and it felt like the Weeping Angels would fit that very well. It was Steven Moffat's idea that we should hint at the Doctor's own room. There was an early version of the script where we actually saw what was in there. But what's scary for one person isn't scary for another – and the moment you define it, it instantly stops being scary for about 70 per cent of the audience. That's why the Doctor sees it but we don't, so it's left to the viewer's own imagination.

Toward the end of the episode, the Doctor tells Amy, 'It's time we saw each other as we really are.' How do you think they've seen each other up to this point?

Amy sees him as somebody who will always save the day. Utterly invincible.

Regardless of the fact that he's constantly leading his companions into terrible danger. Over the years, the Doctor's had companions die – but it doesn't stop him. I touched on something similar in *The Vampires of Venice* [Toby's 2010 episode] and *School Reunion* [from 2006] – by exposing somebody to the kind of extraordinary splendour of space and time travel, you make life back on Earth seem very dull and thin in comparison. But again, regardless of this, the Doctor still does it. So, Amy had seen the Doctor as this infallible

figure, when the reality is that he's reckless, a little selfish, and a little vain. And how does the Doctor see Amy? Even though he's brought Rory into the TARDIS, I still think there's a slight reluctance in accepting that she's a married woman – he still calls her Pond and he can't quite believe she's grown up and isn't a little girl any more. That's why, having broken the minotaur's spell, he calls her Amy Williams – he finally uses her proper married name.

Do you think the Doctor really has a God complex?

Oh, without a doubt! But, to be fair, although that line looks really clever in the script, it was something that I hadn't really planned. It was just one of those lovely moments of serendipity. The title came specifically from the idea of the prison and the minotaur. It wasn't really until I was writing that scene between the Doctor and Rita, when she accuses him of having a God complex, that it suddenly appeared there in the dialogue. I was very pleased when it turned out like that, but it was quite unexpected.

MAKING MONSTERS

Doctor Who demands a lot of its talented monster-makers, from alien beasts to tentacled terrors. Or even, as in *The God Complex*, a huge, hairy, horned Minotaur from the darkest realms of Ancient Greek mythology...

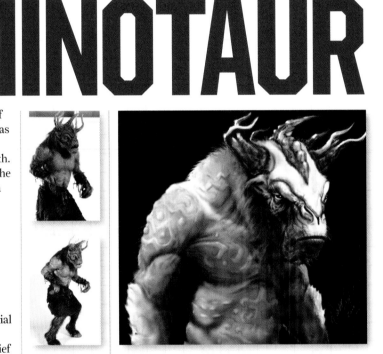

THE MINOTAUR

The God Complex's mighty Minotaur is one of the bigger physical creations *Doctor Who* has attempted. The two-and-a-half metre tall beast is, of course, based on the ancient Greek myth.

'It's such a classic creature,' says Neill Gorton, the head of Millennium FX. 'It's a human body with a bull's head. When you're dealing with something classical, you can refer to illustrations going back 2,000 years to Ancient Greece, when they were painting them on jugs. You can also just put the word "Minotaur" into an internet search engine, or even go and have a look at a bull in a field – and that's exactly what we did. Fortunately, we'd already built a Minotaur for another film, called *Inkheart* (2008), so we had a lot of reference material from working on that one.'

The Minotaur's mythological nature led to a brief misunderstanding between Millennium and *Doctor Who*'s production team. 'The funny thing was, we started off designing traditional Minotaurs,' says Neill, 'because it just said "a minotaur" in the script. Then we had a tone meeting, presented the pictures to Steven Moffat and he went, "Oh, this is great, but we want an *alien* Minotaur. An alien which is Minotaur-ish and has possibly inspired the myth of the Minotaur." So we went straight back to the drawing board.'

It was decided early on that the creature wouldn't be so effective if realised as a computer-generated behemoth. 'Because it interacts up-close with people,' Neill says, 'it would be so much more difficult to do with CGI – you'd suddenly have to shoot in a very specific way. And it's much better as a prosthetic because you can act with it and react to

it. There's a very poignant bit at the end when it's dying and the Doctor's sat there next to it. He's got to be emotive, which can be harder to do with a CGI monster.'

Millennium needed to build virtually the entire Minotaur, as Toby Whithouse's script specified a slow reveal of the creature, including close-ups of horns and hooves. Neill knew that their Minotaur would involve a man in a costume – and a rather tall man at that. 'They wanted it about 2.5 metres tall, with horns scraping the ceiling,' Neill recalls. 'We knew it had to be someone in a costume, so the first thing was to find that person. We have regular performers, like Paul Kasey, but if you want to make them that tall it's rather tricky. We worked on designs but we couldn't start

start sculpting. We sculpted his torso, head and arms all together in clay. The weird hooves added height, which brought Spencer up about another 15 centimetres. The horns on his head took him up another 25 centimetres, too. Then we made a big foam rubber costume which he could slip into. The head was all animatronic. The creature also needed to talk. It originally had lots of dialogue, but then they cut that back so that it just mumbled and then was translated.'

Neill made sure that his Minotaur 'looked old and gnarly. This thing was meant to look millennia old, so we needed an ancient, crunchy-looking face. The animatronic controls allowed us to move its eyes, lips, mouth, so it could snarl, move its nostrils, blink, and move its eyes around'.

There's that word again – animatronic. What does it actually mean? 'With a prosthetic make-up,' Neill explains, 'you stick it to the face and the face moves the rubber additions around. If you furrow your brow, for instance, then the brow will move. But as soon as you get a creature

building the costume until we found someone, so that it would fit properly.'

Neill ultimately recruited actor Spencer Wilding, who was experienced in the field of creature performance, having worn the title costume in 2010's *The Wolfman*. 'Spencer does martial arts and used to be a kickboxing champion. That's a real advantage because the hard thing in these costumes can be knowing what your body's doing on the outside. We tend to use dancers and martial artists inside these things because they've got really good bodily awareness. Dance and martial arts are all about precision and movement, so those people are very body aware without actually having to see'.

'Spencer's two metres tall, so that gave us a bit more height to start with. We already had body moulds for him from another job, so could just

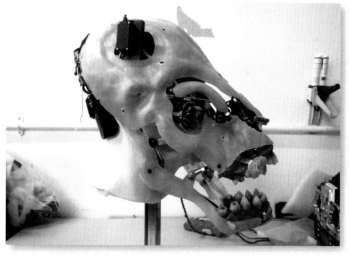

MAKING MONSTERS

>> The God Complex mentions that its alien Minotaur is a 'distant cousin of the Nimon'. This wasn't a creature invented by writer Toby Whithouse, but a reference to an enemy which the Doctor had faced during one of his earlier TV adventures.

The Nimon appeared in the 1979 story *The Horns of Nimon*. The Fourth Doctor and his companions Romana and K-9 battled with these Minotaur-like creatures, which fired energy-blasts from their horns and drained the energy from entire worlds before moving on to new conquests.

Furthermore, actual Minotaurs have twice appeared in *Doctor Who*. In 1968's *The Mind Robber*, the Second Doctor and companion Zoe encountered one in the Land of Fiction, while 1972's *The Time Monster* saw the Third Doctor and Jo defeat a Minotaur which guarded the Crystal of Kronos in the lost city of Atlantis.

with a face much bigger than a human face, the only way to make it move is with animatronics – in this case, radio-controlled ones. It uses small motors operated by joysticks, very much like a radio-controlled aeroplane. If you move a joystick, the flaps on a model aeroplane go up and down. Imagine doing the same thing but with a Minotaur's eyebrow.'

Ah, now we see. 'They're literally the same ones used for model aeroplanes,' Neill continues. 'We buy all that equipment, because the technology already exists and is good, sturdy and strong. The remote control is handy too, because it means you're not tied to the animatronic head by cables. You can stand next to the director and control a Minotaur!'

It took two Millennium operators to control the faith-munching monster for *The God Complex*. 'Each had six channel controllers,'

Neill says, 'so you had 12 channels of movement, including eyes, eyebrows, eye blinks, nostrils, lips, jaw... all of it controlled individually. So they have to work in sync with the guy inside the suit, who can only really do the head movements, to make one seamless performance.'

It sounds like the operator's job is rather stressful? 'Generally, it's fun,' Neill argues, 'but sometimes you've got to do things at precisely the right time and hit your cues. So it's like any actor who has to do a certain movement at a given time. That can be tricky. When you've got a performer who's virtually blind – only able see out through tiny holes – it does get complicated, but you find you get into a rhythm after a while. Then, hopefully, when they shout "Action!", the creature will do all the things it's meant to do, and all at the right time. Thankfully, our Minotaur did.'

THE White Flag

DELIGHTEDLY STICKING BOTH HANDS IN THE AIR, EVERY DAY!

Price: 50 Zaybars (or, you know, just take it for free if you like)

FREE POSTER

Today, *The White Flag* is proud to present a centre-page spread gathering together all 56 variants of the word SURRENDER, along with portraits of all our finest military figures who used those words, pictured before and after their horrendous deaths.

FOR ALL OUR WORTHLESS READERS INSIDE!

The lack of power of words!

Our greatest minds – if such a term may be used to describe members of our insignificant race, not fit to lick the Boots of the Great Balfressic Legion – at the Secondary University Branch-Members' Integral Terminus (or SUBMIT for short) have triumphed yet again. They have produced a 56th word to aid us in unquestioningly handing over power to our glorious new occupiers.

The new word, which goes live across all Vocabular-a-trons from tomorrow nightnoon, is 'plaazari'. As you might expect, it simply means 'surrender', just like the other glorious 55 words which preceded it, such as 'itzeeka', 'malnozo' and of course the unforgettable 'dobbadobbapook'. Citizens are, of course, also within their rights simply to prostrate themselves at the feet of any nearby Balfressic Legionnaire and simply weep openly.

MAPS OF YOUR LOCAL FORCED LABOUR CAMPS! P56-67

WELCOME
TO OUR NEW ALIEN OVERLORDS!

AFTER a full year of awful indpendence, Tivoli is once again occupied by a violently invasive alien force!

There was singing in the streets last night, as the Seventh Balfressic Legion descended on our planet and made it clear they meant business.

Talon

Half an hour after the invasion began, our illustrious President Zellas addressed the nation, speaking very passionately despite being in discomfort, due to the gigantic Balfressic talon pinning him to the floor of his office.

'Citizens,' he told our worthless populace, 'this is a time for rejoicing! For far too long, we have suffered freedom. We have endured a hideous array of choices, in terms of what to do and when to do it.'

Pitiful

President Zellas made reference to our previous rulers, the Quall, describing their departure last year as 'our darkest hour. When the Quall announced that they had become bored with our

EXCLUSIVE by A. A. A. A. BRANCHIA Invasions Editor

so-called "pitiful subservience" and flew back off into the heavens... well, I think it's fair to say that many citizens, myself included, haven't quite recovered from that loss.'

Cave

As the Balfressic talon increased its pressure on his throat, President Zellas giggled, adding: 'I have every confidence in the Balfressic Legion. You only have to look into those squinty red eyes to know that they don't intend to give us even an inch of liberty – unlike the Quall, who would occasionally let us go for strolls and select sandwich fillings. This is a far superior class of oppressor, my people: we can happily cave in, safe in the knowledge that we'll never have to make another stressful decision ever again!'

Chains

Zellas then laughed heartily as he was wrapped in chains, while a nation cheered. Here at *The White Flag*, we very much look forward to being rounded up and imprisoned later today. From tomorrow's issue, please welcome your new editors!

INSIDE! White Flag Etiquette p13 + Win A Horrific Death At The Hands of The Supreme Balfressiarch Himself p55 + Weather p61

EPISODE 12

Closing Time

BY GARETH ROBERTS

THE STORY

The Doctor just wants to keep his head down, lay low for a while. He knows what's in store for him. He knows his destiny lies on the shores of Lake Silencio. He knows his time is nearly up. But the universe won't let the Doctor go just yet...

The Doctor travels to Earth, to the doorstep of his old mucker Craig Owens. The man who never comes back has come back – and Craig is worried. But a spate of mysterious power cuts and disappearing people draws the Doctor into one final adventure. Deep beneath the streets of Colchester lies a spaceship. Inside lurk some of the Doctor's most ancient enemies, growing in power, waiting to strike...

Finally disturbed from their slumber, a battered group of Cybermen prepare to take the world. One by one, they are bolstering their forces with humans from the streets above.

The Doctor stands alone, ready to shatter his enemies' plans. But Craig knows he can't do it by himself – the Doctor can't do anything without his friends at his side. If only he'd admit it.

It's time for Craig Owens to man up and be a hero. Once he's found a babysitter...

Where Have I Seen?

JAMES CORDEN
Craig Owens
Returning as Craig, James is best known for hit BBC sitcom *Gavin & Stacey* and Sky panel show *A League of Their Own.*

LYNDA BARON
Val
Best known for *Open All Hours*, Lynda was Wrack in 1983 *Doctor Who* story *Enlightenment*, and sang 'The Ballad of the Last Chance Saloon' in 1966's *The Gunfighters.*

NUMBER CRUNCHING

6 **CYBERMEN ABOARD THE CRASHED SHIP**

6 IS ENOUGH TO CONVERT THE HUMAN RACE

CLOSING TIME

>> We first met Craig Owens in *The Lodger* (2010), when the Doctor gently nudged him and Sophie together. In that episode, the Doctor shared his immense knowledge with Craig by means of a 'psychic headbutt' – which is why Craig knows the Time Lord so well. >> We learned in *A Good Man Goes to War* that the Doctor can talk to babies, a skill he demonstrates again here with Alfie/Stormageddon. >> Introduced in *The Tomb of the Cybermen* (1967), Cybermats have been used by the Cybermen for a number of purposes. They guarded their tombs on Telos in that story, but later they were used to help the Cybermen infiltrate Space Station W3 in *The Wheel in Space* (1968) and to spread plague aboard Nerva Beacon in *Revenge of the Cybermen* (1975). >> In deleted dialogue, as the Doctor scans for the Cybership outside the shop, he gave Craig a quick guide to the Cybermen: 'They were people. But they "enhanced" themselves with machine parts. They want to make everyone like them.' Which pretty much sums it up. The Cybermen were introduced in *The Tenth Planet* (1966), where we learned they hail from Earth's long-lost twin planet Mondas. They replaced their weak organic parts with machine technology to survive their home world's long exile in the depths of space. The Cybermen seen in *Rise of the Cybermen/The Age of Steel* (2006) – and every Cyber-story to follow, up to *The Pandorica Opens* (2010) – do not share this origin: hailing from a parallel universe they were created by scientist John Lumic. >> The Cybermen in *Rise of the Cybermen/The Age of Steel* were defeated by the Doctor shutting down their emotional inhibitors, leaving them crippled by all the pain and misery they would feel if they were still human. In this episode, the Cybermen are destroyed in a similar fashion: Craig's love for his son '[triggered] a feedback loop into their emotional inhibitors,' the Doctor explains. 'All the stuff they cut out

Fantastic Facts!

of themselves, now they're feeling it.' >> The Alignment of Exedor was named by writer Gareth Roberts by pushing together two words from the Jon Pertwee era of *Doctor Who* – Exillon and Aggedor (from 1974's *Death to the Daleks* and 1972's *The Curse of Peladon* respectively). Months later, idly trying to recall the name of the eccentric would-be alien from US sitcom *Mork & Mindy*, Roberts did a quick internet search and was horrified to find it was Exidor. So don't write in as it was a total coincidence! >> The Doctor's line, 'It's not a rat, it's a Cybermat,' is a paraphrase of a line spoken by the Fourth Doctor in the Target Books novelisation of *Revenge of the Cybermen* by Terrance Dicks. Craig's response about not knowing the names of everything was an ad-lib from James Corden. >> Life imitated art as, mere days after filming completed, Corden became a father for the first time when his partner Julia Carey gave birth to a son, Max. There may have been something in the air as script editor Lindsey Alford, wife of former script editor turned producer Brian Minchin, was also pregnant during production, giving birth soon after to baby Elin. >> The Doctor reminds us 'Silence will fall when the question is asked' – a fact

he learned during *Let's Kill Hitler*. >> The Doctor nicks some TARDIS-blue envelopes from Sophie's stationery stash. He will use them to invite Amy, Rory, River, Canton and himself to witness his death in *The Impossible Astronaut*. He's also given the Stetson we see him wearing in Utah, which came from Craig's mate Shaun's stag night. We met Shaun in *The Lodger*. >> Daisy Haggard's reduced role as Sophie in this story was due to her prior commitment to a play, *Becky Shaw*, at the Almeida Theatre, London. >> In a final scene written by Steven Moffat, we see River Song (on the day she became Dr Song) rifling through eyewitness accounts of the Doctor's final hours – before she is joined by Madame Kovarian (who escaped in *A Good Man Goes to War*), accompanied by the Silence. River's 'owners' have returned to use her in their plan to end the Time Lord's life. Anglican Clerics (again, last seen in *A Good Man Goes to War*) enter with the spacesuit from *The Impossible Astronaut*. The episode ends with River trapped in the suit beneath the waters of Lake Silencio. >> Other story titles suggested by Gareth Roberts – who referred to it during the writing process as *Carry-On Lodging* – included *Everything Must Go*, *The Last Adventure* and, best of all, *Cybermen and a Baby*!

DELETED!

Back at 'base' the Doctor is mixing up a solvent as he prepares to examine the Cybermat. However Craig's biggest concern is the Doctor himself...

CRAIG: Is that really safe?
The Doctor sloshes his mixture -
THE DOCTOR: Completely. I've put newspaper down. I have to crack the brain casing and extract the core program – then I can find out their plan and stop it. That's the sort of thing I do. Too late to change now.
CRAIG: You're ill, aren't you?
THE DOCTOR: What?
CRAIG: My nana. She found out she had cancer, didn't tell anyone, not even my mum. We didn't know until just before she died. She was all crabby and snappy. We thought it was just her getting old -
THE DOCTOR: I am not crabby or snappy!

CRAIG: I'm not stupid, Doctor. I may not have a brain the size of Mercury –
THE DOCTOR: (*Interrupting*) Which is actually a very small planet –
CRAIG: That's it. I'm right, aren't I?
THE DOCTOR: Yes. You're right.
He pulls an empty nappy wrapper from under the table –
THE DOCTOR: Right out of nappies. You forgot to buy more, it was on the list.

DID YOU SPOT?

>> Amy's new career as an advertising model sees her promoting the fragrance Petrichor – one of the passwords to the TARDIS security systems in *The Doctor's Wife*. So does it smell like wet earth then?

BEHIND THE SCENES
GARETH ROBERTS
Writer

This is Craig's second run-in with the Doctor. Do you think he'll ever have the ordinary life he craves?
He has an ordinary life most of the time – he's like the anti-River Song. But he loves the Doctor, and is eternally grateful to him, so I'm sure they'll meet again.

The Cybermats are an odd little creation – creepy, but a bit silly in some lights. How hard is it to make them scary? And was there a temptation to take the mickey?
I think the silly/terrifying axis is a dangerous but good place to be. I like it when innocuous or daft-looking things or people turn out to be absolutely deadly. That's often what *Doctor Who* is all about. It's not taking the mickey, more a unique way of jolting the viewer.

You've done the Cybermen now. Are there any other old monsters you'd like to take a stab at?
Not really. The Cybermen came into it because I wanted a sense of history for the Doctor's final adventure before he keeps his date with destiny. I prefer to invent new creatures and villains, but I always try and do what nobody else is doing – and this year, that meant classic monsters.

UNSEEN ADVENTURES

>> The Doctor has heard about the Alignment of Exedor, when 17 galaxies line up in unison, but he is destined never to witness it for himself, choosing instead to tidy up Craig's flat. We've also missed out on 200 years of the Doctor's adventures since *The God Complex* – his 'farewell tour'. But he gives us no clues as to what it entailed.

Sanderson & Grainger S&G

APPLICATION FOR EMPLOYMENT

TITLE (Mr/Mrs/Other) Doctor – also a Sir (twice) but don't like to boast

SURNAME Doctor   FIRST NAME(S) The

ADDRESS The TARDIS, but currently c/o Craig Owens,

nice big house on Sheckley Street, Colchester, Essex, England,

Earth, Mutters Spiral.. Not sure of postcode.

AGE ~~1107 40ish? Is that too high?~~ 28   GENDER Male so far

ETHNIC ORIGIN ~~Gallifr..~~ ~~Human~~ Normal   POSTITION APPLIED FOR General selling man?

EDUCATIONAL QUALIFICATIONS

– 2.2 in Cosmic Science, Prydon Adademy, South Gallifrey

  Medical Degree, Edinburgh, Earth, 1888 (Joseph Lister will vouch)

– 3 A Levels (woodwork, Hebrew, modern dance) – forced to sit deadly

  exams by robot Principal who had infiltrated Wickham College in 1984

– Won't mention all the ones with robots and teaching machines –

  though am officially a High Brain. But, again, don't like to boast

– Runner Up – "The Robotic Apprentice" (2059 season) – later disqualified

  for a) not being a robot, b) unmasking the SugarTron's scheme to

  enslave humanity live on "The Robotic Apprentice: You're Fired".

PREVIOUS JOB EXPERIENCE	YEARS	PAY	REASON FOR LEAVING
Scientific Adviser to U.N.I.T	Who can say?	Unpaid, but free company car plus facilities to repair TARDIS	Got fed up
Supply science teacher, Deffry Vale School	2006 or 7	Never found out	School blew up
Wine Waiter at quite nice pizza restaurant in London	1 night in 2005	Not a clue. Got good tips though.	Auton invasion
Comissioner from the Provinces	1794	No, But lovely hat.	The French Revolution
Earth Examiner on Vulcan	2020 (is this right?)	No time to ask predecessor, who died in mercury swamp	THE DALEKS!
Saving the universe	The last 900-odd years	NO CHARGE	Own impending death tomorrow, shot by impossible astronaut. (THANKS FOR BRINGING THAT UP)

WHAT DREW YOU TO SANDERSON & GRAINGER ~~The mysterious patina of teleport energy I detected, plus 3 humans disappeared in the vicinity of this store~~ Looks nice. Want to work in a shop. No other reasons. Nothing strange. And I love a big shop.

WHAT QUALITIES DO YOU FEEL YOU COULD BRING TO OUR TEAM? Selling things to people VERY NORMALLY and well and with no hidden agenda. Also protecting shop from invasions, should they occur. Nice smile. Bow tie.

DO YOU HAVE ANY SPECIAL REQUIREMENTS? Name badge. And possibly a big net.

IS THERE ANYTHING ELSE YOU WOULD LIKE TO MENTION IN SUPPORT OF YOUR APPLICATION?

I strongly advise you to employ me to ensure the continued ~~existence~~ success of your ~~planet~~ shop. And I need to start RIGHT NOW please.

The fabulous, fantastic gallery of CHARACTERS THAT *NEARLY* MADE IT INTO CLOSING TIME but didn't for some reason

PRESENTED BY THE WRITER, MR GARETH ROBERTS

THE DOCTOR SAYS: Ssh, it's *not* the Doctor, the Doctor is *dead*, remember? Bang-bang-bang-splash-flipping-heck, boo-hoo, etc. Deader than a doornail, much deader than a dodo and, in fact, with even fewer signs of life than a double biology class on a Friday afternoon.

He does seem to have popped up quite a bit in this book, however – which is odd, considering he's passed on. So from now on I'm making sure that each copy is imbued with a special psychic imprint on every page, so that YOU, as the official owner, can read about him in safety. But to anyone else each instance of his name will change to something less Doctor-y. So, if you lend this book to a friend and they come back asking what *The Brilliant Book of Roy Robins* was meant to be about, you'll know why. It's what the Doctor would have wanted. Had he survived that fatal encounter at Lake Silencio. Where I, of course, as somebody who is not the Doctor and isn't connected with him in any way, was *never anywhere near*. OK? Anyway, before he went up to that great TARDIS in the sky, I'm sure that the Doctor pondered over the life of my – er, *his* – good friend Craig Owens from Earth. Craig seems like a very normal human being person with a very normal human being person's life – except when that rotter the Doctor was around. But who's to say Craig isn't really a complex space-time event with a brain-twisting lifestyle that contains all the hidden secrets and unfathomable mysteries of the universe? (I know, I'm pushing it a bit with this.)

So study this data file of the people who didn't quite make it into the Doctor's definitely final (remember, the Doctor is dead, sniff) encounter with Craig, and see if you can spot any hidden timey-wimey conundrums that the Doctor would have liked to know about if only he was still alive.

PS. You probably won't, it's just for fun.

PPS. If by some chance you do, contact me immediately!

MELINA

Sophie's fourth best friend, who is always having a 'crisis'. Insisted on attending the birth of Alfie, encouraging Sophie at the moment of delivery with helpful comments such as 'Soph, you look absolutely terrible, this is the worst thing anybody ever could ever do!' and 'Don't worry, Soph, the baby isn't actually that fat!' and, bafflingly, 'It's a girl!' Sophie and Melina were away for most of the events of *Closing Time* on a 'peaceful' spa break at Salcott-cum-Virley.

DAVID JENKINS

Melina's current partner. Enjoyed the Saturday night while Melina was at the spa rather too much, and was spotted 'with' Melina's friend Clare (Sophie's third best friend) at the Fox & Goose pub on the High Street on what could have been the final night for humanity but thankfully wasn't. This information was relayed to Melina by an unknown source many consider to have been Clare herself, leading to a lengthy overnight discussion about David's merits and demerits on what was supposed to be Sophie's first night of uninterrupted sleep in five months.

VAL'S NEPHEW

Val's nephew Tom is 41 years old, but retains a healthy interest in collecting motorised toys and vehicles. Val sincerely hoped a Cybermat could be found to add to his collection, which would have been bad news for Tom and his 'housemate' Andrew. 'Tom and Andrew just haven't found the right girls yet,' thinks Val.

THE DOCTOR SAYS: *Which is odd, really, when you think about it.*

JOHN-JOE

The current partner of Sanderson & Grainger saleswoman Kelly. Kelly's desire to meet John-Joe at the arranged time of 6pm on Friday night outside Sanderson & Grainger was thwarted, not by an invasion by the Cybermen, but by John-Joe's failure to remember the arrangement at all. John-Joe often finds himself wishing there was a simple way to 'ssh' Kelly.

THE DOCTOR SAYS: *But of course there isn't. And there never was.*

DON PETHERIDGE AND ANDREA GROOM

Who says love can't blossom over the age of sixty?

THE DOCTOR SAYS:
Certainly not me.
Don and Andrea started at Sanderson & Grainger on the same day as Val, when the store opened in 1971, and spent much of the following 40 years exchanging stolen glances and regretting their marriages to other people. In the few days before the events of *Closing Time*, Don and Andrea finally found themselves acting on their impulses, as if responding to some sense of universal foreboding. Or because Don's wife had run off with Philip Nutt from hardware.

THE KUSTODIANS OF EXEDOR

Ethereal beings composed of pure light after several billion years of evolution, the Kustodians of Exedor are the guardians of the unique space-time alignment of Exedor, a time-locked conjunction of 17 galaxies that many speculate could be the most spectacular thing anybody has ever seen. They changed the spelling of 'custodians' to try and make themselves seem a bit more interesting.

THE DOCTOR SAYS: *The trouble with all that evolution is that it's difficult to communicate with anybody else except by flashing mysteriously. You keep getting mistaken for a traffic light.*

NINA

Local girl who moved effortlessly through the first few rounds of *Britain's Got Talent* with her novelty act involving glittery tassles, the flags of all nations and 15 spinning plates, while she sang along to *The Macarena*. A single mother with a broken nose, a three-legged kitten and a job mopping spills in a local supermarket, Nina shot from obscurity to overnight fame and then (following the events seen in *Closing Time*) to overnight hatred and then to overnight obscurity again, as it was revealed that she was actually married, that her nose had always looked all wonky like that, that she was actually on the checkout at the supermarket and didn't have to mop spills at all, and that her kitten had all four legs, but one had been sellotaped up under its tummy as part of her devious smokescreen.

THE GLAZIER

Glazier Roy Tomlin and his son Tim (of Tomlin & Son Glaziers) were not pleased when a mysterious stranger phoned them early on a Sunday morning with a request that they replace a glass door, damaged, the stranger explained, by an 'emergency Cybermat-battling barrage'. This was until the stranger offered £10,000 to do the job, and instantly transferred the money to Roy's bank account. Roy was later surprised to see the source for the transfer was card number 0000 0000 0000 0001, sort code 00-00-01 and card holder DR A N EXAMPLE.

THE DOCTOR SAYS: *Did you guess who the mysterious stranger in question was? I am not at liberty to say...*

JEFF GREEN
Manager of Sanderson & Grainger

There were absolutely no situations vacant at Sanderson & Grainger's department store, so manager Jeff Green was surprised when he found himself accosted by a man in a bow tie, waving a CV, at 6.30am on a Saturday morning. He was even more surprised to find himself offering the stranger a job at 6.32am on the same Saturday morning. He even made the man's name badge himself as nobody from personnel was in yet.

THE DOCTOR SAYS: *It was no surprise to me, after I explained to Jeff how I'd sold coals to Newcastle, igloos to Inuits, and string vests to Sea Devils. I could not produce the receipts for the latter, alas, as they were all soggy.*

MAKING MONSTERS

Series Six has been a great run for Cybermen fans. Not only did the silver titans make two appearances during the 2011 season, but their old biomechanical friends the Cybermats were reintroduced for the first time since 1975...

THE CYBERMEN AND CYBERMATS

Neill Gorton at Millennium FX is amazed – and slightly scared – to realise that it's been over five years since he helped to reinvent the Cybermen. Back in 2006, three main groups set about reimagining them: Millennium, *Doctor Who*'s CGI effects house The Mill and *Doctor Who*'s own in-house Art Department.

'We wanted a new spin on them,' Neill recalls, 'so in this case, it felt like three departments were better than one in terms of finding fresh ideas and approaches. Concepts were shared, discussed, blended together, and we picked out the ones that worked. I think someone from the Art Department came up with the idea of having the tubes up the arms and down the legs, for instance. But there was no one single drawing that you could look at and see exactly what eventually appeared on screen.'

Neill's team then built their brand new shiny Cybermen and, in the years since Series Two's *Rise of the Cybermen* and *The Age of Steel*, the silver giants have appeared in a fair few stories. Has Neill tweaked them much since that first appearance?

'Only a few small things have changed,' he explains. 'In the 2008 Christmas episode, *The Next Doctor*, we did a new, cooler version of the Cyberleader, which carried the black of the "handlebars" onto the face and gave him a brain-piece like the Cyber Controller. Otherwise, as soon as you had the Cyberleader in a whole group of Cybermen, you couldn't really spot him that easily.'

'Behind the scenes,' Neill adds, 'we've developed a few practical things – how harnesses and clips work best – which helps in how the costumes are put together around the performers. But generally, they've stayed exactly the same.'

This season has seen one significant change in the Cybermen's design, however – the Cybus Industries 'C' logo on their chests has been removed. We first saw the new 'C'-less models in *A Good Man Goes to War*.

'This was done because these Cybermen exist in our own universe,' Neill notes. 'The Cybus models were from an alternative dimension. We simply made a plate which covers the 'C' – if you prised that plate off, you'd still find it there.'

Towards the end of the series, *Closing Time* saw the towering giants endure a makeover – or perhaps

MAKING MONSTERS

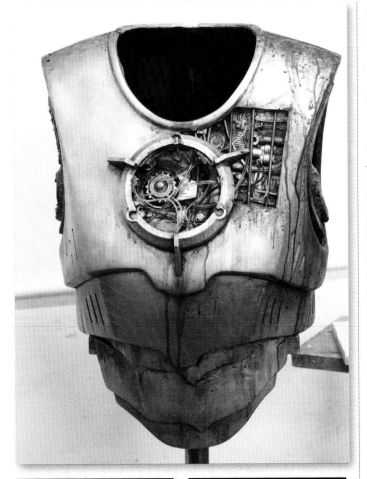

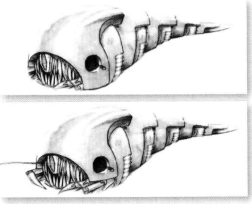

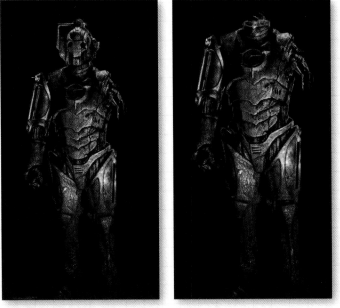

a 'makeunder' would be more accurate... 'The story involved this bunch of Cybermen who have been stuck underground in a crashed ship,' says Neill, 'and have been cannibalising parts to keep going. So they've got plates missing, panels hanging off and wires spilling out. It wasn't really a change to the original design – it just needed to look like these bashed-up Cybermen have been repairing themselves from any old thing they've found lying around.'

'To be honest,' Neill admits, 'there was also a practical side to it. When Steven Moffat said the script needed a more broken-down and damaged look for the Cybermen, we laughed and told him "Well they already are!" These suits have had a lot of use over the years and need constant repair. Whereas normally we'd be trying to make them look shiny and new, with this story it was great – we could just make them look worse!'

Back in 2006, Millennium FX built ten fibreglass suits, plus two 'rubbery' stunt suits, which could be bounced around without getting damaged. 'Slowly but surely,' Neill says, 'that's been whittled down until we're left with just a handful. Some have been broken and damaged, some are on display in exhibitions... We actually cheated a little this year because we built new all-rubber suits for the *Doctor Who Live* tour in 2009, so we put those in the background at the start of *A Good Man Goes to War* to make up the numbers.'

In Episode 12, of course, there was no need to swell the ranks, as a small, rag-tag group of the creatures was all that was required. 'Because the Cybermen in *Closing Time* were all broken down, we also had some Cyber-arms lying about to attack people. And then of course, at the end, Craig (James Corden) is about to be turned into a Cyber Controller. The props department built new

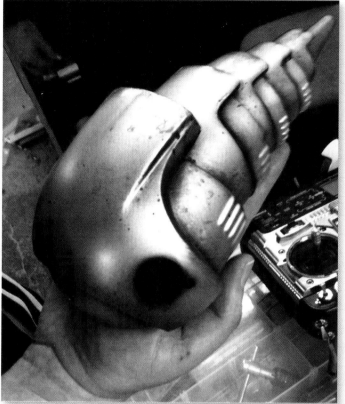

MAD MATS

How CG brought the Cybermats to life...

While Millennium FX designed and built the Cybermats, BBC Wales's own visual FX department helped them make an even bigger impact with some cunning computer graphics.

'The script stated that the Cybermat leaps up and attacks both Craig and the Doctor,' recalls VFX supervisor Craig Higgins, 'so we created a CG Cybermat which could jump up and fly through the air. We also created a crackle of electricity around its mouth, like a taser'.

'We used digital photographs of Millennium's physical model for reference,' explains Craig, 'and made sure empty backgrounds were shot for our Cybermat to be placed into and attack. Our team really enjoyed being able to bring the Cybermats back to life – and to make them look even more dangerous than before.'

Cyberman pieces which they could then attach to a big rig they'd built around him.'

Closing Time also brought Neill's team a totally new challenge. 'Cybermats are fun!' says Neill of these newly returning creations, which first appeared during the 1967 Second Doctor serial *The Tomb of the Cybermen* (then again the following year in *The Wheel in Space*, and finally in 1975's *Revenge of the Cybermen*). 'When you look at them in the old *Doctor Who* episodes, you realise there's a lot that can be done with them,' Neill says. 'We'd all seen the design which was recently done for the *Doctor Who* Adventure Game, *Blood of the Cybermen*. That was quite a nice design, but not exactly what we wanted. Still, it gave us a bit of direction – we wanted these Cybermats to look more high-tech.'

Neill didn't go back and look at old *Doctor Who* episodes for reference. 'We don't tend to do that,' he explains, 'unless there's a very specific reason. When the decision is made that the Cybermats are not going to look exactly like the originals, it makes sense to go at it with a fresh perspective. Whereas with someone like Davros, he is still the same character from the old stories, so you're

trying to do a continuation of sorts and make it feel uninterrupted.'

Neill wanted the new Cybermats to reflect current Cyberman technology. 'When you see our Cybermat, you might not notice straight away, but if you look at it from above, you'll see that the head was designed to echo the face of the Cybermen themselves, right down to the same blue light in the mouth. We then gave them more of an organic maw, as suggested in the script – those nasty piranha-like teeth. The Cybermen are made up of human beings, so you get the idea that the Cybermats might be made up of animals, or some other small alien creature that's been Cyber-converted.'

Neill's team created two different versions of the Cybermats to do everything which Gareth Roberts' script required of them. 'They had to scuttle around and attack people, basically,' Neill says. 'So we made a radio-controlled version which could whizz along the floor, and then we made a cable-controlled version that you could hold and the tail would thrash around and the teeth would snap. As the victim is hanging onto it and fighting with it, it looks like it's really trying to bite them. Fun, eh?'

The Wedding of River Song

BY STEVEN MOFFAT

THE STORY

Time is dying. It's stuck, like the needle on a scratched record, at 5.02pm on 22 April 2011. More than that, all of time itself is concentrated in that split second. All of history, all the moments that ever were and ever could be, squeezed into one pinprick of a moment. Reality can barely contain it. The universe is falling apart at the seams.

And all because the Doctor didn't die.

River Song never killed him on the shores of Lake Silencio. She did the impossible. She shattered reality to save the man she loved.

With the universe a swirling mess of contradictions and impossibilities, the Doctor finds the friends he thought he'd lost – Amy and Rory and River, all part of a massive operation to fix time itself. There, surrounded by captured Silents and their slaves, humanity is trying to put history back on the right track.

All it would take is for River and the Doctor to touch. They're at the very centre of the explosion that's ripping through the universe – if they so much as hold hands, all the damage would be undone and time could resume its proper course. The universe would be saved.

All with just a touch. Or a kiss...

Where Have I Seen?

IAN McNEICE
Winston Churchill
Ian, who reprises his role as Churchill, has appeared in many other top British TV shows, including *Lewis*, *New Tricks* and *Jonathan Creek*.

MARK GATISS
Gantok
Mark has written four episodes of *Doctor Who* and played Lazarus in *The Lazarus Experiment*. He is also known for *The League of Gentlemen* and *Sherlock*.

NUMBER CRUNCHING

Forever **5:02:57** Never **5:02:58**

THE WEDDING OF RIVER SONG

>> Charles Dickens (played by Simon Callow, reprising his role from 2005's *The Unquiet Dead*) is interviewed about the upcoming Christmas special of an undisclosed TV show. 'It involves ghosts,' he says, 'and the past, the present and future, all at the same time' – which is a perfect précis of Dickens's *A Christmas Carol*, which also (confuddlingly) was the inspiration for last year's festive *Doctor Who* special, um, *A Christmas Carol* (2010). >> The Doctor's old pal Winston Churchill was last seen, briefly, in *The Pandorica Opens* (2010) – and before that, in *Victory of the Daleks* (2010). Now, both he and the Holy Roman Empire have survived into this version of the 21st century. >> Silurian scientist Malohkeh, Winston's personal physician, was first seen in *The Hungry Earth/ Cold Blood* (2010). >> The *Teselecta* – from *Let's Kill Hitler* – is back, still commanded by Captain Carter. It's first seen posing as Gideon Vandaleur, envoy of the Silence, before it takes the Doctor's place on the shores of Lake Silencio. >> The Headless Monks, from *A Good Man Goes to War*, keep the unneeded heads of their members in the Seventh Transept – where the Doctor finds the shady dealer Dorium Maldovar. Or part of him, anyway. Since his own 'conversion' (*A Good Man Goes to War*), Dorium's head has had a lot of time to think about the Silence and their plans for the Doctor... >> Dorium describes the Silence as 'a religious order of great power and discretion', who 'don't want [the Doctor] to remain alive.' The Silence want to 'avert' the Doctor's future – in other words, kill him – because 'on the fields of Trenzalore, at the fall of the Eleventh, when no living creature may speak falsely, or fail to give an answer, a question will be asked – a question that must never, ever be answered.' The implication seems to be that the Doctor is heading toward a future confrontation at Trenzalore, when he will be asked 'the oldest question in

Fantastic Facts!

the universe'. And what is this question that terrifies the Silence so? Need we look any further than Dorium's horrified screams at the end of the episode: 'Doctor who?'? >> The death of the Doctor – or his double – on 22 April 2011 is a 'fixed point' in time, a moment that cannot be changed, or... well, just look what happens! The concept of immutable history stretches right back to *The Aztecs* (1964). In that story, the First Doctor's companion Barbara – a history teacher with little experience of time travel at this point – wants to persuade the Aztec people to give up human sacrifice. The Doctor pleads with her to stop, explaining 'You can't rewrite history – not one line!' Many years later, the concept of fixed points in time was introduced: moments of history so important that not even a Time Lord could change them. The resurrected Captain Jack Harkness was one (2005's *The Parting of the Ways*, 2007's *Utopia*), the fate of Adelaide Brooke's Mars expedition was another (2009's *The Waters of Mars*). Perhaps even the Aztecs' slavish devotion to sacrifice, and their subsequent fall at the hands of Spanish invaders, was a further example. *The Waters of Mars* shows us that, even when a Time Lord attempts to alter a fixed point, time itself will try to paper over the cracks, with history unfolding much as it would have done anyway. What River does here, though, is something no one has ever managed

to do before: she actually *breaks* a fixed point. But, as we can see, the consequences are horrific. >> The Doctor mentions that, somewhere out there in the universe, Queen Elizabeth I is 'still waiting in a glade to elope with me'. In *The End of Time* (2009–2010), the Tenth Doctor implied that he had married Elizabeth I in the months between the end of *The Waters of Mars* and the beginning of that story. But perhaps he never actually went through with the wedding, leaving the Queen to wait for ever in that glade. This would certainly explain the older Queen's reaction to him at the end of *The Shakespeare Code* (2007). >> The Doctor learns of the sad death of Alistair Gordon Lethbridge-Stewart, a stalwart of the *Doctor Who* universe, played by Nicholas Courtney. Lethbridge-Stewart (then a Colonel) first appeared in *The Web of Fear* (1968), in which he and the Second Doctor fought Yeti in the London Underground. He next appeared, promoted to the rank of Brigadier, in *The Invasion* (1968) – and he, the Doctor and a platoon of UNIT troops (the organisation appearing here for the first time) clashed with the Cybermen. From *Spearhead from Space* (1970), he became a fixture in the show, standing at the Third Doctor's side during his exile on Earth. He has cropped up occasionally throughout *Doctor Who*'s history since then – most recently in *The Sarah Jane Adventures: Enemy of the Bane* (2008). Nicholas Courtney died in February 2011, and this episode's salute to the Brigadier stands as a tribute to his huge contribution to *Doctor Who*'s success. >> It may have been River's hand holding the gun, but she wasn't the one who pulled the trigger on the Doctor at Lake Silencio: her spacesuit, at this point, was controlling her movements. The River in the spacesuit – the one who causes all the problems in this episode – was the one we saw at the end of *Closing Time*, being spirited away by Madame Kovarian. The episode confirms that

River was sentenced to imprisonment in the Stormcage for the Doctor's murder – but that she most likely can't remember having committed the crime. ❯❯ As he and Churchill find themselves under attack from the memory-proof Silents, the Doctor covers his arm with tally marks – a tactic used in *Day of the Moon*. ❯❯ The Doctor reminds us that Amy 'grew up with a time rift in the wall of [her] bedroom' – as seen in *The Eleventh Hour* (2010). 'You can remember things that never happened,' he adds, referring to the climax of *The Big Bang* (2010), where Amy brings the Doctor back from the oblivion of non-existence by remembering him. ❯❯ We learn that Kovarian's eyepatch, and those worn by her colleagues and Amy's forces, is an 'eye drive' that 'communicates directly with the memory centres of the brain', acting as external storage. By using them, a person can remember their interactions with the Silence – or, rather, the eye drive does the remembering for them. Talking of the Silence, Amy asks why 'the human race [aren't] killing them on sight any more', and the Doctor points out, 'That was a whole other reality' – one where *Day of the Moon*, and its Silence-busting TV broadcast, happened. ❯❯ River used her hallucinogenic lipstick on both President John F Kennedy and Cleopatra. The lipstick was introduced in *The Time of Angels* (2010). ❯❯ River and the Doctor ponder the many theories about them. 'Am I the woman who marries you,' she wonders, 'or the woman who murders you?' Well, strictly, neither! ❯❯ In last year's *Brilliant Book* one of the Dream Lord's teasers about Series Six was '502 but never 503'. This was actually a false teaser, made up by Gareth Roberts. But Steven Moffat then plucked it from the book and used 5.02 as the frozen minute of the alternate reality, where it's never 5.03. So it *was* false when the book was published, but became true later. If you see what we mean. Timey-wimey indeed...

MAGIC MOMENT

The time has come for the Doctor to face up to his destiny – but River won't let him go quietly...

RIVER: You've touched so many lives. Saved so many people. Did you think, when your time came, you had to do more than ask? You have decided the universe is better off without you. The universe is not agreeing.
THE DOCTOR: River. No one can help me. A fixed point has been altered, time is disintegrating...
RIVER: I can't let you die –
THE DOCTOR: But I have to die.
RIVER: Shut up! I can't let you die without knowing you are loved. By so many, and so much. And by no one more than me.
THE DOCTOR: River. You and I, we know what this means. We are ground zero of an explosion that will engulf all reality. Billions on billions will suffer and die.
RIVER: I'll suffer if I have to kill you.
THE DOCTOR: More than every living thing in the universe?
RIVER: Yes.

UNSEEN ADVENTURES

❯❯ The Doctor and River mention their encounters with Cleopatra, queen of Ancient Egypt. River reckons she was a 'pushover', and the Doctor agrees. (But then, River was pointing a gun at her at the time.)

BEHIND THE SCENES
STEVEN MOFFAT
Writer

Bringing to life a world of glittering skyscrapers, steam trains wheeling through the sky, and giant brooding pyramids must have been a challenge for the crew. Do you ever wonder if you're going to ask for too much?
This crew, this team – hand on my heart, you can't ask for too much. Our producer Marcus Wilson just heaves a sigh and says, 'OK, leave it with me...'

Considering everything she has been through, and how her feelings for him nearly destroyed reality, do you think River Song can ever have a normal relationship with the Doctor?
Love isn't a normal relationship – that's why it's got a name. Also, you have to remember, she's a specially engineered psychopath and it never really goes away – she loves her mum and dad, and her fella, but the rest of the universe can go hang. She falls in with the Doctor's moral code because she loves him, not because she especially feels it – bad girl, turned good (kind of). So now the Doctor has a wife, whom he married in an alternative timeline, while miniaturised inside a robot replica of himself, who goes on to have a reverse order relationship with him, while serving time for his murder, before dying to save his life, before he even meets her. Makes *On Her Majesty's Secret Service* seem like a decent honeymoon.

And finally: Doctor who? Care to give us any clues?
No.

Cleopatra
Edit my profile

Works at **Queen of Egypt**
Studied **Being Queen of Egypt**
In a relationship with
Mark Antony

 Cleopatra became friends with Winston Churchill
5.02pm

 Cleopatra posted three pictures to the album
"Conquest of Gaul" *5.02pm*

 Winston Churchill wrote on Cleopatra's wall,
'Lovely to see you as always, ma'am. You really can
dance!' *5.02pm*

Napoleon Bonaparte sent Cleopatra an Asp
5.02pm

Cleopatra became a fan of **Van Gogh** *5.02pm*

Van Gogh likes this. 👍

Cleopatra is playing **Live Chess** with **Stalin** *5.02pm*

Cleopatra joined 'Can I get 6,000,000,0000 people
to join this group before 5.03pm???' *5.02pm*

River Song wrote on Cleopatra's wall:
'Thank for the pyramid, sweetie!' *5.02pm*

 Cleopatra became a fan of **Silurian Medicine**
5.02pm

Cleopatra is reading **Murder on the Sky Orient
Express** *5.02pm*

 Cleopatra became a fan of 'I'm not being funny
but I think this is all the Doctor's fault!' *5.02pm*

P103   ANALOGUE SPY 103 **22 APRIL 17.02:57**

ANALOGUE SPY

SCOWELL TEASES BIG FUTURE FOR DINOSAURS
By Chris Alien

Sir Scowell, the elusive showrunner of monster
ratings hit 'Dinosaurs Have Got Talent', today
exclusively teased the future of the show
to the staff at AS Towers.

   Speaking at a press conference, Sir S said
that following up the smash success of the
dancing T-Rex was no easy challenge, but he was
confident that new stars would emerge during the
audition stage, currently being held in specially
constructed fighting pens at the Wembley Dome.
'We'd all like to see a diplodocus get through
to the finals,' Scowell admitted, 'but they
literally get torn apart in these early heats.'

   He quashed rumours of squabbles on the judging
panel by confirming that, returning to watch angry
reptiles fighting, would be emissaries from both
the Antipodes and the Emerald Isle.

ALSO BEING READ NOW
- Speaking Clock Retires
- Today's Weather at 5.02pm
- Shakespeare appointed new boss at 'EastEnders'

---

22 April **151**

'THE ONLY WAY IS ESSEX!' SAYS LIZ

**Elizabeth I, regularly
voted most popular
Queen of England
in offline polls, may
finally marry the Earl
of Essex.**

   Rumours have been emerg-
ing of a liaison ever since the pair
were spied partying together on
the King of Spain's yacht at this
year's Cannes Festival.

   'Although Liz might have the
body of a weak and feeble woman,'

By our Royal staff,
**SIR JOHN
FALLSTAFF**

friends close to Gloriana told
us, 'she finally has the love of an
Englishman.'

   The Earl of Essex was quick to
confirm their on-again-off-again
engagement. 'Our love is real,'
he insisted. 'It's, like, not for the
cameras.' He was speaking at the
launch of Sir Francis Drake's new
perfume, Potateaux.

ANALOGUE SPY

'DIVORCED, BEHEADED, SURVIVED!' STAR HENRY SPEAKS ABOUT MORE WIVES?

By our television editor, E M Forster

King Henry VIII today told reporters of the agony of sharing his household with six wives and a palace full of TV cameras. 'To be frank, this isn't what I was expecting,' the monarch complained. 'When the cameras turned up it was fun at first, but it's getting a bit intrusive now.'

Denying rumours of a rift with Anne Boleyn since her dramatic beheading at the end of the last series, the randy Royal insisted, 'Anne and I are as close as ever. Her head sits right on my bedside table.'

ALSO BEING READ NOW

- Holmes to host 'Detects Factor' for ITV1
- Emily Bronte, Joan of Arc for 'Loose Women'
- Da Vinci teases more 'Code'

ANALOGUE SPY

UNITED AGAINST THE UNICORNS

By Sir Reginald Dimbleby, Politics Editor

Dick Whittington, the Mayor of London, today assured the public that it has never been safer from attack by mythical beasts.

'Verily,' he told a press conference at Turn Again Tower, 'the likelihood of being eaten in the open air by a Cyclops has never been less. We have a seen a 28 per cent fall in the chances of being attacked by Unicorns and Satyrs in one of the Royal Parks since the reign of my predecessor, Lord Boris. Increased patrols by the Hip Young Gunslingers – the special patrol group organised by Winston Churchill's Head of Law Enforcement, Chief Inspector J. Burchill – and regular air patrols by the Red Arrows have added considerably to feelings of public safety.'

ALSO BEING READ NOW

- No Borgia marriage insists Wyatt Earp
- Jane Austen teases 'Emmerdale' massacre
- Tobias Vaughn unveils new IEpad

ALL THE YEAR ROUND
Girls! Gossip! Great literature!

A GHOST STORY FOR CHRISTMAS
By CHARLES DICKENS

THE SIGNALMAN IN THE SKY

'Halloa! Above there!'

When he heard a voice thus calling to him, he was standing at the door of his rooftop observation post, with a flag in his hand, furled round its short pole. One would have thought, considering the nature of the air, that he could not have doubted from what quarter the voice came; but instead of looking down to where I stood, perched on the top of the rails nearly twenty storeys down from him, he turned himself about, and looked up the Line, looping above him into the clouds. There was something remarkable in his manner of doing so, though I could not have said for my life what. But I know it was remarkable enough to attract my notice, even though his figure was foreshortened and shadowed, leaning over the parapet as it was, and mine was far beneath him, so steeped in the glow of that eternally angry sunset, that I had shaded my eyes with my hand before I saw him at all.

'Halloa! Above!'

(cont. p93)

PROF. T. WITTER'S INSTANTANEOUS MESSAGING SERVICE

Charles Dickens
@therealBoz

Writer. Father. Amateur magician.

Oof. Blocked. In fact – Dedlocked!

@Jedward_The_Talented_Twin_ Terpsichores We just found some pants! In our pants drawer! Thats just so many pants!! [Retweeted by @therealBoz]

Sorry for the long silence, peeps. Busy, busy, busy finishing Bleak House. Hope you like it when it's on TV!

@CharitableGents Please RT: Some of us are endeavouring to buy the poor some meat and drink. It's at this time of the year that want is most keenly felt. [Retweeted by @therealBoz]

@therealBoz from @LittleMatchGirl Just got to end of Old Curiosity Shop. HOW COULD HE DO THIS TO US?? CJHD must go NOW!!! #LittleNellfail

@therealBoz from @Wcollins Stuck too. Thinking of doing a sort of stolen diamond plot. What do you reckon? Been done?

@Jedward_The_Talented_Twin_ Terpsichores PANTS UPDATE! We found some more down the back of the sofa. Watch out for our new song 'We Found Some Pants!' [Retweeted by @therealBoz]

@therealBoz from @HuffamFan Whywhywhy didn't Pip and Herbert Pocket get it on? Get some of that into BH! OMG! #flailing. #whatlarksehpip

Chancellor Sugar needs to watch that Heap fella. His humble act isn't fooling anyone. #apprentice

@LittleMatchGirl from @WildeMan One must have a heart of stone to read @therealBoz's death of Little Nell without laughing. [Retweeted by @therealBoz]

@therealBoz from @TurkeyBoy67 Walk-er!

@therealBoz from @Gamp66 Quilp was SO much better in the pilot.

Very good, @WildeMan. I wish I'd said that.

@therealBoz from @WildeMan You will, Charlie, you will.

@therealBoz from @TheGelth Pity Us!

Not falling for that one again, @TheGelth! Blocked! Just like me, alas...

'I'm not writing for *diehard fans*. I'm writing for the *other 100% of the audience*'

He's the power behind the police box, the man who dictates the Doctor's destiny. And he could do with a holiday! Time to meet showrunner **Steven Moffat**...

In the rooftop bar of a private members' club on London's Shaftesbury Avenue, Steven Moffat is telling the *Brilliant Book* about Peter Jackson and Steven Spielberg's next big project, *The Adventures of Tintin*. It's July 2011, and this hotly anticipated movie will be out in cinemas later this year. Steven wrote the original script in 2008, and then he turned down the chance to pen further Tintin movies in favour of taking over the reins from Russell T Davies on *Doctor Who*. Doesn't he ever wonder, 'what if...?'

'People do it *for me* all the time,' he laughs. 'My agent and my wife will point out, "Essentially, you could be making more money from doing less."'

Which is true.

'Yes, it is. But could I make more money having as much fun as I am on *Doctor Who*? I don't think so.'

The first thing you need to know about Steven Moffat is that he's

very busy. One of the UK's most successful writers and producers, he's currently responsible for two hit BBC shows: *Sherlock*, which he co-runs with Mark Gatiss, and something called *Doctor Who*. He's supposed to be at home right now, writing the 2011 *Doctor Who* Christmas special, but he needed to get out of the house ('this special is doing my head in,' he admits), and knew that he owed the *Brilliant Book* a drink and a chat, so...

Tell us about the 2011 Christmas special then, Steven.
It'll be very, very Christmassy. I like proper Christmas specials. I like them to be about Christmas, to be set at Christmas, to have snow and Christmas trees in them. I think it's rubbish if they don't. Especially if you have a huge kid audience. That's what they expect. Never mind that – that's what *I* expect.
How far are you into the script?
Well, it's not finished yet.

Do you want some help?
Well... no.

Because we have some ideas.
[Laughs] OK, go on.

What about *Silent Night*, featuring the actual Silence.
Hm, yes, *Silent Night* is a nice title. The Silence are good monsters. As with the Weeping Angels, their *modus operandi* is kind of cumbersome, but I think they were a success.

Or what about *The Boxing Day Invasion*, in which the Doctor misses the usual Christmas Day shenanigans and just, sort of, has an all right Boxing Day?
Ha! It'd be a hard one to have a good strap-line for, wouldn't it? 'Nothing much happens... a day late!' But as a budget-saver, it's marvellous.

Well, you can have those ideas. They're yours now. Is there anything you can reveal about the *actual* special though?
I can say that Rory and Amy won't be in this year's Christmas special – it'll just be the Doctor, with guest characters – which takes us out of that ongoing, quite-complex soap opera.

At the end of the 2011 series, it sort of felt like you were 'resetting' the show. The Doctor is now, for the first time in ages, just a madman with a box again.
We're going to explore that properly next series. The Doctor's project is to sort of erase himself from history, because there are only so many times you can stand and boast at Stonehenge before you just create more and more deadly plans to destroy you. We've had a lot of fun with the Doctor as a quasi-celebrity – you're this wandering gypsy scientist, and suddenly you discover you're a legend. What's that going to do to you? It's a nice story to tell, but it gets repetitive, so he has to stop. I mean, I'm exaggerating the extent of the problem for the sake of this answer. In most episodes, the Doctor still just turns up out of the blue. That's why we still need the psychic paper, because he's such an intruder and a stranger to almost everyone he meets.

This series, more than any other, rewards careful viewers across all 13 episodes. Was that a very deliberate move?
I think it's always a good thing to assume you have an intelligent audience. It's not such a big deal to push that a bit.

There's so much packed into many of the episodes in this series, were you worried it might be overwhelming to the viewers?
To be honest, I was a bit nervous, because I know my own love of Byzantine complexity. I worry that I do it too much. I have to keep pulling myself back. But it's worked. I don't know if it would have worked even two or three years ago. When *Doctor Who* came back [in 2005, after a 16-year hiatus], in a series that now probably seems to us all quite simple, it was the only fantasy show around. People had to get used to the grammar of it. Now, having paved the way for other shows, *Doctor Who* has to stay out in front. It has to be the show that makes people say, 'Whoa, what's going on?' I like it when people say that. When people say, 'I had to talk to my kids' or 'my kids had to talk to me about what was going on', I'm thinking, 'Why is that bad? Show me why that's wrong.' If you look at something like *The West Wing* [a US political drama which ran from 1999 to 2006], which is probably my favourite thing ever... I'm not sure I've ever understood a single episode! I don't

> **THE DOCTOR'S PROJECT IS TO ERASE HIMSELF FROM HISTORY**

understand enough American politics for a start. Also, all the characters are much cleverer than me. But they all seem to care about whatever's happening, so I'll care too. So long as somebody says, 'Never mind that, we have to get over there right now,' then I'm happy. I think that's the way people absorb television. All the explanations in *Doctor Who* are there if that's your bag, but they're not essential to your enjoyment of it. An awful lot of storytelling isn't really about making people understand – it's about making people care.

What surprised you most about the 2011 series?
If I'm really honest, I was worried about *The Doctor's Wife*. I worried that it was too 'out there'. There had been rewrites late in the day, and I worried about it being shot in a quarry, I worried about the TARDIS interior being reduced to a couple of corridors... but when I finally saw it through other people's eyes, I thought, 'This is absolutely brilliant!' It turned out to be a fantastic episode.

This year's series has been more arc-driven that usual...
Yes, and I don't think *Doctor Who* will ever be as arc-driven again. But even then the arc stuff only occupied, maybe, two minutes a week.

What are the pros and cons of doing an arc-driven season?
The thing I worry about – though maybe this is a good thing to worry about – is when you've got an episode that doesn't advance the main plot very much, there's a danger that you downgrade it in importance. In that case, you start to worry that the frame is swamping the picture. That's one obvious downside. The other downside, I suppose, is if you did it again. When it's a brand new, shiny thing to do with *Doctor Who* for one year, people get into it and think, 'Wow, look what they're doing this season. They started with the Doctor dying!' If you did it every year, then it would become tedious.

As a writer it must be hard to ensure the whopping great reveals, like River turning out to

be Amy and Rory's daughter, live up to expectations.
It's almost impossible not to disappoint the absolute diehard enthusiasts – people like me – who examine every line, every moment, and think about it between episodes. I'm not writing for them. I cannot. I'm writing for the other 100% of the audience. The other thing I think is, with the whole business of a surprise or a twist, you always have to play fair. You have to give the audience a really good shot at guessing it, or there's no thrill in it. If you guess it in advance, it shouldn't spoil the thrill at all when it turns out you were right. The moment you have downtime between episodes, there's not a hope in hell that a sizeable bunch of the audience won't work it out. Kids mostly got it. My little boys got it. If you actually sat down and thought about it the way a child does, there's a mysterious woman, there's a mysterious girl, and there's a mysterious pregnancy – well, *durr*!

Now, the BBC has commissioned another 14 episode of *Doctor Who* for 2012... or possibly 2013. Do you know what happens in them?

Yes, quite a lot of them, because the writers are already off and running. I've got a broad picture of the next run of 14. This series, I was thinking, 'People love the Doctor nipping back in time and turning out, as in *Flesh and Stone*, to be a future Doctor, so let's do some more of that in 2011.' But now I'm thinking, 'We had more public interest from *Let's Kill Hitler* – just those three words – than any trailer we've ever done, so let's do a series like that, where we really *slut it up*.' That's what I've been saying in my writers' briefings just this week: 'Write it like a movie poster. Let's do big, huge, mad ideas.' Every week, we should say, 'Next week: THIS!'

What's in store for Amy, Rory and River? Do you have ends in sight for any of those characters?

You always have to have a good ending, so I do have an end game for all of them.

But Amy and Rory will be back next series?

Yes.

And River?

That's dependent on Alex Kingston. We reveal who River is this series, but then you think about it and you realise that you've learned nothing. She may or may not be married to the Doctor, depending on whether that was actually a marriage ceremony, or whether it counts if he's inside a giant robot replica of himself.

You were rather having your cake and eating it there.

[Laughs] Absolutely. But the real question you're asking isn't, 'Who is she?' The real question is, 'Are they an item?' And the Doctor's answer

is, 'None of your business!' River is a useful character, to go back to her *Time of Angels* [2010] mode, or even her *Silence in the Library* [2008] mode, when she just rings up the Doctor and says, 'I think this looks fun. Let's go and do it.' And I like what she does to the Doctor. She loves him so much, but she loves him like a wife – she knows all his foibles, but she's still passionate about him – and he obviously adores her, and you sort of don't know what happens when they're alone. People ask me and I say, 'I don't know,' and they think I'm lying. I say, 'But I'm only the biographer. What makes you think the great man tells me everything?' Just because the Doctor is fictional, doesn't mean I know everything about him.

Let's talk about spoilers, because –

[Cutting in] Because I've been ranting about them this year. Or *droning*.

In a radio interview you accused fans who leak plot details of an act of 'vandalism', and said you hoped they'd go away and be fans of something else.

I don't regret saying that at all. I would say it again. I owe it to all the people who work so hard making this show. We threaten people's jobs on *Doctor Who* over secrecy. We say, 'If you give this away, you'll be hauled in front of a disciplinary committee.' If we're going to be that mean with the people we work with, you bet I'll be mean to fans who do the same. No one should be leaking our plots online. They just *shouldn't*.

Some people seemed genuinely surprised that leaked storylines upset you.

Well, we'd never said it in public before. We'd never said, 'This really upsets us. It's horrible.' We'd hidden our feelings. But why should we? Why not just say, 'If you love this show, please don't do that to us'?

> **DOCTOR WHO ISN'T ON AT THE TIME PEOPLE WANT IT TO BE ON**

Once you've made it as plaintively, pathetically clear as that, hopefully people realise that what they're doing hurts us.

On the other hand, the press was really well behaved this year as far as spoilers were concerned.

The press was brilliant. Absolutely brilliant. It was the first time we've ever had press phoning up and saying, 'How much do you think it's safe to give away? We think it would be more exciting if...' They did a brilliant job of teasing about the episodes. I'm all in favour of teasing.

So how do you respond when the press are rather less well behaved?

Do you respond? I don't think you should, because then they'll print whatever it is again. So long as the press are printing stories about us, we're clearly OK. Even if they're printing stories about our ratings supposedly falling. The day we know our ratings really *are* falling is the day they don't bother to run that story.

So what's the truth behind the 'less *Doctor Who* in 2012' story?

The truth behind the delay next year is: why are we killing ourselves, and risking compromising the show, in order to go out in the middle of the summer? I'm sick of it. I'm sick of standing in the blazing sunshine, with a barbecue fork in my hand, knowing that *Doctor Who* is coming on any minute. While our catch-up performance and iPlayer performance are admirable and extraordinary, they do suggest that *Doctor Who* isn't on at the time that people want it to be. It's not even about the ratings; it's an aesthetic thing. Six o'clock on a sunny Saturday is the middle of the afternoon, whereas six o'clock on a winter or autumn Saturday is dark and exciting. When the sky gets darker, kids should be thinking, '*Doctor Who* is coming on!' The show is all about people running down corridors, with torches. You want to be able to see it without the sunshine streaming through your window and onto your TV screen.

So *Sherlock* isn't being favoured over *Doctor Who*?

Of course not. We're making three more episodes of *Sherlock*, and 14 more episodes of *Doctor Who*. You do the maths! The break won't hurt us at all. We'll go out at a better time of year, and I might actually get two weeks off. If people are saying, 'Steven Moffat is a bit tired,' I don't mind, because my reply would always be, 'Well, you go and have two hit shows, and see what it's like!'

Is this a bad time to ask what plans you have for *Doctor Who*'s 50th anniversary in 2013?

[Laughs] Right now I can give you one word: scale.

Can't you give us some more words? Oh, go on..

Epic, huge, massive, indulgent... all your treats at once. The BBC is committed to the 50th anniversary, everyone is committed to it... and I guarantee you it's going to be the best year ever to be a *Doctor Who* fan. We're going to be in production for longer than ever, just to do everything that we intend to do.

And beyond that? Do you think we'll still be seeing Steven Moffat and Matt Smith's names on the *Doctor Who* credits come the 60th anniversary?

I don't know. I don't know what's in Matt's head – ever – but I sort of dread having to take that decision myself. Even though I'm more tired than I've ever been, I don't feel any impulse to leave. A series of *Doctor Who* going out with absolutely no involvement from me? It would probably be a relief to everybody else, but it would be an utter, *utter* shock to me. I used to read [Fourth Doctor actor] Tom Baker in interviews saying, 'But what else could I do?' That's what I think myself right now, as a writer – 'How could any job be better than *Doctor Who*?' So I'm not comfortably contemplating the idea that one day I'll have to leave. It's honestly the best job in the world.

The Doctor's guide to *FASHION*

Hello. The Doctor here again. As I always say, you are what you wear. No, that's not what I always say at all. But it's true. Well, kind of. Anyway...

Everyone in the universe knows how cool I look these days, so I wanted to share the secrets of my wonderful wardrobe with you lot. Aren't you lucky? And what's more, you can cut the clothes out and pin them on me if you want. Oh no, hold on, you don't want to ruin your copy of the *Brilliant Book*, do you? I mean, how would you know what's on pages 159 and 162 with a great big me-shaped hole in them? So here's an idea – invent a cloning machine, pop your book in, and Bob's your uncle. Well, unless your uncle's called Roy. Or Malcolm. Or even Humphrey. Cool name, Humphrey.

Anyway, this is an artist's impression of me in my underthings. I'm not saying it's accurate. Some things a Time Lord never reveals. So get snipping and cover me up, pronto!

STETSON

Stetsons are nearly as cool as bow ties! Just think about it – John Wayne, Clint Eastwood, JR Ewing, Deputy Dawg. Need I say more? Only if you're Amy or River, seemingly.

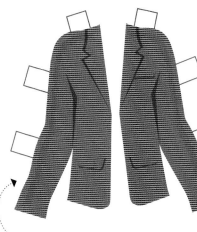

BOW TIE

Bow ties are cool. Everyone knows that. Always have been, always will be. Just ask Magnus Pyke or Albert Einstein or almost any teddy bear. Who wants a long dangly thing that can get caught in the office shredder, when you can have one of these compact beauties?

TWEED JACKET

I love tweed. Smart, hardwearing, and easy to find at your local charity shop. This little number has marvellously deep pockets. Great for keeping all sorts of stuff in – sonic screwdrivers, psychic paper, jelly babies, maps of Bristol, napkin rings, string, a cuddly toy. Bigger on the inside, you see.

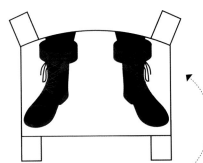

BOOTS

Trainers are all very well and good but there's nothing like a sturdy old pair of boots. Ideal for rough, gravelly alien terrain. And for clomping down corridors. Don't step in pools of acid, though. Which is just good advice generally, now I think about it.

Dress the Doctor – as long as it's in something he's chosen!

FEZ

What's not to like about a fez? Even the name makes you smile. Fez! *Fe-ezzzz!* Go on, try it. See, you're grinning already, aren't you? Unless you're Amy or River.

BRACES

Who invented braces, eh? Marvellous chap. Or chapess. Sort of vertical garter belts for fellas. And they're great for twanging, too. Mine were once twanged by a rather angry Drahvin. But that's another story.

TROUSERS

Some call them jeans, some call them trousers. I call them jousers. No, not really, that'd be daft. I've got 14 identical pairs just in case I drop curry or mercury or something down one. Devil to get out, curry.

SHIRT

Very important, shirts. Without them there'd be nothing to go under your bow tie. Think about it.

OVERCOAT

The newest addition to my wardrobe. Everyone needs an overcoat. Though it took me a while to realise that. You see, it can get chilly when you're trying to seal up an ancient evil in its frozen catacombs. It can get even chillier when you're shopping in Bromley. And it's green, too. I don't mean it's eco-friendly, I just mean it's, er, green.

'I wear a ~~~ now! s are cool!'

I love hats. Who doesn't love hats? Here's a few I'm considering for future us...

BERET

Very Parisian. Perfect for selling onions. And for Frank Spencer impersonations. I shall definitely be bunging on a beret any day now.

DEERSTALKER

Love those flaps! Ideal headgear for stalking deer. Or being stalked by the Deer People of Damafen 5. Don't want to get mistaken for Sherlock Holmes, though. Maybe save this one for fancy dress parties.

'FASCINATOR'

The easiest way to blend in at Ascot or other posh occasions. And easy to slip into your pocket afterwards. I think it's called a fascinator. Don't know why. I imagine there's a fascinating reason.

ASTRAKHAN

Hold on, haven't I worn this one before? Who cares! It's vintage, and vintage is cool right now. Nothing wrong with popping back in time and stealing from yourself, is there? Shut up, River.

THE BRILLIANT BOOK 2012

WAS EDITED BY **CLAYTON HICKMAN** AND DESIGNED BY **PAUL LANG**

IT WAS WRITTEN BY **JASON ARNOPP, DAVID BAILEY, BENJAMIN COOK, NEIL GAIMAN, MARK GATISS, JAMES GOSS, MATTHEW GRAHAM, TOBY HAYNES, CLAYTON HICKMAN, RUPERT LAIGHT, PAUL LANG, DAVID LLEWELLYN, TOM MacRAE, STEVEN MOFFAT, GARETH ROBERTS, STEPHEN THOMPSON** AND **TOBY WHITHOUSE**

AND WAS ILLUSTRATED BY **MARK BUCKINGHAM, NIKKI DAVIES, LEE JOHNSON, PAUL LANG, STUART MANNING, BILL MUDRON, BEN MORRIS, JON TURNER** AND **BEN WILLSHER**

THIS BOOK WOULD NOT HAVE BEEN POSSIBLE WITHOUT THE HELP OF **MURRAY BARBER, NATALIE BARNES, LEE BINDING, KATE BUSH, ARTHUR DARVILL, ANTHONY DRY, ANNABEL GIBSON, KAREN GILLAN, NEILL GORTON, CAT GREGORY, CAROLINE HENRY, DAVID JØRGENSEN, ALEX KINGSTON, STEVEN MOFFAT, STEPHAN PEHRSSON, GARY RUSSELL, EDWARD RUSSELL, CAROLINE SKINNER, MATT SMITH, TOM SPILSBURY, ALEX THOMPSON, STEVE TRIBE, DAVE TURBITT, SUE VERTUE, PIERS WENGER** AND **BETH WILLIS**

IT IS RESPECTFULLY DEDICATED TO THE MEMORIES OF **NICHOLAS COURTNEY** AND **ELISABETH SLADEN**

1 3 5 7 9 10 8 6 4 2

Published in 2011 by BBC Books,
an imprint of Ebury Publishing.
A Random House Group Company

Copyright © the authors, except script extracts copyright © their respective authors

The authors have asserted their right to be identified as the authors of this Work in accordance with the Copyright, Designs and Patents Act 1988

Doctor Who is a BBC Wales production for BBC One
Executive producers: Steven Moffat, Caroline Skinner and Piers Wenger

BBC, Doctor Who and TARDIS (word marks, logos and devices) are trademarks of the British Broadcasting Corporation and are used under licence. BBC logo © BBC 1996. Doctor Who logo © BBC 2009. TARDIS image © BBC 1963. Licensed by BBC Worldwide Limited.

Daleks created by Terry Nation. Cybermen and Cybermats created by Kit Pedler and Gerry Davis. Silurians created by Malcolm Hulke. Sontarans created by Robert Holmes. Judoon and Ood created by Russell T Davies.

All rights reserved. No part of this publication may be reproduced, stored in a retrieval system, or transmitted in any form or by any means, electronic, mechanical, photocopying, recording or otherwise, without the prior permission of the copyright owner.

The Random House Group Limited Reg. No. 954009
Addresses for companies within the Random House group can be found at *www.randomhouse.co.uk*

A CIP catalogue record for this book is available from the British Library.

ISBN 978 1 849 90230 4

To buy books by your favourite authors and register for offers, visit *www.randomhouse.co.uk*

Commissioning editor: Albert DePetrillo
Editorial Manager: Nicholas Payne
Project editor: Steve Tribe
Production: Phil Spencer

Printed and bound in Italy by Rotolito Lombarda SpA.

BBC Books wish to thank the following for providing photographs and for permission to reproduce copyright material. While every effort has been made to trace and acknowledge all copyright holders, we would like to apologise should there have been any errors or omissions.

All images copyright © BBC, except:
page 22 (top left) © filonmar/istockphoto.com
(bottom right) © Richard Cano/istockphoto.com
page 29 (bottom right) © Milos Luzanin/istockphoto.com
page 31 screen grabs courtesy of Cat Gregory
pages 32-35 courtesy Millennium FX, The Mill
page 45 (map) © brett lamb/Istockphoto.com
page 47 (top right) @ NASA
page 52 (background) © edge69/istockphoto.com
pages 74-77 courtesy Millennium FX, The Mill

page 92 (bottom right) © Linda Steward/istockphoto.com
page 102 (background) © Mike Clarke/istockphoto.com (bottom right) © Rob Fox/istockphoto.com
page 119 (inset, centre) © Getty Images
pages 124 and 125 © Toby Haynes/ Stephan Pehrsson
pages 130-132 courtesy Millennium FX
pages 140-141 courtesy Melina Pena, David Jenkins, Bill Evenson, Kikuyu Wills, Nathan Leigh, Mark Heatley, Jeff Elston
page 141 (top right) © Laur-Kalevi Tamm/istockphoto.com
pages 142-145 courtesy Millennium FX, BBC Wales Visual FX department
pages 150-152 (background) © JVT.istockphoto.com

All production designs reproduced courtesy of the *Doctor Who* Art Department.

Doctor Who series photography by Adrian Rogers and Steve Brown.

Thanks to *Doctor Who Magazine* and *Doctor Who Adventures* for additional images and artwork.

Original illustrations:
pages 17, 23, 41, 49, 57, 67, 79, 85, 101, 107, 115, 127, 135, 147 – Lee Johnson
pages 20, 28-29, 63, 93 (top) – Ben Willsher
pages 54, 82, 104-105, 160-161 – Ben Morris
page 55 – Jon Turner
pages 60-62 – Mark Buckingham, Todd Klein, Charlie Kirchoff
pages 90 (top), 91, 92 – Stuart Manning
page 93 (bottom) – Bill Mudron
pages 102-103 – Mels Zucker
pages 110-113 – Nikki Davies

The Doctor

River Song
Stormcage Containment Facility